"Why don't I get y [...] **and when I get ba** [...] **something you think I should know about you."**

Could Jasper see that she was offering him an olive branch? A chance to begin their marriage as it should have been? Asking him to love her was too much, Emma Jane knew that. But surely peaceful coexistence wasn't so far out of their reach.

After what seemed like ages, Jasper's lips turned upward into the smile that was rumored to melt every woman's heart this side of the Divide. Emma Jane had never been one of the girls to giggle and swoon over Jasper's famed good looks, but if he gave her many smiles like that, she could easily find herself wanting to.

"All right. Don't put any pickles on my sandwich. Mother seems to think they're my favorite, but I really can't stand her pickles." He gave her a wink, then settled back into the chair.

No pickles. The simple request seemed to be the beginning of a friendship.

Danica Favorite loves the adventure of living a creative life. She loves to explore the depths of human nature and follow people on the journey to happily-ever-after. Though the journey is often bumpy, those bumps refine imperfect characters as they live the life God created them for. Oops, that just spoiled the ending of Danica's stories. Then again, getting there is all the fun. Find her at danicafavorite.com.

Books by Danica Favorite

Love Inspired Historical

Rocky Mountain Dreams
The Lawman's Redemption
Shotgun Marriage

Visit the Author Profile page at Harlequin.com.

DANICA FAVORITE

Shotgun Marriage

⟨H⟩ **HARLEQUIN**® LOVE INSPIRED® HISTORICAL

Recycling programs
for this product may
not exist in your area.

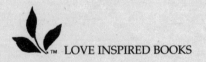

™ LOVE INSPIRED BOOKS

ISBN-13: 978-0-373-28356-9

Shotgun Marriage

Copyright © 2016 by Danica Favorite

www.Harlequin.com

Printed in U.S.A.

Love is patient, love is kind. It does not envy, it does not boast, it is not proud. It does not dishonor others, it is not self-seeking, it is not easily angered, it keeps no record of wrongs. Love does not delight in evil but rejoices with the truth. It always protects, always trusts, always hopes, always perseveres.

—*1 Corinthians* 13:4–7

For Camy Tang and Cheryl Wyatt,
thanks for being such great friends,
coconspirators (not that we admit to anything,
of course!), and for walking this road called life
with me, and all its ups and downs. I love you guys!

Chapter One

Leadville, CO, 1881

"Did you hear he spent their wedding night in a brothel..." The whispers came from one of the pews to Emma Jane Logan Jackson's left. But as she looked in the direction of the sound, all she saw were pious young women seemingly engrossed in their Bibles.

Jasper reached over and patted her hand. "Ignore them," he said quietly, clasping the fingers that rested in the crook of his arm and giving them a gentle squeeze. Odd to be receiving this small amount of comfort from the virtual stranger she'd just recently married. He'd barely talked to her, let alone touched her, since their wedding two weeks ago.

Ignoring the gossip was easy enough for him to say. He was Jasper Jackson, son of the richest man in Leadville. But Emma Jane? She'd spent her whole life the laughingstock of town.

Smoothing the delicate fabric of the pale blue silk dress her mother-in-law had purchased for her, Emma Jane remembered all the times she'd wished for finer clothes to wear to church. She'd been wrong in thinking a new dress would keep the other women from talking about her. Whether it had been the poorly mended hand-me-downs, her father's drinking, her mother's antics in trying to make their family more respectable and even Emma Jane's own awkwardness, people always found a way to make fun of her.

All she'd ever wanted was to find respectability in the town's eyes, but even with marriage to Leadville's most eligible bachelor, it eluded her.

"I thought getting married was supposed to stop all the talk," Emma Jane whispered back.

Jasper squeezed her hand again. "It will be all right. Eventually some other scandal will hit town, and they'll forget all about the circumstances of our nuptials. Soon enough, they'll be begging to be invited to tea because they can't resist the Jackson fortune."

His emphasis on the words *the Jackson fortune* made Emma Jane stop and look at him. Her strikingly handsome husband, with his dark good looks, seemed almost bitter, like he resented having so much wealth. Surely being well-to-do was a good thing. With her father's rising and falling fortunes, she knew both what it was like to be in plenty and in want, and frankly, she'd much rather have the plenty.

"What do you expect from a marriage practically forced on him by a scheming…"

Emma Jane turned in the direction of the voice, but all she saw was a group of women demurely peeking behind their fans. She squared her shoulders, straightened her back and gave them all a tight little smile. The only scheming going on was among the other women and their nasty gossip.

Jasper tugged at her hand again. "It's not worth it. They're just jealous because they aren't Mrs. Jasper Jackson."

More of the bitter tone as he emphasized *Mrs. Jasper Jackson*.

"You seem…" Emma Jane struggled for a descriptor that might induce her reticent husband to talk to her about it.

His lips turned upward in a smile that looked to be more painful than the effort was worth. "It's no secret that every woman in town wanted to marry me." He snorted. "Or, at least, they wanted to marry my fortune."

Then he looked down at her, his dark brow creasing. "I'm sorry. I know our marriage benefited your family financially. I didn't mean to insult you."

She couldn't give an answer to that, even if he'd wanted her to. The truth was, her family had insisted on the marriage, more for the funds it would bring to their coffers than any cares for Emma Jane's reputation. Her father had gambled away her sister Gracie's hand to settle a debt, and the only way to save Gracie from marriage to the town's most odious man had been for Emma Jane to marry into wealth. Her mother had come up with a scheme for Emma Jane to trap Jasper into marriage, but Emma Jane hadn't been able to go through with it.

Fortunately for the Logan family, Emma Jane's clumsiness took over where her conscience wouldn't let her act. She'd ended up trapped overnight in a mine with Jasper. Emma Jane's reputation at stake, marriage to Jasper was the only solution. Her family caused such a fuss that the Jacksons were glad to give them whatever funds necessary to avoid any further embarrassment. Emma Jane's family left town shortly after the wedding, pockets full of Jasper's money.

No wonder he was bitter.

Jasper cleared his throat. "It just would be nice, you know, if people cared about what I wanted to do with my life."

"Forgive me," Emma Jane said softly, pulling her hand out of his arm, then she tugged at the lace edging on the sleeve of her dress.

She hadn't considered what their marriage had cost Jasper. Nor had she thought about what he'd wanted. Her parents had browbeat her into the marriage, and because it was what Emma Jane had always done, she'd meekly agreed.

"No, forgive me." Jasper took her hand again and settled it back into the crook of his arm. "It was a thoughtless remark. You had as little choice in the matter as I did. Honestly, my frustration isn't even about that. I just can't stand the way everyone is so concerned with trivial matters."

Now *that* Emma Jane could understand. "We should find our seats," she said, tugging at her husband's arm.

"You go on. I see the sheriff has arrived."

Jasper's brow furrowed, and the line between his eyes had deepened. His thick, dark hair flopped over, seeming to have ignored the way he'd slicked it back earlier this morning.

"Is everything all right?" She followed his gaze and noticed Sheriff Calhoune standing on the other side of the church.

"We're tracking down some of the bandits who got away the night of the brothel fire. I'm hoping he has some leads. This town's not safe with scoundrels like them on the loose."

The brothel fire. Jasper had spent their wedding night helping their friend, Will Lawson, rescue an innocent young lady from the clutches of a gang of bandits. During the rescue, the brothel had gone up in flames, creating chaos in their community. With Jasper's scornful words about no one caring about what he wanted, it seemed wrong to prevent him from speaking with the sheriff. Even if church was about to start.

"I'll see you at our seat," she said.

Jasper gave a quick nod before turning away.

Polite strangers, that's what they were. And while part of her yearned to know more about this enigmatic man she married, she couldn't bear to impose on him any more than she already had.

"Don't be a bother, Emma Jane." Her mother's words echoed in her head. Day and night, she'd worked so hard to not be. But because of her, Jasper was in a marriage he didn't want. How could she ask him to give more than he already had?

The sound of giggles to her right drew Emma Jane's attention. A beautiful baby girl, with golden hair and dressed in a pretty lace dress, bounced on a woman's lap.

"Your baby is darling," Emma Jane said to the woman, who gave her a smile in return.

"Thank you."

"What's her name?"

"Hannah."

"What a lovely name. I'm Emma Jane…" She paused at the introduction. No longer Logan, it didn't seem right to call herself Jackson, either.

Would being married ever seem normal?

"Pleased to meet you. I'm Pamela Woodward." The baby reached in Emma Jane's direction. "Would you like to hold her?"

Emma Jane automatically took Hannah in her arms, breathing in the soft powdery scent. Her heart warmed as the baby immediately snuggled up to her.

Hannah pulled at the collar on Emma Jane's dress, and Emma Jane gently took the baby's tiny hands in hers. Such a sweet child.

Which was when it hit her. Married to Jasper, there would be no children. He'd told her, just before they were married, that theirs was to be a marriage in name only.

"If it isn't the town harlot, stealing other women's beaus and tricking them into marriage." Flora Montgomery nudged Emma Jane as she passed, giving her a haughty glare, then turned to the baby's mother. "It's very brave of you, letting a woman like her hold your baby. But perhaps you haven't heard…"

With the pain of not having children heavy in her mind, Emma Jane handed the baby back to her mother. "Thank you for letting me hold Hannah. She is a dear."

She turned to leave to avoid making a scene, but Flora blocked her path.

"You haven't heard about our *dear* Emma Jane, have you?"

Pamela's eyes narrowed. "I've been in Denver, visiting my parents."

"After the church picnic, we were caught in a terrible storm," Flora said. "Jasper found shelter for us at a nearby farm. When we were supposed to be getting ready to bed down for the night, Emma Jane lured him outside, then pushed him into an abandoned mine. She jumped in, and when they were found the next morning, her dress was in tatters."

"I did no such thing!" Emma Jane had gone for a walk to clear her head after listening to Flora's taunts. Well, all right, she'd run out of the barn crying. But Flora had been particularly cruel, telling the other girls that Emma Jane was going to be sold into a brothel. Not that Emma Jane would ever admit to Flora how those horrible rumors had affected her. For whatever reason, Flora had always picked on Emma Jane—had done so ever since they were in school together. Though Emma Jane had often wished she knew what she'd done to offend the other girl, mostly Emma Jane wished Flora would just leave her alone.

Emma Jane straightened her shoulders. "I'd gone for a walk and fallen into an abandoned mine. I had no idea Jasper was out there. He heard my cries for help and, in trying to rescue me, fell in, too."

She looked at Pamela, hoping she'd be sympathetic. "Truly, it was all just a terrible accident, and nothing untoward happened. Pastor Lassiter married us himself, and he would never have done so had any real harm been done."

The woman nodded slowly. But Flora wasn't finished yet. She gave Emma Jane a nasty smile, baring the points of her teeth before turning to the baby's mother. "I'm sure that's what Emma Jane would like people to believe. But Mrs. Jackson told me herself. The Logans would have ruined them. They told the sheriff that Jasper..." Flora lowered her voice. "Took liberties."

"Jasper would never do that!" Emma Jane stared at

the other girl, horrified that she would spread such vicious lies about Jasper.

"Of course he wouldn't." Flora's voice lacked any kindness. "No man would even consider you in that way. You are, after all, most unfortunate in your appearance."

The pitying look Flora gave Emma Jane made her realize that not even the finest dress would ever make her pretty. After all, Flora was the very picture of everything a woman ought to be, with her golden blond curls and bright blue eyes. Emma Jane's hair was also blond, her eyes blue. But the blond was stringy and streaked with brown, and the girls used to tease her that it must be dirty. And her blue eyes had brown flecks in them that Flora had said came from being evil.

Even though Emma Jane knew in her head that Flora's accusations weren't true, it didn't make the cold lump in the pit of her stomach go away.

Flora was right about one thing, however. She had nothing to attract a man like Jasper into wanting to be her husband.

Still, the dig on Emma Jane's appearance was not enough for Flora, whose eyes glittered with a kind of blood lust.

"But what I don't understand is why you went along with the lies, unless, of course, you were telling them yourself."

A sickeningly sweet smile followed Flora's last statement, and she turned her attention back toward Pamela. "Jasper was so disappointed about being railroaded into the marriage that he spent the night…" Flora looked around, then lowered her voice. "In a place of ill repute."

The fact which every woman in church was still whispering about. But they didn't have the whole story.

"He was helping Will Lawson—a lawman—rescue an innocent young lady from the clutches of an outlaw." Emma Jane spoke louder than was polite, but hopefully some of the other gossiping women would finally hear the truth.

"So you say." Flora flipped open her fan, then smiled at Pamela. "I just thought I'd warn you so you understood why none of the good families in Leadville are extending invitations to this woman. Bad company corrupting good character and all that."

With a final nasty grin, Flora flounced over to her seat in a pew a few rows up. Emma Jane gave the woman they'd been talking to a weak smile. "I'm sorry you were dragged into this. I sincerely appreciate your kindness to me, and I assure you that I've been nothing but honest with you."

The woman's noncommittal murmur spoke volumes. Flora's words had poisoned any hope Emma Jane had of even being able to delight in someone else's child.

Then Emma Jane spotted Mrs. Jackson heading in her direction.

"Stop dawdling." Jasper's mother took Emma Jane by the elbow. "We are to be an example for the rest of the church, and you're making a spectacle of yourself."

"Yes, Mrs. Jackson."

Face heated, she sat in the Jackson pew where Mrs. Jackson indicated, trying to enjoy the feel of the velvet cushions rather than the hard wooden benches the rest of the church endured. Mr. Jackson, Jasper's father, leaned into Emma Jane. "Where's Jasper?"

"He went to talk to the sheriff," she answered, further conversation being cut off by the sound of the organ's first chords.

After the hymns, Pastor Lassiter spoke, sharing the need for the church community to continue to rally around the women who'd been displaced in the brothel fire. While some of the women had moved on to other houses of ill repute, many had nowhere else to go.

Emma Jane tried to focus her attention back on the pastor's sermon, but she found herself unable to think beyond the poor women who'd been left homeless. Like Emma Jane, they were deemed unworthy and unlovable by the rest of society.

And yet, not one of them judged Emma Jane for the disgraced circumstances of being forced to marry. They all treated Emma Jane like she was a real lady, worthy of respect. Emma Jane had even become friends with a colorful woman named Nancy.

Emma Jane twisted around to see if Nancy had shown up at the church yet. The so-called fallen women often arrived after the service started, leaving before it ended to avoid ridicule.

Marriage hadn't brought Emma Jane any closer to finding respectability, but perhaps helping with the pastor's ministry, people would finally see her as a good Christian woman. Maybe then she would finally have the acceptance that had eluded her for most of her life.

Jasper Jackson stood at the back of the church, listening as Pastor Lassiter concluded his sermon. He hadn't intended to miss church, but he'd been caught up in talking to the sheriff to figure out their next move.

The newly acquired badge heavy in his pocket, Jasper couldn't help but touch it one more time. Him. A deputy. All his life, he'd wanted to do something important, but every time he tried to find his significance, his mother cited the need to carry on the Jackson legacy. She'd sob and tell him she'd been lucky to have even him, and he couldn't spoil it by…well, she'd have a fit of vapors for sure when he shared his news.

But this time, he would not be swayed.

A woman had died saving Jasper's life the night of the brothel fire. In the heat of an argument with the bandits, Jasper had acted foolishly, and the bandits started firing on them. Mel pushed him out of the way, getting shot in the process. Mel. A woman of the night. Not the kind of woman a man owed any kind of honor to, but she'd done the most honorable thing a person could do—she'd taken a bullet meant for him. He'd promised Mel that he'd find and rescue her sister, Daisy, from the gang of bandits that held her. The same gang who'd killed Mel.

No, his honor wasn't at stake. It was his very soul. Or at least it felt that way as church let out and his new bride, Emma Jane, approached, her delicate features unmarred by the thoughts that plagued him. He had to admit that she was a lovely woman. He'd done the honorable thing by marrying her, but until he completed his mission in keeping his promise to Mel, he would have no peace in his own heart.

"Hello, Jasper." Emma Jane gave him a weak smile. "Your mother—"

"There you are!" Before Emma Jane could finish her sentence, his mother stepped in between them. "Why didn't you sit with us?"

Jasper cringed. The Jacksons weren't typically confrontational, especially in public. But the only way he was going to be able to share his decision without encountering hysterics was to do it now.

"The sheriff was here, so I went to talk to him about the latest news on the bandits. I thought it would be a few days, but he decided to swear me in as a deputy today."

He never imagined that Emma Jane Logan's face would be the one to keep him calm. Until he realized that she wasn't Emma Jane Logan anymore. Jasper exhaled slowly, trying to let go of the inevitable tightness in his chest that always seemed to come at the reminder of his marriage. At least she didn't appear to be standing in the way of the one decision he'd gotten to make about his own life.

Of course, Emma Jane had what she wanted—his name and fortune. Though she'd insisted that the events leading to their marriage were not intentional, he couldn't forget the sound of her mother congratulating her on a job well-done. The woman had practically cackled with glee as she'd told Emma Jane that luring him to the abandoned mine had been masterful.

Marriage to Emma Jane would have been a whole lot easier had he continued to believe it was all an accident. He'd even thought, in their time at the church picnic, they'd become friends. But friends trusted each other, and Emma Jane should have trusted him when he'd told her that he'd find a way to save her family without her having to get married. Perhaps, in supporting his cause, Emma Jane could make up for taking away one of the most important choices a man had in life.

A stolen glance at his parents revealed they'd both turned odd shades of red—to be expected, of course—

but part of him wished they'd have come forward to say they were proud of him.

No, it was Emma Jane who first spoke up.

"After everything that happened with the brothel burning down, I can understand your desire to bring justice." She gave a small smile. "I've been thinking I should do more to help Pastor Lassiter's ministry to the women rescued from the fire."

Her words shouldn't have surprised him. After all, aiding the less fortunate was what their church was about. Or, at least, that's what people said their church was about. He'd seen many of the young ladies pay lip service to helping others, but none ever seemed to put those words into action. Except Emma Jane. He didn't know her well, yet he could remember seeing her a number of times at other church events, helping out.

"Nonsense," his mother snapped. "We'll give the pastor some money, just as we always do, and that will be that."

Then she turned her attention to Jasper. "I hardly know what's gotten into you. Your unfortunate marriage, chasing bandits—I can't imagine what you'll do next."

He recoiled at his mother's description of his marriage. Especially when he noticed the pained look on Emma Jane's face. Why he was so concerned about his young wife's feelings, he didn't know, especially when the larger issue at stake was his ability to follow his dreams. No, his mission was bigger than a dream. Innocent lives were at stake.

Ignoring his mother, Jasper turned to his father. "I am alive today because of the noble sacrifice of a woman who only wanted her sister to be saved. If I don't help bring these men to justice, who will? If I continue to live with no other purpose than to entertain Mother's guests, then really, what was the point of a woman dying in my place?"

Then, taking another deep breath to dispel the inevitable lump that filled his throat when talking about Emma Jane, Jasper addressed his mother. "It would do you credit to remember that if it hadn't been for Emma Jane pushing me out of the way of the mine caving in, I'd be dead. She put her safety in jeopardy for mine, and I will always be grateful."

His life had been saved twice in a matter of weeks. By women. Perhaps, as much as he reminded his mother of his debt to Emma Jane, he needed to remind himself of it, as well. She risked her life for him. If marriage was the price he'd had to pay, so be it.

"Regardless of what happened in that mine, we both know you'd have had to have married her, anyway," Constance snapped.

Jasper swallowed. True, of course, but Emma Jane's sacrifice had somehow made his own more palatable. Even if the mine hadn't caved in, they would have both been gone long enough that their returning together— after being out alone in the pitch-dark—would have caused tongues to wag. But once they'd been trapped in the mine, marriage had been a foregone conclusion.

And as he watched Emma Jane's lower lip quiver, he couldn't help but wonder how much she regretted the cost of their marriage.

"What's done is done," Jasper said quietly, looking at Emma Jane. "And it's time we made the best of it."

His words didn't erase the sadness from her eyes, and while Jasper wished there was something else to be done, he knew that the distance between them wasn't going to be bridged by a few words.

As grateful as he was for Emma Jane saving his life, the sting of her betrayal was still too deep, the pain too fresh. When she'd approached him at the church picnic and told him that her mother wanted her to marry him to restore the money her father had lost in a poker game, he told her that he'd help her find a solution that didn't involve marriage. Emma Jane had said she was willing to trust him. But she'd lured him out to the abandoned mine, anyway. Obviously, she'd heard him say he needed to go clear his head, and gone out on her own. Of course he'd answer her cries for help. She couldn't have known how dangerous it would be, or that the rains would have weakened the ground to cause a cave-in. He wasn't even sure that she'd known the mine was there.

Regardless, Emma Jane had to have known that being alone with him, outside in the dark, was enough to compromise them both. For that, he blamed her.

So why, as tears shone in Emma Jane's eyes, could he not bring himself to hate her?

Maybe it was because, as he had just told his mother, they couldn't do anything about the past. All they could do was move on. Jasper was trying, he really was, and maybe someday he could hold more firmly to his resolve to look ahead rather than be afflicted by questions he would probably never find answers to.

"We should take this conversation somewhere more private," Jasper's father said, gesturing toward Pastor Lassiter's empty office.

Jasper looked around, realizing for the first time that while many of the churchgoers had exited, there were still enough people milling around that seeking privacy was a wise decision. He followed his father into the pastor's office, waiting until his mother and Emma Jane had entered the room before closing the door behind them. Pastor Lassiter wouldn't mind if they used his office while he was busy conversing with folks leaving the church.

"I meant what I said about making the best of our marriage," Jasper said slowly as he moved toward Emma Jane, stepping in between her and his mother. "But you have to understand that my mission to save Daisy takes precedence right now. Her life is in danger, and every moment that I spend here is a moment closer to her demise."

Emotions he didn't understand flickered across Emma Jane's face as she straightened her shoulders and nodded. "You have my full support."

Then she hesitated, looking down at her Bible, as if she were hoping it would... Jasper shook his head. What could the Bible do for her? It wasn't going to save anyone's life.

Emma Jane sighed and looked up at him. "But... I'm tired of pretending that the whispers don't bother me. I'm tired of people thinking I've driven you away. I..."

"I'm sorry you're bothered by all the talk." Jasper cut her off, trying not to sound cold, but what else was he supposed to say? Everyone thought that being a Jackson was a wonderful thing, but all it did was put you in the limelight, where everyone always had something to say about your life. And by something, it never meant anything good.

Jasper took a step back. He'd intended for their marriage to ease Emma Jane's problems, not make them worse. The only reason he'd married her was because after being alone together overnight, her reputation would be ruined, and no decent man would have her. Apparently, their marriage hadn't had the desired effect.

"I'm sorry, Emma Jane." He held out his hand to her, then captured her gaze, ignoring his mother's indrawn breath. How had he never noticed before that Emma Jane's eyes were such an exquisite shade of blue, with little flecks of brown dancing within?

"I'd hoped that our marriage would be enough to keep people from talking." He looked back at the ground, unable to face the way her wide-eyed expression asked questions of him he wasn't ready to answer.

"I don't know what to do about it right now. Even if I stay, people are going to find something to talk about."

He sent a glare in his mother's direction. "The best thing for Emma Jane right now is for everyone to stand beside her in my absence. You can support me, thereby supporting her, or…"

Or *what*? Jasper let out a long, frustrated sigh. His mother would do exactly as she pleased, which didn't do anything to help Emma Jane. Leaving him trapped in the conundrum of dealing with Emma Jane's hurt feelings or following his calling to rescue Daisy and bring the bandits to justice.

Why did doing the right thing have to put him in such a difficult position?

"It's all right, son." His father stepped forward, placing one hand on Jasper's shoulder, the other on Emma Jane's. "Your mother and I haven't done all we could in easing your wife's transition into our family."

He gave Jasper a squeeze, then moved back and addressed Emma Jane. "I apologize if we haven't been as welcoming as we could have been. Such a hasty marriage didn't give any of us time to properly prepare, and that's no excuse. I'll do what I can to address any talk."

Jasper couldn't help but notice his mother still remained near the door, her back stiff and unyielding, her mouth pursed tightly. There would be an argument between his parents later, and yet again, Jasper was responsible.

Why did so much have to rest on his shoulders? So many things for him to be held accountable for, and yet the one thing that mattered most—saving the life of an innocent woman—seemed to be directly at odds with it all.

He heaved another sigh, then took Emma Jane's hands in his, wishing her hands didn't feel like ice, like they needed him for warmth. "I don't know what you want from me."

"I just want you to talk to me," Emma Jane said quietly. Her shoulders rose and fell. "I know ours isn't a love match. But I at least thought we could be friends. That we *were* friends. Instead, I find that you have shut me out completely."

Her words weren't supposed to sting. All of this was her fault. They were once friends, and they could be friends still, but she had to trap him into marriage. So why was he the one who felt bad?

"I'm not sure what to talk to you about."

"You could have told me that you were leaving our wedding reception to help Will rescue Mary's sister Rose from the bandits. Mary knew, so why didn't you fill me in, as well? I understand you wanted to help them. Mary and Will are my friends, too. And now, trying to bring the rest of the gang to justice and find this Daisy person? Why can't I help?"

A whole list of reasons, starting with the fact that the only people who knew for certain that Rose had run away, and not been kidnapped, were Will, Jasper and Rose's family. Jasper had been asked not to apprise anyone of that fact.

Fortunately, there was one equally important reason. "These are dangerous people. The only reason Mary came along that night is because she followed me. She wasn't supposed to be there. These men are the kind to shoot first, ask questions later. I won't have you risking your life."

Emma Jane gave him a mournful look. One that almost made him feel bad for excluding her. But she didn't understand how dire the situation was.

"I just want you to let me in. To talk to me like we did before our marriage."

Jasper wanted that, too. But it seemed like there was too much at stake to waste effort on social niceties. They'd had good conversation, sure, but conversation did nothing when it came to saving lives.

"There's no time for that. The search party is leaving soon—with or without me. Once this business is settled, then we can talk."

The Emma Jane he'd always known was a little mouse. But when she straightened her shoulders, Emma Jane looked like a tiger.

"I can help."

With the ferocity in her eyes, Jasper almost believed her.

"Emma Jane, you're just a…"

He wanted to say "woman," but the truth was, his life had been saved by two women. He had no illusions about females being the weaker sex. But against these men, a person who didn't know how to fight, to survive and to kill if needed—that person was dead. Emma Jane could do none of those things.

"A woman who happens to be friends with the women rescued from the brothel. Women who were privy to the bandits' secrets. So do not condescend to me about what I can and cannot do."

She stepped aside, including his parents in the conversation. "I have tried to do what has been asked of me. But I am tired of sitting and pretending that having insult upon insult heaped upon me does not bother me. I am Mrs. Jasper Jackson, for better or for worse. And as such, I will assist my husband in bringing these bandits to justice. And when that happens, I will walk through this town with my head held high, and not a soul will dare look down upon me."

A few tense moments ticked by. Then, with a steely look far more threatening than even his mother's fiercest glower, Emma Jane stared directly at his mother. "Including you, Mrs. Jackson."

Everything in him wanted to applaud Emma Jane at her words. As far as Jasper knew, no one had stood up to his mother before. At least, not with that level of vigor.

But Emma Jane was not finished, because then she turned her attention on him. "You will let me help you. If you do not include me in your plans, I will do my part, anyway. Even if it means going to the sheriff directly."

Jasper didn't doubt her words. No, this ferocious spitfire, a woman with whom he was entirely unacquainted, meant business. Just as Mary had snuck out and followed him to the brothel that night, he knew Emma Jane would do the same—and more.

They'd barely gotten Mary and her sister Rose out

alive that night. How much more danger would Emma Jane face? It seemed an impossible choice—include Emma Jane in a potentially dangerous mission, or risk having her go behind his back and get mixed up in something potentially more precarious?

Chapter Two

"I need to go." Jasper had prolonged his leaving long enough. Almost too long. He'd only meant to tell everyone of his plans, not have the impassioned discussion that ensued.

"Hopefully, this lead takes us to where the bandits are hiding. Then it will be over and all will be well. I just wanted a chance to say goodbye, you know, in case. If all goes well, I'll be home by supper."

Emma Jane stepped forward and gave him an awkward hug. "Stay safe."

The rush of emotion in his chest came on harder than the force of the worst blizzard he'd endured. His wife's hug was all warmth and completely unexpected after Emma Jane's fervent speech about joining him.

"Promise me you won't try to help me with this case while I'm gone. We can talk when I get back."

He could see her hesitation as she shifted her weight and chewed on her lower lip. Those eyes looked at him in a way that made him believe that things would, in fact, be all right.

"I promise."

He wasn't supposed to care about Emma Jane Logan, er, Jackson. But he'd forgotten that underneath all that awkwardness lay a woman with deep compassion for others. If only she'd had compassion for the fact that he'd have liked to have chosen his own wife—a woman whom he actually loved.

In that, Jasper envied his friend, Will, falling head over heels for Mary. Their marriage would be a real marriage, full of happiness and love. What did Jasper have to look forward to?

Nights sitting by the fire and talking? That had been pleasant enough before he'd been forced to marry her. But what of the rest of their lives? And children? How were they supposed to have children when they didn't share the kind of feelings needed for the begetting of children?

Jasper jerked away. All this time, he'd remained in Emma Jane's embrace. How had he forgotten himself? Memories of their time trapped in the mine flooded back to him. Just before Emma Jane had shoved him out of the way of the rockslide, he'd kissed her. But then the rockslide hit, and while he'd been saved, Emma Jane's heroism had left her with a nasty bump on the head. Jasper had considered it a sign.

Kissing Emma Jane Logan had nearly killed them both.

Now that she was Emma Jane Jackson, Jasper had no intention of repeating the experience. He had more important things to think about than romance. Even if he couldn't get the memory of the soft press of her lips against his out of his mind.

"I should get going," he finally said, shifting awkwardly.

His father stepped forward and gave him a tight embrace. "Stay safe, son."

And then, almost as if his father feared the worst, he said slowly, "I can't pretend to like what you're doing, but I understand."

Henry's voice quavered slightly. "I don't want there to be any regrets between us. So know I love you and I'm proud of you."

Jasper should have been pleased to hear those words, but something in him ached, knowing he hadn't yet done anything to be proud of. He exhaled roughly. He'd save the joy in hearing the words for when he knew Daisy was safe.

His mother, though, held no such sentiment. Red-eyed, she stared past him at Emma Jane.

"If he dies, I will blame you. He never had such foolish notions about chasing bandits until after he met you. And I promise, you will rue the day…"

"Enough, Constance." His father took his mother by the arm.

After a glance at Emma Jane's stricken face, Jasper, too, had had enough.

"None of this is Emma Jane's fault. If you listened to me at all, you'd know that I've been wanting to do something meaningful with my life for a long time."

Jasper held out a hand to Emma Jane, and she took it, her gloved fingers seeming so small in his. He'd married her to protect her, and here, with his mother's hostility, he had to wonder for the second time today if it had done any good.

Was he wrong for trying to be more than what he was?

But could he live with himself if he didn't? Could he

continue looking himself in the mirror if he were nothing more than a dandy, taking in social entertainments but contributing nothing but gossip to society?

Squeezing Emma Jane's hand gently, he gazed down at her. "Thank you for supporting me. I know this isn't the marriage either of us wanted for ourselves, but I'm grateful that you're standing by me and I promise to do the same for you."

The tears glimmering in her eyes were unexpected, and they stirred something in his gut he hadn't been prepared for. Was it sympathy? No, something deeper. Like maybe the friendship that had begun before he'd realized Emma Jane had set him up wasn't completely dead.

He swallowed the rising emotion and let go of Emma Jane's hand, turning to his mother. "Emma Jane is my wife. She is a Jackson and should be afforded every courtesy the name entails."

Henry coughed. "Jasper is right. What's done is done, and even if we could undo it, it would only bring more scandal to the family. We need to make the best of things."

Jasper noticed he gave Constance a slight squeeze before letting her go. The small affection between his father and mother made him even more grateful for his father's support.

Which made Jasper feel even worse. As difficult as his mother could be, he did love her. After all, he'd spent years playing her society games, entertaining the young ladies she deemed suitable and generally tolerating all of her misguided attempts at arranging his life. Perhaps he shouldn't have been so accommodating, then she might be more understanding of the desires of his heart.

At least his father appeared to be more understanding. He looked at Emma Jane with an expression of warmth that convinced Jasper that things would eventually work out. "Emma Jane is also right. We should be doing what we can to support Jasper. Doing everything we can to assist him will keep him much safer than if we're working against him."

Jasper's father held out his hand to Jasper. "I promise not to interfere. And if there are resources I can provide, say the word, and it's yours."

This time, the victory felt real as Jasper shook his father's hand. Even though Jasper could tell his mother was holding back tears. A Jackson did not cry in public, but he knew his mother would be home and in bed with a headache later, the acceptable excuse for sobbing her heart out.

He should feel bad, and part of him did, but he was used to his mother brandishing tears to manipulate people's feelings. More important, though, were the tears that needed to be shed for a woman who had no one to cry for her.

That had to be his focus. Not guilt over everyone else's overwrought emotions.

Jasper looked over at Emma Jane, then back at his father.

"Keep Emma Jane safe." Then he took another deep breath. "I'm sure everything will be fine, but if something should happen to me, take care of her."

"I will."

Two words, as solemn as the wedding vows he'd spoken. His father would keep the promise, just as Jasper would keep his.

"I don't need to be kept safe," Emma Jane huffed, but her tigress look faded as his father met her eyes.

An unspoken agreement seemed to pass between them as his father turned his attention back to Jasper. "I'm going to get your mother home. I'll let you have a private moment to say goodbye to your bride."

His parents turned away, leaving Jasper alone with Emma Jane.

"I think we've said all we need to say," Jasper stated tersely.

"I meant what I said about helping you."

"You can't ride out with us."

Emma Jane nodded slowly. "I wasn't asking to. But I'll be talking to the women, and I will get information to assist you."

Her plan seemed harmless enough, but that was precisely the problem. Nothing about the people he pursued was harmless, and even if the women here knew something they could use, Emma Jane knowing could put her in danger.

"Please don't." He took her hands in his. "I know you mean well. But they will kill you, Emma Jane. If they think you know anything that can hurt them, they will kill you."

He hated being so blunt with her, but he didn't know any other way to put it.

"Don't you remember?" she said, too lightly to be anything than covering up her pain. "Everyone thinks I'm an idiot. The only perceived threat people see in me is that I've dashed the marital aspirations of every woman in this town. Instead of fearing that the bandits will kill me, you should be more fearful that one of your adoring fans will do it so they can take my place."

A little harsh, but as he remembered the vitriol aimed at Emma Jane since their wedding, she probably wasn't too far off the mark. Every woman in town wished them ill. No, not them. *Emma Jane.* She'd snatched the town's most eligible bachelor out from their noses. Despite their marriage, the rumors and innuendoes hadn't stopped.

"I'm sorry," Jasper said quietly. "I wish it were easier for you."

Oddly enough, he spoke the truth. Emma Jane hadn't been the first to try to trap him into marriage. Every girl in town had, at some point, contrived some scheme to attempt to compromise herself with him. Emma Jane had merely been the one to succeed. And they all hated her for it.

"It will be," Emma Jane reassured him with a small smile. "Once I help you bring down the bandits, everyone will see that I am a credit to you. A credit to this town. A woman worthy of respect."

"You don't need to put your life at risk for that. I promise you, Emma Jane, once this is all over, I will do everything I can to fix things. But for now, you have to trust me. Your respectability is not worth your life. Continue to occupy yourself with the pastor's ministry, but don't get involved with this case."

She appeared to consider his words, nodding slowly.

"I really do have to go." Then he locked eyes with her, squeezing her hand. "The most important part of marriage to me, the part ours is lacking, is trust. Trust me, and stay out of this. If you do this, our marriage will have the foundation it needs for us to have a future. Do you understand?"

Emma Jane's eyes filled with tears as she nodded again. Maybe there was hope for their relationship, after all.

As they started to turn to leave, Mary and Pastor Lassiter entered the office.

"I was just coming to find you," Emma Jane said, a happy smile finally filling her face.

As much as everyone talked about Emma Jane's unfortunate appearance, Jasper couldn't help but think that many of them had never seen Emma Jane smile. When she smiled, it lit up her whole face, and even her eyes sparkled. Jasper had escorted many of the town's beauties, and not one had a smile like Emma Jane's. Jasper shook his head. These thoughts had no business popping up. Not when he had so many more important matters to think of.

Pastor Lassiter returned her smile. "I'm glad to have run into the both of you. Your wedding was such a rushed affair, and then everything that happened with Rose, I fear that I haven't done my duty by the both of you."

"We understand, Pastor," Jasper said smoothly. "I've also been occupied. The remaining bandits still need to be caught, and I've accepted a deputy position to help make it happen."

Pastor Lassiter's brow furrowed. "You should be spending your time getting to know your bride. Emma Jane's a lovely woman, and she needs the support of her husband right now."

Why was everyone so worried about Emma Jane? She'd gotten what she wanted—the Jackson name. In the meantime, there were some very bad men on the loose, and another young woman potentially in danger.

"Emma Jane will be fine. We have the rest of our lives to get to know each other." Jasper didn't want to add that since there was no love between them, they'd need all that time—and more—to bridge the gap between them.

But if they could build the trust he asked for, perhaps, as Pastor Lassiter had said the day of their wedding, love could grow.

"People are talking," the pastor said slowly. "I don't like to give credence to gossip, but in Emma Jane's case, the longer you remain absent from your wife, the worse it will be for her."

The pained expression on Emma Jane's face almost made him feel guilty. He'd been busy for most of the time in the days since their wedding, but he'd seen how people had treated her at the wedding and at their reception. None of the women from good families even spoke to Emma Jane, and all of the men had apologized to him for the behavior of their wives and daughters.

But it would blow over. Gossip always did. Soon enough, people would be clamoring for invitations for tea with Emma Jane, and they'd be looking for her sponsorship at their events. The Jackson name and fortune had that effect on people.

Ignoring the prickle at the back of his neck, Jasper replied, "No one ever died from gossip. The longer we delay in finding and rescuing Daisy, the more her life is at risk. As I said, my wife will be fine."

But something tugged at him as he remembered talking to Emma Jane when they were trapped in the mine, and how hurt she'd been by all the women mocking her dress, whispering about how her father had gambled away all their money, and worse—her sister's hand in marriage.

Maybe no one had ever died from gossip, but he'd seen how it had broken Emma Jane's heart.

"I'm sorry." He held out his hand to her. "I'm so used to people talking about me, I suppose I hadn't considered much about how it might be hurtful to you. But I have to go with the posse today. They're counting on me. I should be back by supper—we can talk then. I promise we'll figure something out."

The lines in Emma Jane's forehead disappeared, even though Pastor Lassiter still looked concerned. But it was the best he could do for now. If the bandits weren't stopped, how many others would be in danger? He'd do what he could to make more of an effort with Emma Jane. Maybe he'd talk to his friend Will about how to balance life as a lawman and making time for family. Of course, Will's engagement was as new as Jasper's marriage, but surely the other man would have some advice. He only hoped that Emma Jane had the wisdom to stay away from the case.

The humiliation of sitting and listening to the women mocking her in church was nothing compared to the fact that Jasper didn't seem to take the gossip she faced seriously. But of course it wasn't he who was called the names. A woman finds herself in a compromising position, and she is all sorts of evil. But what of the man? No one spews insults at him or tries to tell him that there is something wrong with him. Since their wedding, Jasper was perfectly able to carry on with his life with no ill effects.

Emma Jane watched as her husband justified his actions to the pastor. Jasper honestly didn't think he'd done anything wrong. But as Jasper pointed out that a woman's life was in jeopardy, how could Emma Jane argue? It seemed selfish to speak up and say that Pastor Lassiter was right—she did need him. Both in defense against the women at church and with his mother.

Jasper bowed his head slightly. "I'm sorry, Pastor. I really am. But I do need to get going. The posse is leaving soon, and I need to be with them."

Then, without waiting for anyone's response, Jasper turned and walked away.

It shouldn't have hurt, since Emma Jane knew he was leaving, but the farther he went, the bigger the empty space in her heart became.

Mary came and put her arm around Emma Jane. "It will be all right. Hopefully, they catch the bandits soon and they won't have to keep rushing off. Will seemed confident that they were close to finding them. Their most recent lead was promising, he said."

Far more information than Jasper had given Emma Jane. Was it wrong to envy her friend and the open communication Mary and Will had?

"I hope so." She turned to Pastor Lassiter. "In the meantime, I believe you were saying that the church needed additional assistance with the women you're caring for right now. What can I do to help?"

Though the pastor's brow remained furrowed, he gave a smile. "It's as I keep telling everyone, Emma Jane. You have a good heart. Once the Jacksons figure that out, they'll be grateful to have you in their family. You've already done so much, and I'm proud to have you in our church. As for what you can do…"

Mary stopped him. "Oh, no, you don't. First, we haven't eaten. While I'm sure the Jackson chef is wonderful, you can't tell me that the food is nearly as good as the wholesome meals Maddie fixes. And then Emma Jane and I are going to sit down and catch up on everything that's gone on around here lately. After that, you can put Emma Jane to work. It'll be waiting."

Emma Jane had always admired Mary's take-charge attitude. But now, faced with a friend who actually cared about her, Emma Jane couldn't help the tears that filled her eyes. She hadn't realized just how hard it had been on her own. Though she and Mary had only recently become close, Emma Jane couldn't imagine how she'd managed all these years without Mary's friendship. She'd thought she'd found that kind of confidant in Jasper, but since their marriage, he felt more like a stranger. No, worse than a stranger.

"None of that." Mary gave her a quick squeeze. "What did I tell you about tears ruining your complexion? You'll feel better once you've gotten some food in you."

Pastor Lassiter grinned. "And people wonder how *I* manage with all the people in my home. They should see how well the people in my home do all the managing for me."

They all chuckled together as they exited the church, then rounded the corner to the parsonage. Mary's younger brother and sisters were chasing one another in the backyard, playing some kind of game. The giggles filled Emma Jane's soul. She hadn't heard laughter at all since she'd been staying in the Jackson mansion. Even in her own home, laughter had often been missing. But here, at the Lassiter house, where Mary and her siblings were staying until their house could be built, merriment abounded. If Emma Jane could have one wish about her future with Jasper, it would be that their home would be more like this place than where they'd both grown up.

Emma Jane shook her head. She shouldn't be thinking such things. She had to believe that she and Jasper would find their way…somehow.

But how were they supposed to do that when he kept shutting her out? He said that it was for her safety, but that was what men always said to women. Jasper and Will had made Mary stay behind the night of the brothel fire for her safety, but Mary had followed them. And even though she had been in danger, Mary herself had told Emma Jane that it had been her quick thinking that had saved them. When the bandits had them all trapped, Mary distracted the bandits by throwing the lit lamps at them, giving Will, Jasper and herself time to get away.

Even now, word about Mary's bravery was getting out around town. She was a hero.

As they walked toward the parsonage, Emma Jane couldn't help but wonder if a heroic act of her own might make the town look at her differently.

So what could Emma do that wouldn't upset Jasper…?

"Mary!"

The youngest little girl came running up to them, and Mary swung her up in her arms. "How's my sweet little Nugget?"

"Hungry! You've been gone ever so long, and Maddie said we couldn't start eating until you and Uncle Frank got here."

Emma Jane couldn't help but smile at the child's honesty. She'd heard that the younger Stone children had taken to calling Pastor Lassiter "Uncle Frank," but experiencing it for herself warmed her heart. Just last winter, Pastor Lassiter's wife and all of his children but Annabelle had succumbed to the illness that had run rampant through their community. Many families had lost loved ones, and it had seemed horribly unfair to Emma Jane that the good pastor had suffered such a tragedy. Yet here, in the happy chaos of his yard, Emma Jane saw no evidence of loss, but of the joy of living.

If only she could capture some of that for herself.

"They're something else, aren't they?" Pastor Lassiter's voice came beside her.

"Yes, they are." She turned to him, noticing the happiness on his face. "Can I ask you what may be an impertinent question?"

"I'm not sure you're capable of asking an impertinent question." His eyes twinkled. "Ask away."

Emma Jane took a deep breath. "How did you do it? The past year, you've faced unimaginable losses, and yet here you are, still opening your heart and home with such joy?"

"That's a good question."

Emma Jane watched as he looked around the yard, seeming to take in every detail. "I think it's several things. The first is that the human capacity to love is limited by our humanness. But when we allow that love space within us to be filled with the Lord, our capacity to love is limitless."

Put that way, it was easy to understand as Emma Jane pictured the many folks who came through their church and their community, as well as the nearby communities Pastor Lassiter served so tirelessly. She'd wondered how one person could accomplish all of that.

"How do you get the Lord to fill that love space?" Immediately, Emma Jane thought of Mrs. Jackson. Perhaps relying on her own power to love her mother-in-law was where she was making the mistake. Could God give her the strength to love Mrs. Jackson?

"Ask Him. Read your Bible. And let Him work in you."

Then Pastor Jackson turned to her and looked at her intently. "The other thing that got me through was the realization that we must see everything that comes our way as an opportunity from the Lord. We remember to thank Him for the good things, but we also need to take the time to look at the bad and ask the Lord what He's trying to teach us through the situation." Clearing his throat, he waited a beat before saying, "For me, I learned that while it's easy to love the Lord during the good times, we must also cling to Him through the bad. Love Him just as much in the hard times, because the kind of the love that most honors God is the love that endures all things."

Still, Emma Jane couldn't imagine the strength it took to endure all of the loss in Pastor Lassiter's life. He took her hand.

"I know that your marriage, and the events surrounding it, are less than ideal. But don't think for a moment that the Lord has abandoned you. Draw near to Him, and I promise that you will make it through in a way far more profound than you could have imagined. He has good plans for you, Emma Jane, and I am praying you will cling to Him as He sees you through."

Tears pricked the backs of her eyes. No one had expressed such a deep belief in her before. And yet, as she thought back to the pastor's earlier words about the love of God, she realized that he wasn't just expressing his own personal belief about her, but God's belief in her.

"Thank you." Emma Jane squeezed his hand. "I appreciate you sharing your heart with me."

Pastor Lassiter gave a small smile. "If it makes you

feel any better, I will also tell you that there are days I miss my sweet Catherine so much it hurts. It seems brutally unfair that I had to lose her. But as it says in Job, I can't accept only the good and not the bad from the Lord. It's all right to feel that way. Just keep giving it to God, and He will be faithful in standing beside you."

His openness touched Emma Jane deeper than any of his sermons ever had. She wanted that kind of relationship with the Lord. That depth of love and trust. She'd do as he said—when she got home, she'd spend as much time as she could reading her Bible. There wasn't that much else to do at the Jackson mansion, anyway. She might as well spend the time being productive.

However, before she could formulate a response, Nugget came barreling toward them.

"Uncle Frank! Let's eat! Maddie made fried chicken, and I've got my eye on one of the legs."

From matters of the heart to matters of the stomach. Emma Jane couldn't help the joy welling up in her at the absolute delight of being with this family. *Oh, Lord*, she prayed, *please let me find this joy in my own home.*

Chapter Three

Emma Jane's day with Mary had been exactly what she'd needed. Not only had she found incredible peace talking with Pastor Lassiter, but the afternoon spent visiting with Mary had given her a new strength. Their friend Polly, who was also staying at the parsonage with her family to help with the Stone children, had joined them, and Emma Jane could honestly not recall a more enjoyable afternoon. Then the three girls went to the barn, where the women from the fire were staying, and they were able to tend to some of the women's needs. Emma Jane hadn't had much of a chance to chat with her friend Nancy, so she'd promised to come back the following morning.

Which left her sitting in her luxurious bedroom in the Jackson mansion, Bible in front of her, and unable to sleep. The past several nights had been spent in misery, and now she felt so happy it seemed a sin to close her eyes.

Well, that and the fact that Jasper had not returned by suppertime as he'd promised.

Had he been hurt? Killed?

Or was it like all the promises she'd heard all her life from her father, the ones that consisted of "Things will be different this time, you'll see."

Nothing in her life had ever become different, not even when the one thing that was supposed to make a difference, marrying Jasper Jackson, had happened.

Floorboards creaked on the stairs, and Emma Jane jumped up. The Jacksons had already turned in for the evening, and surely by now the servants were already in bed. Which meant it had to be Jasper.

She opened the door and Jasper jumped.

"Emma Jane! What are you doing up?"

"Reading my Bible." She smiled and opened the door wider. "How was your expedition? Was it successful?"

Jasper shook his head. "Another dead end."

"Come in. Why don't you tell me about it?"

Jasper looked at her like she was crazy. "I can't come in your bedroom." He glanced at her nightgown. "You're not even properly dressed."

With a sigh, Emma Jane pulled her shawl more tightly around her. "My nightgown is much more modest than what half the women wear around town. Besides, we're married." She smiled up at him. "I've already been compromised, so it's not as though you can compromise me any worse."

But he glowered at her words. "That's not funny."

Emma Jane sighed. "I'm sorry. I was just trying to lighten up a bad situation. I didn't mean to hit a raw nerve. Can we pretend I didn't make a thoughtless comment, and then you come in and tell me about your progress? I'd like to work on our friendship, if that's all right with you."

When he didn't answer, Emma Jane continued. "Besides, I meant what I said about wanting to help. Since you won't let me *do* anything, at least let me listen. One of the women today said that having someone listen to her troubles was help enough for her."

For a moment, she thought he was going to snap at her or comment about how it wasn't time to work on their marriage, but then he sighed and took a step toward her door. "I suppose I can spare a few minutes."

What happened to the Jasper she used to like? The man who used to like her?

"The chair by the window is comfortable. You could sit there if you like." It sounded strange to her to be so formal with her own husband. Then again, it still sounded strange for her to refer to herself as having a husband.

"I'm glad you're comfortable here," Jasper said as he sat, settling against the soft velvety fabric.

"I'm still getting used to it all, to be honest. I've never had such luxuries, and having a staff is still intimidating."

He laughed. Not the fake laugh she'd heard from across the room at so many social functions where she'd stood in the corner, praying no one would notice her. Rather, it was the same warm sound she'd heard from him when they'd gotten to know each other during the mine cave-in. After their rescue, they'd recuperated at a nearby lake resort because it was closer than returning to town. A stay that had been extended to a week due to a snow storm making the roads impassable.

There, she'd thought they'd become friends. Stuck in a hotel with no one but the proprietors and Will and Mary for company, they'd formed a bond of sorts, and their easy camaraderie had made her wonder why they hadn't gotten to know each other sooner.

Emma Jane hadn't heard that laugh since their wedding.

"I've missed that sound," she said quietly, hoping it wasn't the wrong thing to say. She'd already blundered in mentioning their past, but hopefully this would be a happier reminder.

Fortunately, Jasper rewarded her with a smile. "I guess we haven't had much to laugh about. And I haven't exactly warmed to your attempts at trying to ease the situation. Sometimes I feel selfish for enjoying life when a woman is dead because of me and I've yet to make it up to her."

Back to sober Jasper. And yet, not. Because where he'd once shut her out, here he was opening up.

Could their relationship be turning a new corner as she'd hoped?

Emma Jane sat on her bed, pleased that at least Jasper had made himself comfortable on her chair.

"I don't think she saved your life so you would feel guilty for living." She gestured to the Bible she'd been reading. "I've been reading in John, where Jesus says that He's come so people can have abundant life. I know it's not an exact parallel, but Christ's sacrifice was meant for us to be able to do good with our lives. Surely Mel dying for you was similar."

Jasper stared at her for a moment, and Emma Jane felt silly for saying such things. Her mother and sister used to mock her for all of her "Bible nonsense," and even her father told her it wasn't seemly for a woman to be so familiar with Scriptures.

"I guess I hadn't thought of it that way," Jasper said

slowly. "You used to say things like that in Sunday school, things that made me think. I'd forgotten until now."

Emma Jane felt her face warm, just as it had when their Sunday school teacher had complimented her. The other girls in the class, however, had teased her mercilessly. On top of all of her other faults, she'd been too bold in showing off her knowledge.

"Why are you embarrassed?" Jasper looked at her with an intensity that made her feel even more unclothed than she already was. "You used to say such interesting things in Sunday school, then you stopped."

Then, with a note of what sounded like regret, he said, "And then you stopped coming at all."

"I was tired of being made fun of by the other girls." The words came out almost as a whisper, and her chest burned as she said them.

"I'm sorry. I never noticed."

He truly did sound as though he felt badly for not noticing. But no one noticed Emma Jane. Not unless they found something to tease her about. Except Jasper. He'd never teased her.

"It's all right. I stopped going to most of the church functions and took to reading the Bible on my own. I know it's not seemly for a woman to spend so much time reading the Bible, but sometimes it was all I had."

"Why did you come to the church picnic?"

Back to their shared history and events that they both seemed like they wanted to forget but couldn't.

"My mother made me. I didn't want to go. I knew word of my father's bad night at cards had gotten out. But my mother said it was our only hope."

"Marrying me." His voice came out raspy, like it

hurt to say the words as much as it hurt Emma Jane to admit her shame.

"Yes." And then, because she couldn't help it, "I'm sorry. I never meant any of this to happen."

Flora's words at the church came back to her. "I heard some of the talk that's gotten around about what happened. I want you to know…"

"Stop. Please." He ran a hand over his face. "I thought I could do this. I thought I wanted to get through it, but…"

Jasper let out a long sigh. "I want to understand, Emma Jane. But there's still so much of me that thinks about what was taken away from me, and it's hard to let go. I need you to be patient with me."

Her chest was so tight it almost hurt to breathe. How she managed to get out the words, she didn't know. "Of course. I…"

The rest, she couldn't say. Because as much as she knew that Jasper resented not having a lot of choices in life, the choices he did have were a far sight better than anything Emma Jane had ever had. He acted as though she'd wanted to marry him. Not that she'd wanted to marry anyone else, of course, but just like Jasper had said he'd wanted to choose his own wife, she'd wanted to find her own husband.

Granted, what she wanted was probably a lot more than what Jasper wanted for himself. But for Emma Jane, she wanted a husband who wanted her. Who didn't marry her out of obligation. Who enjoyed spending time with her…and genuinely liked and loved her…

Didn't he realize that, in their marriage, all of her hopes and dreams had been dashed, as well?

She swallowed the lump in her throat. "I didn't mean

for us to quarrel. Perhaps we can talk about something safe. Like what you're reading in your Bible."

Emma Jane forced a smile to her lips, hoping that, at least in this, they could find common ground.

Only, with the dark look that crossed Jasper's face, she knew she'd missed the mark—again.

"I don't read my Bible."

She'd hoped, in marrying a man active in their church, that their faith would eventually bring them together. Apparently, even that hope was to be dashed.

"Why not?"

Jasper shrugged. "I learn plenty from Pastor Lassiter's sermons. I know enough about God that I don't need to keep studying. After all, I've been attending church since I was a child."

Jasper might have grown up wealthy, but as Emma Jane recalled his mother's words earlier about giving money to the church in lieu of helping out, she wondered if he might have grown up poor indeed.

"But Pastor Lassiter talks about the importance of reading God's Word."

Jasper shrugged. "And he reads it to us every Sunday. Why should I do more?"

"Because it deepens your relationship with the Lord."

He looked thoughtful for a moment. "I suppose that's why you always made such insightful comments in Sunday school. How often do you read your Bible?"

"Every day." Emma Jane hoped her words didn't sound too prideful. When she'd made a similar comment to one of the girls at church, she'd chastised Emma Jane for being too full of herself.

Jasper didn't say anything for a long while, and as the silence began to grow uncomfortable, Emma Jane wondered what she could say that wouldn't cause more strife between them.

Fortunately, Jasper's stomach rumbled loudly, and it sent Emma Jane into motion.

"I just realized, the staff has all gone to bed, but if you're hungry, or you want some tea, I could get you something."

Finally. A small smile teased the corners of Jasper's lips. "Mother will be furious if she finds you in the kitchen." Then, in a mocking voice, he said, "Don't you know that is what the help is for? We do not belong in their domain, just as they do not belong in ours."

Emma Jane giggled. "That sounds exactly like her."

"I've heard it my whole life." Jasper yawned at the same time his stomach rumbled again.

"It would be no trouble to get you a sandwich. I spent all night working the night of the brothel fire to make sure everyone was taken care of. Cook and I became friends of sorts, and I think she'll be happy if I get you something without disturbing her."

Jasper sat up slightly. "I didn't realize you spent so much time helping that night."

"Of course. I couldn't sleep, knowing that you, Will and Mary were confronting a dangerous situation. Then, when Mary and Rose came here, telling us of the fire, I had to do what I could. Rose was with the doctor, and poor Mary was exhausted and famished. I had to make sure she had something, and then, with you and Will still out there, I knew that you'd need something, as well. I didn't sleep at all that night."

And then Jasper had been too busy talking to the authorities to talk to her. The only reason Emma Jane even knew the full story of what had happened in the brothel was because Mary had told her. Though that fact hurt, what wounded her even more was the surprised expression on Jasper's face. True, he had been too busy to notice Emma Jane's contributions, but the fact that it didn't occur to him that she'd want to help, well, that seemed like a far greater sin than Jasper's abandonment.

That was the trouble with marrying someone you barely knew. Jasper didn't know that for someone like Emma Jane, the easiest thing to do was to step in and work, because when you worked, you didn't have to talk. Because talking meant that people would notice her and make fun of her. No one ever seemed to pay any mind to the workers. Probably why Jasper had never noticed her, either.

"I'm sorry I never thanked you for your help," he said huskily.

"It was a busy night. Your mother rushed you into bed and had the doctor in there with you so quickly, I'm sure there were a lot of things you didn't notice."

The weariness on Jasper's face seemed to increase as the lamp flickered beside him. She hated continuing to make him talk, but they seemed to almost be getting along. Could they regain ground as friends?

"I think Pastor Lassiter has a point about us needing time together to get to know each other. I don't understand what's fueling your need to help this Daisy person, and you don't understand anything about me." Emma Jane pulled her shawl tighter around her. "Why don't I get you something to eat, and when I get back, you can tell me something you think I should know about you."

At least, with Jasper leading the conversation, it

would keep her from making any more missteps that would drive them apart.

Hesitating before heading for the door, she watched the play of emotions on her husband's face. Could he see that she was offering him an olive branch? A chance to begin their marriage as it should have been? Asking him to love her was too much—Emma Jane knew that—but surely peaceful coexistence wasn't so far out of their reach.

After what seemed like ages, Jasper's lips turned upward into the grin that was rumored to melt every woman's heart this side of the Divide. Emma Jane had never been one of the girls to giggle and swoon over Jasper's famed good looks, but if he gave her many grins like that, she could easily find herself wanting to. However, a man's appearance faded over time, and Emma Jane hoped that what she found beneath was the same man she'd grown to like at the church picnic.

"All right. Don't put any pickles on my sandwich. Mother seems to think they're my favorite, but I really can't stand her pickles." He gave her a wink, then settled back into her chair.

No pickles. The simple request seemed to be the beginning of a friendship as Emma Jane went downstairs to the kitchen. There, she found Cook already at the stove, busying herself with the kettle.

"What are you doing up?" Emma Jane crossed the room and reached for a mug. Though Mrs. Jackson would probably disapprove of Jasper not being served on fine china, the mugs held more, and he seemed like he could use a larger cup of tea.

"I heard Mr. Jasper come home. He doesn't take good

care of himself, so I thought I'd prepare some food for him."

In her short time at the Jackson mansion, Emma Jane had learned that everything was about catering to Jasper—when it wasn't about Mrs. Jackson, of course. But his mother's primary concern, other than reputation, was making sure that Jasper never wanted for anything.

"I should have known. I came down to do the very thing myself."

Cook pointed to a plate on the table. "Sandwiches for Mr. Jasper, just the way he likes."

Emma Jane couldn't help but notice the pickle hanging out the sides. She went over and removed it.

"What are you doing with Mrs. Jackson's prized pickles? Those are Mr. Jasper's favorite."

"When I asked him what he'd like, he mentioned that he'd prefer not to have pickles." Emma Jane hesitated, wondering if she should share his secret.

Cook nodded slowly. "I wondered who'd been leaving pickles in strange places in the dining room. Poor Mr. Jasper probably didn't want to hurt his mother's feelings. Mrs. Jackson prides herself on those pickles, though I don't know a single soul who can tolerate them. I'll keep that in mind for the future."

It was a simple conversation about pickles, but it told something about Jasper's character that Emma Jane hadn't been expecting. As much as he played the role of a carefree playboy, Jasper's compassion ran deep. Rather than hurt his mother's feelings, he'd gone along with the charade of liking her pickles.

As Emma Jane finished preparing Jasper's tea, she thought more about Jasper's compassion. At the church picnic, when everyone else mocked Emma Jane's out-moded dress and the ridiculous way her mother had painted her face to attract attention, Jasper had reprimanded the girls who'd mistreated her in front of him. He'd spoken to her with kindness and treated her with dignity even when everyone else was whispering about her father losing everything at the gambling halls. He'd even promised to help her find a way to get her family out of the mess.

Of course, he hadn't meant to marry her, and he'd said as much. Poor Jasper had only thought to do a good deed for Emma Jane, and she'd repaid him by forcing a marriage he didn't want.

She sighed and put the sandwich and tea on a tray. No, she hadn't forced the marriage. Her parents had. And when she'd tried telling everyone that it wasn't Jasper's fault they'd been trapped in a mine together and that nothing had happened requiring marriage, everyone ignored her.

When she arrived back in her room, Jasper lay sprawled in the chair, his mouth hanging open, snoring softly. His thick dark hair had fallen over closed eyes. The rugged lines had disappeared from his face, and he appeared so peaceful, full of calm and innocence. Looking at him like this, Emma Jane understood why his looks beguiled so many. He seemed so handsome and debonair. So…perfect. Everyone seemed to want that perfection, and yet, the more time Emma Jane spent with Jasper, the more she realized there was so much more to him. Which was strange, because she barely knew him at all.

After setting the tray down on a nearby table, Emma Jane took one of the blankets from her bed and tucked

it around Jasper. She'd have liked to have moved him,
but she wasn't that strong, and she didn't want to disturb
him. He seemed to be sleeping comfortably enough, and
because she'd napped on that very chair a time or two,
Emma Jane knew he'd be fine.

Then, because it seemed like the right thing to do,
Emma Jane bent and kissed him on the forehead. "May
God bless you and keep you."

She crossed the room, turned out the lights, then
climbed back into her own bed and settled into sleep.

Jasper woke with a crick in his neck, feeling more
rested than he had in days, yet not entirely comfortable.
He opened his eyes, then realized where he was. Emma
Jane's room. He must have fallen asleep when she'd
gone to get him something to eat. He glanced around
the room and noticed the tray sitting on a nearby table.

Dear, sweet girl. His stomach rumbled, so he went
ahead and grabbed the sandwich. The tea was cold, but
it quenched his thirst. He ate and drank, enjoying the
meal she'd prepared for him. Even the lack of pickles
on his sandwich warmed his heart. True, his mother
would have done the same and brought him a tray. But
something about the fact that Emma Jane had taken it
upon herself to tend to him was endearing. She hadn't
needed to go to all that trouble.

As if to remind him of her presence, Emma Jane gave
a small sigh as she shifted in her bed. He looked over
at her, noticing that she lay curled up in the blanket,
almost like a child. Her hair lay spread out across the
pillow, a deep honey shade that was neither brown nor
blond, but a combination of the two. He'd heard people talk about how plain Emma Jane's looks were, but

watching her sleep, he thought her quite lovely. True, she didn't have the classical beauty that seemed to be prized in society, but there was something genuinely attractive about her innocent face and lack of artifice.

Emma Jane sighed yet again and mumbled something incoherent. Jasper turned away. He shouldn't be intruding on her private moments of rest.

She'd been kind to him the night before, trying to talk to him and find out what he was really like. For all her faults, Emma Jane was trying to be a good wife. But could she make up for the fact that she'd used him so badly?

He remembered how she'd made a point to tell him that she'd complied with his request, not investigating on her own and relying on him to share information.

Emma Jane was doing her part, and it was time he thought about doing his. Letting go of his resentment of the situation and giving her an honest chance. He'd told her last night that he was finding it difficult. But for as hard as he saw Emma Jane trying, he knew he owed her nothing less.

Jasper folded the blanket Emma Jane had put around him. Her consideration gave him pause. He hadn't known that she'd helped out the night of the brothel fire. Nor had he known that she'd been helping with the women displaced by the brothel fire. In some ways, it shamed Jasper to realize that as angry as he was about his marriage, he hadn't at all thought about what kind of woman he'd ended up with.

Somehow, in all of this mess, he'd found himself attached to a good woman.

As he placed the blanket on the chair, the bedroom door opened.

"Jasper! What are you doing in here?"

His mother's gasp jolted him and, from the startled sound in the bed, Emma Jane, as well.

"Good morning, Mother."

"Answer my question."

Jasper wanted to laugh at his mother's insistence. He was a married man, and still she concerned herself with the propriety of being in a woman's—no, his wife's—bedchamber.

"Emma Jane heard me come in late, and she wanted to be sure I was taken care of." He gestured to the empty plate. "I fell asleep in the chair, and she was kind enough to let me rest."

"She should have alerted the staff." His mother's face was pinched in an unpleasant expression. "Speaking of which, one of the maids says she saw Emma Jane leaving the kitchen last night. I cannot have her interfering with the staff's business."

He knew his marriage had been hard on his mother, who'd dreamed of a big society wedding with a woman of her choosing. But as he'd told her the day before, they had to come to terms with the fact that life had other plans for them.

"Emma Jane was being a good wife," Jasper said in a carefully modulated tone. "I was grateful for her kindness to me."

"I see." She turned her attention to Emma Jane, who'd just woken and now sat up in bed, pulling her covers around her. "In the future, please leave the care of my son to our staff."

Was his mother seriously telling Emma Jane not to take care of him? Did she truly expect that he and Emma Jane were going to continue to live in this house as strangers? But as he saw the tension in his mother's elegant figure, he knew that was exactly what she was thinking. His mother never thought that he and Emma Jane would have a real marriage.

Jasper swallowed. He'd never imagined it, either. But he had hoped that, over time, he and Emma Jane could at least find a peaceful way to live together. Last night, she had reached out to him in an attempt to make that happen.

Constance's edict would only serve to drive a wedge between their already fragile marriage.

"I like Emma Jane's care, Mother. So if it's no trouble to her, then I see no need for her to rouse the servants on my behalf." Jasper looked directly at Emma Jane, hoping she understood that he was on her side.

"I see. However, I do want to stress that your *wife* should not be in the kitchen." His mother turned and sauntered out of the room, leaving the door open behind her.

Although Emma Jane's comment last night about her already being compromised had rubbed him the wrong way, he couldn't help but think it now. What did his mother think she was saving him from? They'd already been forced to marry.

"I'm sorry about that," Jasper said to her. "She'll warm up to you eventually."

"It's all right." Emma Jane stared at the blankets on the bed, not meeting his gaze. "I'm sure it must be hard for her to have you married to someone like me. I'm not exactly the society darling she'd hoped for."

Her words shamed him. Not because she was trying to, but because that's what Emma Jane seemed to truly believe. He thought back to the way the women had teased her at the church picnic, how Flora Montgomery had tried to persuade him not to speak to her because of the scandal surrounding her father's gambling losses. Even at their wedding, which was supposed to quiet all the talk about Emma Jane's fall from grace, he'd heard the whispers disparaging her character.

Jasper knew none of it was true. He'd assumed everyone else would figure out the truth sooner or later, as well. But it hadn't occurred to him that Emma Jane believed herself deserving of the censure.

"Any man would be honored to be married to someone like you," Jasper said gruffly.

Emma Jane finally met his eyes. "You aren't."

He'd forgotten how direct she could be. When they first spoke at the church picnic, he'd admired that about her. Even respected the fact that she'd come right out and said that if he married her, it would solve her problems. But that was before she'd tricked him into compromising her. Before she'd demonstrated her lack of trust in him.

"No man wants to be made a fool of."

He hated the way she shrank back at his words. Emma Jane wanted to be friends and recapture what they'd had before they'd been forced to marry. But how could they get past it, when she had no idea what she'd stolen from him?

A chance to fall in love. To have a loving home. A family of his own. Perhaps he and Emma Jane could get to a place where they could find a way to have children. But there'd never be the same loving glances he saw Will and Mary exchange. He'd never know what it was like to have someone see all the parts of him and love him, really love him, for who he was.

Maybe Jasper had been the fool. This whole mess had started because seeing Will again and meeting Emma Jane had made him want to be a better man. To be known for something other than the wealthy playboy who stole women's hearts. He'd thought he wanted a life of substance instead of playing to society's whims.

Yet here he was, stuck in a marriage of convenience because he'd tried to be the man of honor he wanted to be.

Tears rolled down Emma Jane's cheeks, and he knew he should be sorry for them. Part of him was, but the other part of him still mourned the life he could never have.

Chapter Four

When Jasper finally arrived downstairs, he found his mother in her sitting room, sorting through envelopes. She looked up at him and held out several in his direction.

"Do you see these?"

"Yes, Mother." He tried to sound as accommodating as possible, but he found it more difficult than usual. They often had this conversation about invitations. All the brides she'd hoped to snare for him. Now that he was married, he'd thought these conversations would end.

"All the best families in town, and not one invitation from them. We're supposed to be the pillars of society, and yet we seem to only be receiving correspondence from the lesser-known families."

"So what would you have me do? Throw her out on the street?"

Jasper gave his mother an icy look, then turned to go into the dining room. After the sandwich Emma Jane had so thoughtfully provided, he wasn't all that hungry. His encounter with his mother had stolen the rest of his appetite. But he could put together a few things to take with him on the trail.

Yesterday's dead end had him wondering. Everything seemed too convenient. The promising lead, and then it suddenly fizzling out. Something was off, and he couldn't put his finger on it. Trouble was, since this was Jasper's first foray into law enforcement, no one else in the sheriff's office took him seriously. Everyone assumed that his desire to take down the rest of the gang was a playboy's whim.

His father sat at the head of the table, and while he appeared to be reading his paper, as soon as Jasper entered the room, he looked up at him.

"Go easy on your mother. It's a rough transition."

"You don't think it's rough on me?" Jasper grumbled, pouring himself a cup of coffee as he sat. While he didn't want his father's lecture, he could use some advice on the case. Or at least in getting the other men to respect him.

The glare he got in response made Jasper feel about five years old. Henry folded the paper, then stared at his son. "Your mother has had one thing driving her all these years—her son marrying well so she could gain the daughter she never had. Your choice in wife is not exactly what she had imagined."

"I didn't choose to marry Emma Jane."

Silence rocked the room for several minutes before Jasper's father answered. "You would have left a girl ruined instead?"

Jasper squeezed his eyes shut, forcing himself not to say something he'd regret. Finally, he took a deep breath, then opened his eyes. "Nothing untoward happened. I told you. But society and honor dictated that we marry. I didn't make the rules, I just follow them. Now that we're married, I have to make the best of it."

"So why are you running away all the time? That doesn't sound like making the *best of it* to me." His father's dark eyes bore deep into him, searching for the truth. Henry had been able to make Jasper come clean on even his worst deeds ever since he was a child.

This, however, was not like the entire plate of tea cakes he'd pilfered, eaten, then promptly became so sick he'd never had the urge to touch one of the dainty delicacies again. And yet, telling his father the truth about his intentions was even more important.

"I'm not running away." Jasper sighed. "If anything, my marriage is a complication getting in the way of what I want to do."

He took a long sip of the cooling coffee, then continued. "Seeing Will again made me realize how little I'd done with my life. Everyone admires Jasper Jackson. But for what? My good looks, my last name, the money I'll inherit when you die? I want to do something meaningful with my life."

With everything that had happened over the past several days, Jasper hadn't been able to express those things. Finally getting it all out made the load feel so much lighter.

"When I helped Will rescue Mary's sister, I realized that in fighting for justice for those who can't fight for themselves, there was so much more to the world than just myself."

Emma Jane's image flashed before his eyes. When they'd been forced to marry, she'd told him the only reason she'd agreed to marry him was to protect her younger sister, Gracie. Had Emma Jane not married

Jasper, Gracie would have been forced to marry one of the most execrable men in town. As part of their marriage agreement, Jasper's father had paid off Emma Jane's father's gambling debts. One of those debts was to a man who'd told Mr. Logan that he'd take Gracie as a wife in lieu of cash. Had Jasper had a sister, would he have done any differently to spare his loved one a miserable future?

Perhaps he and Emma Jane were not so dissimilar, after all.

He only wished he didn't feel so conflicted over his marriage.

One piece of his experiences of late continued to ring true, and that was the thing that drove him in his quest. "Even without my desire to be a better man, there's the fact that a woman gave her life for me. Mel didn't have to take the bullet meant for me, but she did. How do you ignore her dying wish to find and save her sister?"

All these days later, he could still smell the residue of gunpowder mixed with Mel's blood. Jasper had foolishly tried intimidating Ben Perry, leader of the gang he was now pursuing, and Ben's men had opened fire. Jasper should have died, but Mel shielded him. How does a man repay such a sacrifice?

Which was why he'd die before giving up on his quest for Mel. Everything in Mel's life had been about giving her sister a better life. He owed it to her to save Daisy. Married to Emma Jane, Jasper accepted that his other dreams of home and family would be denied. But he would make something meaningful of his life.

"Sounds like some powerful motivation," his father said slowly. "Just remember that when a man marries, his life is no longer his own."

Jasper gave him a long, hard look. He'd already spent time living the life his parents wanted. Just when he thought he'd figured out what he wanted with his life, it seemed life had other plans. How was he supposed to balance his dreams with being a husband?

Emma Jane's ears stung as she stood outside the dining room door. There was a reason for the saying that eavesdroppers never heard good about themselves. But this was more than just hearing bad about herself. Oh, Emma Jane knew that Jasper hadn't wanted to marry her, even without overhearing his conversation with his father. But realizing that Jasper felt like she'd taken away his chance to do something meaningful with his life…

Suddenly she felt very selfish for wanting him by her side to protect her reputation. Jasper wanted to do good in the world, and he wanted to help people. For the first time, she truly heard him as he explained to his father what it meant to save this Daisy person.

Taking a deep breath, Emma Jane stepped into the room. "Jasper's right," she said, not bothering to enter the conversation gracefully. "He's doing something important. Working to bring down a gang of criminals, and saving this woman, those things matter. I'll still be here when he's finished with his mission."

She gave what she hoped was a convincing smile as she turned to serve herself breakfast. While the words sounded like the right thing to say, her stomach churned. It certainly didn't feel right.

But what else was she supposed to do? Emma Jane couldn't argue any of Jasper's proclamations without being the worst kind of heartless, selfish woman there was. It already seemed wrong for her to have become his wife, even though she'd had good reason. Why add more selfishness to her sins?

Jasper and Mr. Jackson stared at her as she took her seat at the table.

"He might not come home," Mr. Jackson said slowly.

Emma Jane shrugged and speared a piece of sausage. "He came home last night. He came home from the fire. Perhaps we need to put our faith in God and pray for his continued safety."

It was a trite answer, but what else did Emma Jane have to give? She focused her attention back on her plate, methodically eating, though she had no appetite. It gave her something to do other than acknowledge the gazes focused on her.

Mr. Jackson coughed. "I suppose that's true. The Lord has protected our Jasper many a time or two."

Even without looking at him, Emma Jane knew Jasper was grinning.

"You remember that time I wanted to pet a bull?"

This got Emma Jane's attention. She looked up at her husband, and sure enough, his face was lit up brighter than the midday sun.

"Your mother still needs smelling salts when you tell that story." Mr. Jackson leaned in toward Emma Jane. "He wasn't more than six or seven years old, and we were visiting friends at a ranch. Jasper saw the bull in the pen and thought that red coat of his was the prettiest thing he ever saw, and he wanted to pet it. Trust me when I say, never attempt to pet a bull."

At this, the two men laughed heartily, and even though Emma Jane hadn't been there, she could imag-

ine the anger of a bull at having a little boy chasing him
around and trying to pet him.

More importantly, though, she couldn't help but feel
a surge of warmth at Mr. Jackson's attempt at trying to
include her. He'd defended their marriage in talking to
Jasper, and even though he'd also defended his wife's
cold attitude, Mr. Jackson seemed to be at least trying
to be on Emma Jane's side.

Of course, marriage wasn't supposed to be about
sides, but what else was Emma Jane supposed to think?

"It must have been something, Mr. Jackson." Emma
Jane smiled warmly at him, trying to show that she,
too, was trying to make the best of a difficult situation.

"You really should call me Henry. We're family
now."

Emma Jane wasn't sure which warmed her the most,
the genuine kindness on the older man's face, or his use
of the word *family*. Perhaps things weren't going to be
so bad, after all.

"Mrs. Jackson said…"

"Constance means well. It's just as I was telling Jasper. Give her time, and she'll warm up to you."

Another expression of understanding. Yes, Emma
Jane had to have hope that things could get better.

At that moment, Mrs. Jackson entered the room.
"What is all this tomfoolery I hear in here?"

Emma Jane tried not to shrink back in her chair,
though she did remain silent. Nothing good ever came
of opening her mouth in front of Mrs. Jackson.

"Jasper was just telling us of his intention to continue working as a lawman. I expressed my concern,
but Emma Jane rightly reminded me that we need to
put our trust in the Lord."

Being so endorsed made Emma Jane sit up a little straighter.

"How dare you!" Mrs. Jackson's voice jolted Emma Jane back to reality. "If it weren't for you driving him away by forcing him to marry you, my son wouldn't be leaving us. And you try to explain it away with faith?"

Mr. Jackson put a hand on her arm. "Now, Constance, you know that's not true. Jasper's involvement in the situation is because he feels obligated to repay the woman who saved his life."

"A woman of no consequence."

Jasper rose from his chair. "I would be dead without her. Surely she deserves to be given some consequence."

His dark eyes flashed as he looked from his mother to his father, then settled on Emma Jane.

She felt small under his scrutiny and, for a moment, hated herself for it. She had nothing to be ashamed of. Even if his mother seemed to think so.

"As for your comments about my wife..." Jasper swallowed as he glanced briefly at his father before bringing his full attention back on Emma Jane.

"She has not driven me away. On the contrary, I have not been the best of husbands by neglecting her of late. I only hope that she is willing to continue to be patient as I bring these bandits to justice and find Daisy."

Was that remorse she heard in his voice? Her heart fluttered in her chest. Perhaps his father's words had given him pause to think. To consider Emma Jane as his partner in all of this.

"Of course I can be patient," Emma Jane said softly. She smiled at him, then turned her gaze on his parents. "In fact, as I mentioned yesterday, I am greatly enjoying my work with Pastor Lassiter's ministry. It will occupy my time while Jasper assists Sheriff Calhoune."

Jasper's slow nod gave her the courage to look over at his parents. Mrs. Jackson still wore a pinched expression of someone who'd taken a bite of something most distasteful. But Mr. Jackson murmured approvingly.

"It seems you are both similarly matched in your pursuit of the greater good."

"Associating with people not of our kind." Mrs. Jackson glowered at Emma Jane.

"Who is not of our kind," Jasper asked, taking a step toward his parents. "The pastor? His family? Emma Jane is the model of Christian service."

"You know exactly of whom I am speaking."

Though Mrs. Jackson's glare intensified, Emma Jane found that she did not shrink under it as she normally did. Though her aim in helping Pastor Lassiter was not to receive praise, she could not help basking in the compliment Jasper had given.

"Constance, enough!" Mr. Jackson gave Emma Jane a kind smile. "Constance has always doted on Jasper. This has been a lot of change for her all at once. I hope you'll give her some grace as she learns to adjust to the situation."

Adjust to the situation? Emma Jane took a deep breath. More people asking of her, but not…well, it didn't matter. People didn't do things for the benefit of Emma Jane, anyway. It was always Emma Jane doing for others. But it would be nice sometimes if someone thought to do for her.

"There is nothing to adjust to." Jasper slammed his hand down on the table. "Emma Jane is smarter than any of the ninnies you've paraded through our parlor.

If I had to choose between Emma Jane and any one of the girls you thought I should marry, I'd pick Emma Jane. Now if you'll excuse us, I believe my wife and I are going to visit the church so I can see for myself the good works she is engaged in."

After his discussion with his father earlier, Emma Jane wouldn't have expected his fierce defense. Especially the part about him preferring her to the other girls. He was most likely just being kind, but at least he knew what Emma Jane was up against. Perhaps he was more sympathetic to her plight than she'd first thought.

Emma Jane carefully dabbed her lips with her napkin, then looked up at Jasper.

"I'm sorry," he said, resting his hand on the back of her chair. "I didn't even ask if you were finished. Or if you had other plans for today."

"It's all right. I'm finished." Her cheeks warmed when his hand brushed her back as he pulled out her chair for her.

He was being polite, she knew, but it still felt good to have him give even that small consideration to her feelings. And while she'd always known Jasper to be a handsome man, it seemed the more he showed his kindness, the handsomer he became.

If he kept up such actions, Emma Jane might very well find herself one of the giggling girls fawning over their fans at him. Perhaps it was just as well Jasper was chasing after bandits rather than spending time getting to know her. It wouldn't do to find herself attracted to a man who couldn't possibly fall in love with her.

Chapter Five

"You don't have to stay if you don't want to," Emma Jane said softly as they entered the barn that was serving as a makeshift shelter for the women displaced by the brothel fire.

Her permission for him to leave made it impossible for him to do so, even if he'd wanted to. The contrast between his father's chastisement for not doing more for his wife, and his mother's attacks on Emma Jane, as well as Pastor Lassiter's admonitions for him to get to know her better, made it apparent that this was exactly the place he needed to be right now.

Plus, he still needed to figure out his next move in pursuit of the bandits. It would be foolish to do anything without thinking it through. Yesterday's dead end had proven that.

"I want to." Jasper smiled and pulled her hand more firmly into the crook of his arm. "The voices of reason around us are right. I haven't spent the time I should have on getting to know you. Besides, didn't you tell me just yesterday that you thought your work here could help my case?"

Emma Jane's face lit up. Once again, he was struck by how pretty she was when she smiled. Why hadn't he taken more notice of her before?

"You should meet my friend Nancy. I'm sure she'll give us lots of useful information."

It pained him to see the eager expression on her face. Mostly because he absolutely could not get her mixed up in this case. But also because as quickly as he'd set the intention of spending time with Emma Jane, if he was to question the women, even if one was Emma Jane's friend, he would have to do it without her.

"Once you make the introductions, you'll have to occupy yourself elsewhere," he said quietly. "I can't have you involved with this."

Emma Jane's face darkened, like clouds covering the sun in an unexpected storm. He should have seen it coming, had, in fact, known it was coming. What he hadn't expected was how it twisted his gut and made him feel...

No. He was just doing his job.

"But I thought..." Emma Jane's eyes glistened.

"I know, and I'm sorry."

He took off his hat and ran his hand through his hair, then stared down at the hat. He'd chosen an older hat, one usually reserved for when he went out riding, and now as he stared into the rivulets that carried away his sweat, he wished he could disappear as easily.

But that would be doing Emma Jane an even greater disservice.

He finally looked back up at her, holding his hat in his hands. "Please understand. This gang is ruthless, and if they think you are helping me in any way, they won't hesitate to take you down."

Swallowing, he looked around to be sure no one was listening to their conversation. "They made me a deputy because one of the other deputies quit. The gang had sent him a note, threatening to kill his wife if he kept poking his nose into their business."

What would they do to a woman actively working the investigation? Another deputy, Skeeter Ross, was recuperating from a gunshot wound he'd gotten while chasing them. If his horse hadn't tripped at that exact moment, Skeeter would be dead.

"I can't put you at risk," he said, hoping that beyond those tear-filled eyes lay some level of understanding.

"But they already know we're married. They could still come after me because of your work. What more harm could come if I helped you?"

"Do you know how to shoot a gun?"

"Don't be ridicu…" Emma Jane sighed. "I suppose that's your point. I don't know any of the things needed to be a lawman."

Then she looked up at him with those big, trusting eyes. So innocent. No way could he involve her in the case. "How do *you* know them? I can't see society's biggest dandy knowing how to shoot a gun or capture bandits."

"Will taught me. Back when my father and I first met him, my father thought it would be a good idea for Will to teach me in dealing with riffraff. Because of my father's wealth, I was a target for kidnappings, robberies and the like. My father wanted to be sure I knew how to keep myself safe."

Will had taught him a lot of things, and even though the practical lifesaving pieces were the ones he empha-sized here, the biggest lessons Will had imparted to him were the ones that had more to do with the kind of man Jasper wanted to be.

The man Emma Jane had married was not the man everyone in society believed him to be. How was he supposed to be any kind of husband to her when she had no idea who he really was? When he was still trying to figure it out himself?

"More than that, though." Jasper looked at Emma Jane, who still carried an air of doubt about her. "Will taught me about being a man. About defending people who are weaker than you and fighting for what's right, even if others don't agree with you. I owe a lot to him, and I guess if you want to know about me, then those are the things you should know."

She'd asked that question of him last night, and here in the light of day, the answer was clearer than he'd expected. He hadn't been lying when he'd said those things to his mother this morning about the women she'd hoped he'd marry. Not one of them would respect the answer he'd just given Emma Jane, but he hoped, given what little he knew of his wife, that she would.

And if she didn't, well, he wasn't sure what he'd do. He knew her expectation in marrying him was all about the fortune that would save her family. She'd said she'd hoped to be friends, but what did that look like to a woman like Emma Jane?

Would she still want to be friends once she realized that being a good man, and being a society dandy, had nothing in common?

"Thank you," she finally murmured, her face unreadable. "I suppose that's a start. You said yesterday that you needed me to trust you if our marriage was going to have a chance. So I'll do my part. I'll introduce you to Nancy and a few other ladies, and I'll leave you to your work."

Her acquiescence should have been a victory. But like all of the victories he'd found lately, this one didn't sit well with him.

How was he supposed to balance it all? Will seemed to do just fine, balancing his work with keeping his fiancée happy, but Jasper seemed to flail at every turn. Apparently, his pal hadn't taught him all the lessons he needed. And now, with time running out to find the bandits, and a wife he couldn't please, Jasper was going to have to figure it out all on his own.

Emma Jane hated that her last sentence sounded so peevish, but she couldn't find a way to make herself take it back. Oh, she wanted desperately to leave Jasper to it, but she couldn't help but think of her friend Mary, and how Mary knew all the details of Will's work. Will shared with her, and bounced ideas off her, and even though she had no qualifications as a lawman, Will still respected her opinion.

Then again, Will adored his bride-to-be, so maybe being in love came with different rules than being married.

Fortunately, she spied Nancy sitting in a corner by herself, which gave her the perfect opportunity to help Jasper. Perhaps, if he saw how she could be an asset to him in what he allowed her to do, he would realize that she could lend a hand in other areas, as well.

He'd told her that she needed to earn his trust. She'd do all she could to make him see that he could count on her. That she was every bit as capable as Mary in helping Will. No, it wouldn't make him fall in love with her.

But at least, if they could find a way to work on this case together, they could find enough in common that Emma Jane wouldn't feel so alone.

"I believe I see my friend Nancy, if you'd like to meet her." Emma Jane hoped her smile looked more like she was being friendly than filled with her newfound determination. She'd been told in the past that her determined expression made her look cross.

"Thank you, Emma Jane." Jasper rewarded her with a smile of his own. Before the circumstances leading to their marriage, Jasper had hardly spoken to her, hardly noticed her, much less found cause to offer a smile. Surely this was to be considered progress.

After all, how could she blame him for resenting marriage to her? They'd been virtual strangers, caught together in circumstances beyond their control. And while it was easy to focus on the things they could not control, there was plenty Emma Jane could.

Starting with finding a way to get along with her husband.

Now, filled with newfound purpose, Emma Jane took Jasper's arm and brought him over to where Nancy sat.

"Hello, Nancy." She gave the other woman a smile, though she knew that Nancy would most likely not smile back.

"Emma Jane." Nancy looked up at her and, as Emma Jane predicted, did not return the friendly expression.

Nancy had never had cause for the niceties of society, being on the fringes on account of her occupation as a woman of the night. And though Mrs. Jackson would be scandalized by it, Emma Jane found it refreshing to be around someone who let her be herself.

"I would like to present to you my husband, Jasper

Jackson. He's expressed a particular interest in wanting to meet you."

"I'll bet he has," Nancy sneered. "I suppose you'll be warning me off about putting notions in your wife's head."

The smile that formed around Emma Jane's lips came of its own accord. She couldn't help but like the direct way Nancy spoke. Then, remembering to be agreeable to Jasper, she quickly replaced the mirth with a more solemn expression.

It wouldn't do to offend him so soon.

However, instead of being offended, Jasper chuckled. "I can see why Emma Jane likes you. A straight shooter. I like that myself."

Still, the hostile expression on Nancy's face remained.

"If you're a friend of Emma Jane's, then that's good enough for me," Jasper continued. "I was hoping to discuss another matter with you."

Nancy's eyebrows rose, but she didn't say a word.

"I've been recently deputized, and I was hoping you could give me information about the gang we've been chasing. Everything I've found has led to a dead end, and I was thinking, who knows these men better than the women who, um…"

Then Jasper turned beet red and turned his head away.

Nancy snickered. "We didn't exactly talk when I spent time with them, if that's what you're wondering."

"Be nice," Emma Jane said, giving Nancy an admonishing look. "It won't do you any good if you keep chasing folks away with your wild talk. Jasper needs your help."

Emma Jane had never spoken so boldly before, but as her heart thudded in her chest, it felt…well, it felt like the time her sister had dared her to use the rope to swing into the lake. Scary, but good. Jasper's earlier defense of her to his mother echoed in her head. He'd spoken up for her, and even though she knew he didn't fully accept her, she had to believe that if they kept speaking up for each other, then maybe…

She glanced at Jasper, who was still beet red. Surely they could at least become friends.

"I can't help him," Nancy said, looking around. "It's bad enough I'm associating with church folks. If word gets out that I was talking to the law…"

"We can protect you." Jasper looked fully recovered from the embarrassment over Nancy's frank talk.

"Dream on, rich boy. I'm sure it's all fun for you, playing with guns and chasing bandits. But it's not a game to the men you're after. They're ruthless killers, and it won't be just your body they leave in their dust."

Nancy looked at Emma Jane so hard it was almost like having a gun pointed right at her. Jasper seemed afraid that Emma Jane would be targeted by the gang, and Nancy confirmed it. Emma Jane swallowed. Perhaps she'd been too hasty in pushing her desire to work with Jasper on the case.

"And what about the innocent women they'll keep hurting if they're not stopped? What about…"

"If you're talking about Daisy, you need to let her go. I've heard talk that you're searching for her, and I can tell you right now that it's a lost cause. Forget about her and move on."

Emma Jane didn't know Jasper very well, but the emotions darkening his face told her that he'd do anything but forget about Daisy. In fact, she'd guess that Nancy's words only served to make him more determined to find her.

"And what if I can't?" His body was tense, his fists balled at his sides. This was not the society dandy everyone admired. If any of the women who giggled over their fans at him could see him now, Emma Jane wasn't sure they'd recognize him.

If she had to choose, she'd say she liked this Jasper better.

"Then I guess you'd better kiss that pretty wife of yours goodbye."

Nancy turned to look at Emma Jane, then her face softened. "No offense. But if he pursues this case, you're going to be the one to suffer for it. I know you meant well in coming to me, but you're putting every woman you introduce your husband to in danger. And you're signing your own death warrant."

A chill rattled through Emma Jane, and she pulled her shawl tighter around her. Part of her wished she'd left well enough alone and let Jasper go about his business. But another part of her—something boiled deep within her. Where an instant ago she felt cold, now she was on fire.

A gang so dangerous that anyone who tried to stop them would be threatened like this? What would they do if they weren't stopped? Who else would they hurt?

Frankly, they sounded like a bunch of bullies to Emma Jane. The same kind of tormentors who'd mocked her in church, whispering behind their fans, whether it be about her family's debts, her father's gambling and public intoxication, her patched dresses or, now, her hasty forced marriage.

"So you would let them continue to control you," Emma Jane said quietly, realizing as the words came out that she needed to hear them just as much as Nancy. She had wasted far too much time cowering the way her friend was doing.

And nothing in her life had gotten better.

She looked over at Jasper, who gave her a slow nod. As if he…approved of her. Emma Jane swallowed. "I don't want to put you in danger, Nancy. I don't want to be in danger. But if we run in fear from this gang, these bullies, then we will always have to run."

She turned her attention to Jasper. "I'll do everything I can to help you stop them."

Emma Jane had spent her whole life trying to make herself agreeable enough to get people to like her. To get her mother to approve of her. And now, as she was encouraging Nancy to stand up to the bullies, she found that she could no longer do it.

She wanted Jasper to like her, to be her friend, so that somehow their marriage could have a reasonable sort of existence. But he needed to learn to like her for who she was, not the agreeable persona she tried to adopt.

Perhaps the biggest bully, the worst enemy, was not the threat of this gang plaguing the town. Rather, it was the ever-increasing pressure to fit in a mold that simply wasn't her.

So what did that mean for her marriage?

Chapter Six

"I'm sorry I couldn't have been of more help," Emma Jane said quietly as she slipped her hand into his arm.

"It's all right." He patted her arm softly, looking around the barn at all the women milling around.

Why, after all this time, had none of the other deputies come to talk to these women?

Then he spied Will in a corner, talking to a figure in the shadows. Of course his buddy would be here.

"No, it's not all right," Emma Jane huffed, pulling her hand away, then turning to stop in front of him and face him. "Why won't she help us? Doesn't she see that, either way, we're all in trouble?"

She looked so earnest, and in that innocent expression, he finally understood why all the lawmen in town didn't respect Jasper's intentions to rescue Daisy and stop the gang. The answers to her questions were not that simple. And, unfortunately, Emma Jane's passionate desire for justice meant that she was more apt to go into a situation hotheaded without thinking it through.

He glanced in Will's direction. Had his friend ever tried telling him those things? Would he have listened?

So how did he get Emma Jane to listen?

"You're right," he told her honestly. "It's not all right. But Nancy is also right. I don't want to needlessly put anyone else in danger. So what do I do?"

Emma Jane looked confused. She shifted her position slightly, glancing around before bringing her attention back to him. "I don't know. But I feel like I have to do something. I've just…"

She turned her attention to the ground, for all the fascination that dirt might hold.

"I've not had much experience in standing up to bullies before."

Which is when it hit him. Harder than any bullet that he feared.

He'd seen the way the other women in town picked on Emma Jane. Flora Montgomery in particular seemed to take great pleasure in tormenting his wife. How many times had he told the other woman to be nice?

This wasn't just about the gang that had Daisy in their clutches, but Emma Jane learning to stand up to people like Flora Montgomery.

She was using chasing down the gang as her line in the sand.

Except the two situations were not the same.

Flora Montgomery wasn't going to cause Emma Jane bodily harm. But this gang would.

"I'll help you stand up to the bullies." Jasper took both of her hands in his. "But I need you to help me, as well."

Those deep blue eyes of hers locked on to his. The little flecks of brown mesmerized him, as they always did when he took time to notice.

Hopefully, the expression meant that she'd trust him.

"I think we've already determined that I'm not cut out for being a lawman," Emma Jane said, kicking at a small rock on the ground.

"Hey." He pulled one of his hands out of hers, then used it to lift her chin, forcing her to meet his eyes once again. "You may not make a great lawman. But you have many other fine qualities. And I look forward to discovering each and every one of them."

"But I want to help. And I feel completely powerless to do so."

"Then do as I asked you. Stay out of it, and if you see or hear something in your work, let me know, but don't try and do anything about it yourself."

Truthfully, he wasn't giving her any power. But he hoped that she knew that he saw...well, he didn't even know what he saw. Potential, maybe? He knew as little of Emma Jane as she knew of him.

Yet the more he learned of her, the more he realized that there was a greater level of goodness in her than he'd originally suspected. But how did he balance that with the questions he did have of her character? That was the trouble with trusting someone you barely knew. As much as he wanted to believe in Emma Jane wholeheartedly, he didn't know enough about her to know if he *could* trust her.

What was Emma Jane's true plan here?

The fear and uncertainty in her eyes, it looked a lot like she did the day she trapped him into marriage.

Wanting to trust him? He'd like to think so. But it was clear that she didn't. Did she lose faith in him after the church picnic somehow and decide to take matters into her own hands? Would justice in this situation not happen fast enough for Emma Jane, leading her to do something they'd all regret?

"I'm not a child," she fumed. "I know what's at stake. I've agreed to what you need from me. You don't need to patronize me."

"I'm sorry. I just don't know how to convey to you how dangerous this gang really is. There's so much you don't know."

"So tell me." Those luminous eyes of hers bore into him, and while he'd been noticing their beauty, he also couldn't help but notice their intelligence.

Every single society miss he'd ever courted all blushingly waved their fans at him and blithely agreed to whatever he wanted. Even Flora Montgomery, who sometimes made a show of standing up to him, mostly responded by pouting but always complying with what he asked.

And yet…he had more respect for Emma Jane than he had for all those other women put together.

Jasper hesitated before opening his mouth to speak. How did a man balance confidential work with talking about it with his wife? Will would know.

As if he knew the direction of Jasper's thoughts, the other man caught his eye, making a motion with his head. Whatever conversation he'd been engaged in now over, Will was indicating he needed to talk to Jasper.

"Will needs me." Jasper breathed out a long breath, hating the way Emma Jane looked at him—as if he was using Will as a convenient excuse to push her away. Mostly because she was mostly right to think it.

"Of course. You've spent a lot of time with me, and I appreciate it. I know you have work to do."

Dismissed. Polite, but with an undercurrent of pain

that made him wince. Not because she was trying to hurt him, but because she was trying so hard not to sound like he'd hurt her.

Had it been any one of the simpering misses he'd courted, he'd have been able to walk away. But he was a husband now, and Pastor Lassiter's warnings about their relationship rang in his head. He had to make his wife a priority. Even though his duty lay elsewhere.

"I didn't mean..."

"I know what you meant. You don't have to dance attendance on me, there's plenty here to occupy my time."

If it weren't for the tone of her voice, he might have believed her. And then there was the flash of her eyes. The brown flecks dimmed the main blue color, and in them, he read...

Who was he kidding? He didn't know her well enough to be able to read her eyes. But he wasn't a fool.

"I know you're displeased with me right now, Emma Jane. We're supposed to be spending time together to get to know each other and build a foundation for our marriage. And yet, I have this case..."

Jasper glanced in Will's direction. Mary had joined him, and they appeared to be conversing while looking at the two of them.

"Well, it looks like Mary has joined Will, so why don't you come with me to say hello?"

Emma Jane appeared to relax slightly as she nodded, her face looking more peaceful than it had since they began this conversation. Had she been that upset by him leaving her?

So many things he still had to learn about being a husband. All men had to learn them, he supposed solemnly, but it seemed so much harder with a wife he didn't want. Swallowing the resentment that had once again risen up, Jasper offered Emma Jane his arm. He was trying so hard to forgive her and move on, to figure out a way to make their marriage work. But how could he rid himself of this bitterness once and for all?

As they approached Mary and Will, Mary smiled warmly. Though the couple were an appropriate distance from each other, and no one could accuse them of impropriety, the connection between them was obvious. A person only had to glance at them to know they deeply cared for one another. Their bodies were tilted in toward each other, and their attention never strayed far from one another for long.

And when they looked at each other, it was obvious they were in love.

If only Jasper could have had that for himself.

People once said he was the luckiest man in all of Leadville, with the ability to marry any of the beautiful women in town. But what none of them understood was that when he saw the love between Mary and Will, he hadn't wanted to settle for anything less.

Beside him, Emma Jane let out a sigh, one so soft it was barely discernible. A quick glance in her direction made the breath in his throat catch. The longing in her eyes was unmistakable.

He'd been the recipient of many a wistful glance in his day. But this was not the look of a woman in love. Rather, he immediately recognized it to be something else. Emma Jane wanted the same thing he did—to have the same kind of love Will and Mary shared.

They might want the same thing, but unfortunately, neither was going to get it from the other.

* * *

"Did you see how fast Jasper scrambled up the roof to get away from Emma Jane?"

The familiar twitter of Flora's voice burned Emma Jane's ears.

Oh, she knew Flora was just trying to make trouble, but what was the point in causing problems for a woman who was already married? It wasn't as though Jasper was going to wake up one morning, realize it had all been a terrible mistake, divorce Emma Jane and marry Flora.

But Flora didn't seem to understand that.

"I heard from Jasper's mother that they aren't even sharing a bedroom," Flora's companion said in a whisper too loud to be surreptitious.

"Of course not." Flora cackled, her voice carrying in Emma Jane's direction, almost as though she'd turned in Emma Jane's direction as she spoke.

But Emma Jane didn't look up from the shirt she was mending. As women of the night, none of the women in the barn owned anything proper, even if it hadn't all burned up in the fire. Church members had donated what they could, and she, along with others, worked to make them fit.

She held up the shirt to the light, examining her handiwork. In that, no one would find fault. Her stitches were tiny and even.

"I hope you're not thinking of taking that for yourself," Flora said, dropping a pile of clothes in front of her. "It is last season, but I'm sure it's finer than anything you've ever owned."

Emma Jane's face heated. Her throat constricted, preventing her from saying anything as she put the shirt into the pile of clothes she'd finished mending.

"Then again, you're used to cast offs, aren't you? I believe many of your school dresses came from the church, didn't they? I'm sure I've even seen you wearing one or two of mine."

She tossed her golden curls and looked down her nose at Emma Jane. "You're so fortunate that Mother insists I always wear the latest fashions. My clothes are always in perfect condition when we donate them, since I never wear them but more than a few times."

Flora turned to her companion and laughed in that high-pitched, fake way of hers.

"It is such a chore being fashionable."

As the other girl turned more into the light, Emma Jane recognized her. Sarah Crowley, who had often vied with Flora for Jasper's attention. Apparently, nothing united two rivals like a common enemy. Her.

"It's also a chore doing penance for so many of your crimes against humanity."

Emma Jane swiveled at the sound of Polly MacDonald's voice.

"Honestly, I don't know how you sleep at night." Polly glared at the other two women. "You should be ashamed of yourself for the way you're talking about Emma Jane."

Polly picked up the pile of clothes Emma Jane had been mending. "You did a fine job, Emma Jane. Sarah might need a lace machine to make such beautiful trim, but I declare this cuff is exquisite."

She held up one of the gowns Emma Jane had repaired.

"The old lace was torn too badly to fix, and it seemed wrong not to have lace on that dress. So I improvised."

Improvising was something Emma Jane had to be good at. Flora was right in that a lot of her clothes had been cast offs. Unfortunately, that meant clothes from girls who were taller, shorter, fatter and thinner than she was.

"And that is why Flora is so nasty to you." Polly glared at the other girl. "She knows that you're far cleverer than she is, and that rankles. You always got better marks in school, and every one of us was green with envy at all the times you were chosen as an example of excellence."

Flora snorted.

Then Polly leaned in toward the other girl. "Now that Emma Jane is married to Jasper, you're even more jealous. I saw how you tried to get him to kiss you at the church picnic. Even though you told everyone he stole a kiss, I saw him spurn you."

The image of Jasper sitting in the mine came back to Emma Jane. He'd looked so anguished at the mention of his romance with Flora. Everyone, including Emma Jane, had assumed they were a couple. Jasper had denied it, but everyone had heard Flora's bold declarations of stolen kisses.

Maybe Jasper deserved a little more credit than Emma Jane had been giving him.

Sarah nudged Flora. "Is that true?"

"Of course it's not. She's just making up lies to make that creature feel better."

"That creature is Mrs. Jasper Jackson," Polly declared hotly. "And she's a good woman, far more virtuous than the likes of you."

Flora tossed her head. "As if you'd know anything about womanly virtue. I don't know why you're taking up for her, but I'm sure when word gets out, your already meager invitations will dwindle down to nothing."

Polly looked down at Emma Jane. "As long as I'm on Emma Jane's invitation list, I couldn't care less."

Emma Jane closed her eyes and swallowed, willing herself to speak. Why, oh, why, could she never speak up against bullies? But Polly was speaking up for her, and she deserved Emma Jane's support.

She smiled weakly up at Polly. "Of course. You're always welcome in my home…"

"We'll see what the real Mrs. Jackson has to say about that." Flora turned on her heel and walked away, Sarah trailing behind her.

The *real* Mrs. Jackson. That was the real problem, wasn't it? Jasper's mother refused to accept Emma Jane, and based on what the gossips were saying, everyone knew it.

Polly shifted her weight. "I, um…I should probably apologize to you."

"For what?"

"For not taking up for you before. Even at the church picnic, when Mary stood up for you, I told her she was crazy for supporting you. I think we were all too afraid of Flora's pernicious tongue to do anything." Tears filled Polly's eyes. "The truth is, we've all been victims of Flora's treachery, and we weren't brave enough to defend ourselves. I think everyone was just relieved that she'd found you to pick on and was leaving us be."

Emma Jane's heart constricted. The pain she'd been suffering all these years…her own eyes filled with tears.

"I was so caught up in what she was doing to me, I hadn't realized that I wasn't alone," she said, more to herself than to Polly.

Would things have been different had Emma Jane reached out? Had she looked around at the other girls in her class and at church? Could Emma Jane have seen that she wasn't the only one suffering?

"We all should have stood up to her a long time ago, and again, I'm sorry that it's taken me so long to do so on your behalf."

"I should have stood up for myself," Emma Jane whispered, knowing that, even now, she wasn't sure she had the courage.

Polly sighed. "None of us did, either. We all went along with whatever she wanted us to do, knowing that if we displeased her, we'd face her wrath."

"How does one person get so much power?"

Tears streamed down Emma Jane's face, not just for all the abuses she suffered at Flora's hands, but also for the pain streaked across Polly's face.

"What's going on here?" Jasper came up behind Polly, his brow furrowed. "Why are you crying?"

Emma Jane swiped at her face with her sleeve before remembering that she had a handkerchief. There hadn't been money for such finery in her home, but when she'd married Jasper, Mary had given her several with her initials. Where she'd found the time to embroider them, Emma Jane didn't know, but that small gift meant the world to her.

As Emma Jane used her handkerchief, Polly said glumly, "We had a run-in with Flora."

"Polly was good enough to stand up for me, but I'm afraid it only incensed her more."

Jasper's scowl deepened. "I wish I'd never paid a lick of attention to her. I know her father is my father's best friend, but the longer I know her, the more I wish I'd never courted her, even if it made my parents happy."

More of the bitterness she'd seen from Jasper made sense. And, as Emma Jane replayed the times she'd seen Jasper with Flora at local assemblies, she now understood his detachment.

Then Jasper looked down at her, a muscle ticking in his jaw. "I'm sorry she's still being cruel to you, Emma Jane. I've wished a thousand times that I'd paid more attention and done more to make her stop tormenting you."

Actually, Jasper had done a lot more than most in stopping Flora's nastiness. Whenever Flora had picked on her in front of Jasper, he had always chastised her. In fact, the more Emma Jane thought about it, the more she realized that any time someone gossiped or said a cross word about someone in front of Jasper, he was always quick to quiet the talk.

As much as Emma Jane had said she didn't really know him, she was finding that she knew him quite well, after all. The more she realized the finer points of Jasper's character, the more grateful she was indeed that he'd married her.

"It's all right," Emma Jane told him softly. "As I recall, you've always stopped any talk that you've heard."

"For all the good it's done." Jasper sighed, then gazed at her with what seemed to be real compassion. "Look, I know I seemed harsh yesterday when we talked about how much the talk bothers you. But I've had to deal with it my whole life. I do my best to stop people when they're gossiping about others, but they just keep right on when my back is turned."

He glanced in the direction of Flora, who'd been joined by a few more of her cronies. "My reputation as a playboy is not undeserved. But a lot of the stories about me are either grossly exaggerated, or simply untrue."

Then he looked back at Emma Jane. "I apologize for any of that talk as it applies to you. I regret kissing every single one of those girls, and I truly regret the way it makes everyone look sideways at you."

Emma Jane hadn't realized that Jasper, too, might have been the victim of malicious gossip. And even though his admission of kissing other girls would lower his value in some people's eyes, it gave her even more hope for their relationship. Jasper was the kind of man to admit to his mistakes.

Of course, his admission also pointed out one glaring fact about their relationship. Not once had Jasper even tried to kiss her. Sometimes she thought she had a memory of a kiss while they were in the mine, shortly before the rockslide hit. But Emma Jane knew it was mere foolishness. If such a kiss had happened, why hadn't Jasper mentioned it? And if it was as good of a kiss as had been in her dreams, why hadn't he repeated it?

No, kissing Jasper had only happened in her imagination.

Clearly, if the man liked to kiss as much as his reputation claimed, and even in his own admission, his failure to kiss his wife meant only one thing.

He had absolutely no interest in Emma Jane.

Chapter Seven

The trouble with Jasper's sweet apology was that when he excused himself a few moments later, Emma Jane found it hard to refuse. Building a bridge between her and her husband wasn't going to happen in a single afternoon. Polly, too, had left her, needing to check in with her mother and catch up on her duties at home.

Emma Jane looked around for Nancy. She hadn't realized that having Jasper talk to her friend would put her in a bad position. Even though Emma Jane wanted Nancy to do the right thing, she knew all too well the difficulty in standing up to bullies. What Nancy needed most of all, what had helped Emma Jane, was having a real friend.

She spied Jasper, huddled in a corner with Will. After catching his eye, she gave him a quick wave, and he nodded at her. A simple acknowledgment, but in some ways, it marked a step in a positive direction for their relationship. How many times had Emma Jane waved at him in the past only to have him not notice her?

Warmth filling her heart, Emma Jane went into the stable area, where she knew Nancy liked to spend time.

They'd discovered a mama cat and her kittens a few days ago, and knowing Nancy, she was probably checking on them.

The stable was quiet, deserted. No Nancy, but at least Emma Jane could check on the kittens and read a little in her Bible. She was grateful for the small book Pastor Lassiter had given them as a wedding gift. It was perfect for carrying around, and it gave her the opportunity to read to some of the women here in the barn. Though some objected to hearing about religion all the time, Emma Jane noticed how many appreciated the comforting words of the Psalms. She slipped into the stall where the cat had made a place for her little family to sleep. Mama cat was gone, probably in search of food. The soft straw she and Nancy had found to give the cats a comfortable bed would make a nice place to sit and read.

She pulled out her Bible and opened it to the Twenty-third Psalm. A well-worn page, but all the women seemed to come nearer when she read it. Just like Emma Jane, they were all probably in their own private valleys of the shadow of death. Everything in their lives had changed overnight, and many of them had no idea what would happen next. Only the solace of the Lord would get them through. One of the kittens mewed, and she looked to see it had fallen and was stuck in the hay. Just as she reached for it, one of the barn doors banged open.

"I saw you talking to the law, Nancy."

"I didn't tell them nothin', Ray. You know better than that. Haven't I kept all of your secrets? I've given you an alibi plenty of times, so you needn't fear me."

"What about that wife of his? You two seem awfully

cozy to me. Betty said you've been spending a lot of time with that woman."

Emma Jane shrank against the walls of the stall. Nancy had warned her that their friendship might cause trouble for her. Had looked fearful when Jasper had tried speaking to her. A shiver coursed down Emma Jane's spine. Had she needlessly put her friend in danger in hopes of winning over her husband?

"So I listen to some do-gooder read me Bible stories. What's it to you? I'm just biding my time until a place at the Silver King Saloon opens up. If that means letting some poor woman think she's doing a charitable deed, it doesn't hurt a soul."

Some do-gooder? Poor woman? Emma Jane's heart sank as Nancy so callously denied their friendship.

But Nancy had been the one to ask Emma Jane to read from her Bible, and as Emma Jane recalled, she'd told her that she'd turned down the opportunity to work at the Silver King Saloon.

What was going on?

The voices came closer.

Emma Jane could see Nancy clearly now, as the young woman was nearly even with the stall door. Nancy glanced over, barely looking at Emma Jane, but she understood as Nancy closed the door. She was trying to protect Emma Jane.

"Well, I don't like it." Ray stepped in toward Nancy, so close their faces were almost touching. "That posse last night got a little too close for my liking, and I'm thinking we have a traitor in our midst."

"It's not me." Nancy started to move away from the stall, but Ray grabbed her arm.

"Betty says…"

"Maybe you ought to be asking Betty what she's saying to that deputy she's had as a customer all these months," Nancy said.

Ray snorted. "Who do you think our inside man is?"

Jasper had told Emma Jane he suspected the bandits had someone in the sheriff's office working for them. Now she could confirm his suspicions. It felt good to know that she'd be able to help him *and* keep her promise to stay out of the case. After all, she would be doing exactly as he'd asked—reporting back to him on what she heard.

As much as she wanted to jump in and tell Ray that Nancy was telling the truth, that she hadn't told Emma Jane or Jasper anything, she remembered Nancy's warning about how dangerous these people were.

Nancy, though, didn't appear to be afraid. She lifted her chin and looked Ray in the eye. "Well, maybe he's working both sides. Wouldn't be the first time, you and I both know that."

Emma Jane heard a strange clicking sound.

"I know it all too well. Which is why I'm getting rid of any leaks."

"You can't think..." Nancy's face crumpled as she took a step back. "I would never..."

"I don't think. I know."

A gunshot rang out, and then a thud. Emma Jane squeezed her eyes shut. The image of what had happened burned against her eyelids. Even if she scrubbed with the strongest lye, nothing could ever remove the memory of Nancy's last moments.

The kitten she held in her arms mewed.

"Who's there?"

Emma Jane let the kitten go, encouraging it to scamper in the direction of the man who'd just killed Nancy. He wouldn't harm a kitten, but if he looked in the stall, she knew he wouldn't hesitate in killing her.

The kitten cooperated, but the man didn't seem to notice. Instead, he kicked open the door to the stall next to her.

Emma Jane's heart thudded against her chest.

He would search her stall next.

Maybe if he thought she slept through the whole thing, and hadn't heard anything, he'd leave her alone. But if he knew she'd been conscious, he'd kill her for sure.

She curled up in a ball, arranging the straw around her, like she'd been using it as a makeshift bed, closed her eyes and prayed.

The stall door, which had been slightly ajar, banged as he opened it all the way. Even with her eyes closed, she could feel his gaze on her.

"What are you doing? We've got to get out of here." An unfamiliar male voice broke through the silence.

"Seems we've got a witness."

"Looks like she's asleep. We've got to get out of here. Folks in the street heard the gunshot and are trying to figure out where it came from."

"There's gunshots around these parts all the time. We've got to take care of her."

Emma Jane heard the strange click again. Now she knew. It was the sound a gun made just before someone shot it. She swallowed, saying one last prayer.

Please, don't let this be my final prayer.

"Then they'll be on to us for sure. Let's go."

A heavy boot nudged her. "It's that do-gooder."

Footsteps crunched the straw nearby. "Jasper Jackson's wife. We can't kill her. Not with the Jackson power and money."

Shouts came from the street. The voices grew closer.

"What if she heard? At the very least, she can finger me for Nancy."

"We'll take her with us. Maybe we can use her as leverage. That rich boy needs to learn he picked the wrong hobby in poking his nose into our business."

This time, the man kicked her. Hard. Emma Jane winced at the pain.

Quickly, she yawned, hoping she was convincing in pretending that she'd just woken up.

"What's happening?"

Dark eyes glinted against the sunlight streaming through the crack in the roof.

"You're coming with us."

The shiny barrel of a gun—the gun used to kill Nancy—pointed at her face.

Emma Jane stood slowly, her heart thudding so loud, it echoed in her ears. If she took her time, the voices she heard might make it. And then they could catch these evil men in action. Her throat was so dry, she couldn't have screamed for help even if there wasn't a gun pointed to her head.

"Hurry it up. I'm not afraid to use this. Just ask your friend." He pointed toward the open stall door. Nancy's lifeless body lay beyond.

Seeing Nancy dead somehow made the situation seem all the more dangerous. Jasper had warned her. Nancy had warned her. And now Nancy was dead.

Tears pricked her eyes at the senseless loss. As much as she wanted to cry for her friend, there was no time for that, not when she had to figure a way out.

Emma Jane scooted forward, letting her Bible settle in the straw. Would they notice it when they found Nancy's body? Would they realize Emma Jane was in trouble?

Selfishly, she wanted to keep the Bible with her. Until now, she'd never had a Bible of her own. She always had to use the family Bible. It had brought her so much comfort already, and she had a feeling that, with these men, she'd need it.

But if it helped Jasper find her...

"Let's go!"

Ray grabbed her by the arm and jerked her to her feet. The Bible remained where she'd left it as Ray pulled her out of the stall.

His partner waved his gun at her.

"You don't have to die. But if you yell, fight or put up any kind of fuss to draw attention to us, we will kill you. Live or die, it's your choice."

Strangely, Emma Jane didn't fear dying—not in this moment. Oh, she knew without a doubt that these men would kill her if they thought she was a threat. But something in her told her that if she just went along with them, she would be safe. Let them think she was cooperative, and somehow, some way, she would find a way to escape. If only she could convince her trembling limbs to believe in that hope.

Jasper removed his hat and ran his free hand through his hair. It seemed most of today had been a waste. Neither he nor Will had any leads, and it seemed like the bandits were toying with them. Even the gunshots they'd heard earlier seemed to be nothing but hotheads coming out of the saloon. Jasper sighed. The trouble with the lawlessness running rampant was that one never could tell if a gunshot was something serious or was just idiots fooling around.

At least things with Emma Jane seemed to be improving. He looked around for his bride.

The women were gathered in the main room of the barn, waiting for the noon meal. Knowing Emma Jane, she was probably helping set up.

Except, as he glanced at the women carrying dishes to and fro, he didn't see her. Mary, Polly and several other women who helped with the ministry were all present. He walked over to where Mary had just set a platter of bread on the table.

"Have you seen Emma Jane?"

Mary looked up, her brow furrowed. "No. I thought…" She turned toward the barn door, where Polly was bringing in a large pot. "Where's Emma Jane?"

Polly groaned and Jasper rushed toward her. The pot looked much too heavy for the woman to be carrying it herself.

As he took the pot from her, Polly said, "I have no idea. She wandered off to the stalls a while ago. There's some kittens she likes to play with."

Then Polly frowned. "But that was ages ago, and I can't imagine why she's not helping us. That's not like Emma Jane."

"Oh. You're looking for Emma Jane?" Flora sidled up to him, a nasty smirk on her face. "I saw her ride off with two men earlier. Guess she's as loose as we all suspected."

It took every ounce of effort not to dump the contents of the entire pot, which smelled like a hearty stew, on the horrid girl. With Herculean control, Jasper set the pot on the table.

"I'm sick of your lies, Flora Montgomery. Emma Jane never did a thing to you. She's a good woman, with more kindness in her pinky than you have in your whole body. You might be jealous that I married her, but let me set the record straight. There is nothing on this earth that would have induced me to offer for you."

Flora blanched, and for a moment, Jasper felt awful for his cruelty. But when had she ever felt bad for her malicious words about anyone else?

"It's true," Flora insisted. "Sarah Crowley saw it, too, didn't you, Sarah?"

Sarah walked over, wiping her hands on her apron. "I'm afraid so. I'm sure there's a reasonable explanation why she'd ride off with two men who were not her husband, sitting on a horse with one of them, and her ankles bared for all to see."

The looks she and Flora exchanged said that they clearly believed that only Flora's theory could be true.

Will joined them. "What kind of horses were they?"

Flora made an unladylike noise. "As if I would pay attention to any such thing. I have work to do, so if you'll excuse me."

She flounced off, her head held high, and by the exasperated groans from Mary and Polly, it was clear that Flora hadn't been doing any work at all. Jasper knew all too well that Flora often showed up to make an appearance at charity work so people thought she was helping, but she often just stood around, completely useless.

"What about you, Sarah?" Jasper narrowed his eyes at her, taking over Will's investigation. Something wasn't right, even if no one else seemed to care.

Before answering, Sarah looked away, her gaze settling on Flora, who wore such a deep scowl Jasper could hardly fathom why the other girl was considered so beautiful. Disgust filled him once again at the reminder of how he used to flirt with her.

How could he have thought a woman with Flora's character held any value? An image of Emma Jane popped into his head. She might not have been considered one of the most beautiful women in town, but...

He shook his head. Dwelling on her characteristics wasn't going to help him find her.

Sarah leaned in and lowered her voice. "Flora thinks it's unladylike for me to have such admiration for horses, but the only reason we saw Emma Jane was because I'd been staring at what a beautifully matched pair of chestnut roans they were. I have not seen such fine horseflesh. I have to go."

Then she straightened and turned, rejoining Flora.

Will nudged Jasper. "Where have you heard talk of a matched pair of chestnut roans?"

A flash of memory hit. "Didn't Eric Abernathy come into the sheriff's office the other day, ranting about his brand-new horses being stolen?"

Will nodded. "That's right! I remember now. He'd just had them brought over from back east. He was madder than a newly woken bear that no one would form a search party to help find them. We just didn't have the manpower."

"I'm sure it's the gang." Jasper frowned. "But why would they take Emma Jane?"

A shout sounded from the stalls. "It's Nancy! She's dead!"

Jasper and Will ran in the direction of the voice. A

woman stood by the door to the stables, sobbing. "I just told Ray... I didn't mean..."

"Ray? He was here? What did you tell him?" Jasper glowered at her, grabbing her by the elbow. How had he missed one of the gang members in town?

"He'll kill me, too." The woman jerked from his grasp, then ran off.

Jasper started to go after her, but Will's voice stopped him. "Don't waste your time. Come here. I found something."

As he stepped over the body, Jasper's gut clenched. Another woman. Dead. Nancy had warned him that talking to him would get her and Emma Jane killed. Was this the result of Jasper's actions?

Will held up a Bible. "Recognize this?"

Jasper pulled it out of Will's hands without even looking at it. He didn't need to. "Emma Jane hasn't gone anywhere without it since the wedding."

The memory of her sitting in her bed in her nightgown, reading that Bible, came back to him. So innocent. Emma Jane hadn't been part of this fight. All she'd wanted to do was the right thing, to help, and now she was in grave danger.

Why hadn't she listened to him and just stayed out of it? Knowing Emma Jane, she probably went to talk to Nancy on her own and somehow got caught up in this mess. Clearly, his wife hadn't realized how dangerous the people they were dealing with were. She should have trusted him.

"You think she saw the murder and they took her to keep her quiet?" Will motioned toward the body.

Jasper swallowed the lump in his throat. "Why didn't they just kill her?"

"A Jackson?" The tone in Will's voice reminded him of how Will had come into his life. After Will had saved Henry's life, Henry had asked Will to teach Jasper how to protect himself. Growing up, there'd been a number of kidnapping threats.

He'd just never imagined that, as an adult, those threats would still be there. Despite everything Jasper had done to learn to protect himself, he'd forgotten one important lesson. Passing those lessons on to his wife. Especially a headstrong one who didn't trust him to do the right thing and took matters into her own hands.

"I never thought…" Jasper's head spun as he realized the danger Emma Jane was in.

"Emma Jane is tough. You told me yourself that, during the mine cave-in, she possessed an inner strength you admired. She'll get through this, too."

Jasper nodded slowly, his gaze drawn back to Nancy's body. What would they do to Emma Jane? His gut churned at the thought. Was this because she was a Jackson, or was this Nancy's warning coming true? Or had Emma Jane somehow become more involved in trying to solve the case?

He looked around for clues, for any signs of struggle, but other than the dead woman lying at the entrance to the stall, the barn looked exactly as it should.

Will walked over to the other side of the stall area, leading out to the street.

"Over here!"

Jasper quickly joined him, looking at the place Will indicated on the ground.

"There haven't been any horses staying in this barn since we put the women up in here. Two sets of horse-shoe prints. That has to be the kidnappers."

The prints left a clear trail as far as Jasper could see. Fortunately, the barn was at the edge of town, and the trail went straight into the brush, where other horses weren't likely to tread on them. Easy enough to follow.

"I'll get the horses." Jasper started toward where he'd left his mount without waiting for Will's response.

"We should get the sheriff first."

Jasper didn't pause. "You get the sheriff. I'm going after my wife. I'll leave tracks so you can catch up."

Chapter Eight

"What were you thinking, bringing him here? Bad enough you brought the woman, now him?"

Emma Jane looked up from the fire, where she'd been heating up a soup she'd cobbled together from the meager ingredients she'd found in the cabin. She'd realized pretty quickly that fighting the men would drain her of any energy she'd need to survive and, eventually, escape. For now, she'd make the best of things, and if cooking supper was part of it, at least she wouldn't go to bed hungry.

Two men were dragging an unconscious Jasper into the cabin. His hands were tied behind his back, and a handkerchief had been tied around his mouth.

"Jasper!"

She started toward him, but the leader of the gang, the dark-haired man who'd objected to Jasper's presence, pointed his gun at her. "You get back to tending that meal. I've still got half a mind to kill you, but so long as you're useful, I might let you live."

Emma Jane tried swallowing the lump in her throat, but it remained lodged in place. How had Jasper come to be here? Her heart sank and turned over in her stomach as she realized that he'd probably come after her, putting himself in danger in the process.

The men dropped Jasper on the dirt floor, his body thudding on the ground. A trail of dried blood had clotted down the side of his face. For a moment, Emma Jane's breath caught. But then his chest rose and fell slightly. It was enough to let her take a breath, but not enough to ease the tightness in her chest.

"He's injured," Emma Jane said quietly but not moving. "Supper should be ready soon. Let me tend to him."

"He'll be fine. Just a knock on the head." Ray, one of the men who'd kidnapped her, nudged his partner. "Might have been a little harder than we intended, but we got the job done."

"What job?" Their leader walked over and smacked Ray on the side of the head. "Seems to me every job I give you gets messed up. You were supposed to go into town to take care of Nancy. You come back with *her*."

He pointed at Emma Jane, giving her a dark look. "I do not need another woman in this place."

As if to remind them of her existence, the other woman began coughing again. When Emma Jane had arrived, the woman had been coughing up a storm, delirious with fever. She'd felt so bad for the poor woman and had been doing what she could to make her more comfortable.

The woman also had a small baby boy, now sleeping inside an old crate near the fire. When Emma Jane had arrived, the baby was nestled in with his mother. With the woman's raging fever, Emma Jane worried that the baby might get sick. She'd put together a makeshift bottle from odds and ends she'd found in the cabin, and one of the men, Mack, had given her some goat's milk. Not the best solution, Emma Jane knew, but with the way the baby had gobbled up the milk, she'd probably saved the baby's life. Already color was returning to the baby's cheeks, and he had stopped whimpering. Mack commented that it was the first time the baby had quieted in days.

Emma Jane went to the fire to stir the soup. Tasting it, she deemed it fit to eat. Perhaps if the men had a little food in their bellies, they wouldn't be so cantankerous. Which meant that maybe they wouldn't be so eager with their guns.

A nearby shelf held some bowls, and as Emma Jane dished out the soup, the men continued arguing.

"I told you, she was there when I did it. I didn't want her talking. I'd have shot her then, but Jimmy said killing a Jackson was a bad idea."

"And you didn't think to check for witnesses before doing it?" The leader blew out an irate breath as Emma Jane handed him a bowl.

"You didn't put anything in this, did you?"

He eyed her warily, and for a moment, Emma Jane wished she had put poison in the soup. Of course, she had no idea what she could have used as one. It wasn't as though there were bottles labeled Poison lying around.

"No." She handed another bowl to the one called Jimmy. After all, she owed him her life. Were it not for him, Ray would have killed her.

"Prove it. Take a bite out of my bowl."

Emma Jane did as he asked, looking him in the eye as she took a spoonful of his soup.

Satisfied, the man grunted and waved her away. "As I was saying, Ray, you're a disgrace. I gave you a simple job, and you fouled that up. But that doesn't explain how you ended up bringing him here."

Ray pointed at Jimmy. "Ask him. He's the one who had that idea, too."

Jimmy set down his soup. "Same reason we grabbed the girl. There's no way we'd get away with killing a Jackson. We went back to clean up our tracks, and he had started tracking us. Figured it was easier to knock him out and take him prisoner than it was to spend the rest of our lives running. You kill someone with that much money and power, there's no way you'll ever stop running, even if you do make it to Mexico."

"I'm not afraid of no Jackson," Ray declared.

"You should be." Jimmy stood, then pointed at Jasper. "We might have the law around here handled, but his father has the money to buy more law than we can. I know a guy who tried robbing him once. Trust me when I say that you cross a man as powerful as Jackson, you'll wish you were dead."

His answer seemed to satisfy the leader, who stood. "We'll continue this conversation outside. No need for big ears to learn the rest of our plan."

He looked pointedly at Emma Jane, but she didn't care. If the men left the cabin, she could tend to Jasper's wounds.

Before she could reach Jasper, the baby let out a small cry. Emma Jane picked him up, noting immediately that he was wet. A good sign, considering how weak he'd appeared when she'd first begun tending him.

"I wish I knew your name, little fellow." Emma Jane stroked his head as she laid him down and changed him. Mack had given her some old shirts to cut up and use for diapers. For an outlaw, Mack seemed like a pretty decent guy.

Satisfied the baby was comfortable, Emma Jane set him back in the crate, then moved it closer to where Jasper lay.

After untying him and removing the handkerchief from his mouth, she moistened one of the clean cloths. She wiped the dried blood on the side of his head. Fortunately, the wound itself seemed small, and as Emma Jane pressed the cloth to it, no fresh blood came out.

Jasper moaned. Emma Jane's heart jumped and her breath caught. Was he waking up?

"Jasper?"

His eyelids fluttered open. "What happened?"

He struggled to get up, but Emma Jane stopped him. "Slowly. You took a nasty hit to the head, so you might be dizzy standing up."

When they'd been trapped in the mine, some of it had caved in and knocked Emma Jane unconscious. From what she remembered of her recuperation, she'd been dizzy off and on for days afterward. Jasper would need to take it slowly, but from the gleam in his eyes, Emma Jane figured he wanted to do anything but.

"Where are we?" He looked around the cabin, almost frantic in his motions.

"Shh...calm down. We're in the bandits' cabin. You're safe."

"Safe?" Jasper's head jerked up, then he pulled himself into a sitting position. "We've got to get out of here."

Just as quickly as he'd gotten up, he put his hand to his head. "Everything's spinning."

"You need to lie down and rest. There's a pallet by the fire. Let me help you over there."

He stumbled as he tried to stand, and from the way he grunted, Jasper seemed to realize the futility of not following Emma Jane's instructions. She helped him balance, then led him to the pallet.

"I made some soup. We'll see how you do with the broth, but your stomach might be upset."

One more thing she remembered from her own head injury. As much as she'd wanted to eat, she'd struggled to keep things down for the first day or so.

"You made soup?" Jasper looked up at her as he sat on the pallet.

"It was all they had ingredients for."

He continued to look at her with incredulity.

"Oh. You didn't realize I could cook, did you?" Emma Jane smiled as she sat down beside him. "I suppose there isn't much use for my cooking skills with all your help at the house, but when Father was in a bad place and we had to let the servants go, I ended up doing all the cooking."

The infant began to fuss. "Let me get the baby, and we can finish talking."

"Baby?"

"Oh." Emma Jane continued toward the little boy. "I have much to catch you up on."

She picked up the infant and held him up for Jasper to see before making her way to the rocker. "When I got here, the woman who'd been taking care of things was quite ill. No one was taking care of her poor little baby. The bandits were quite put out by the situation, so I pitched in to help."

"You did *what*?" Jasper ran a hand over his face. "Emma Jane, these are bandits."

"Bandits who are in a foul mood because they haven't

had a hot meal since their woman took sick. They said they were going to let me go as soon as they finished their last job. They're going to Mexico when this is all over. They just need me out of the way for a while so I don't go to the sheriff before they get the last job done."

It sounded so much simpler when she explained it. Some of it, Emma Jane took a lot of pride in having figured out for herself.

"They told you that?"

Leave it to Jasper to sound annoyed with her when she'd done quite a good job, if she did say so herself. She'd been taking care of a sick woman, a baby, gotten supper ready and had done a little tidying in the cabin. Not bad for an afternoon's work. And, while doing all that, she'd figured out what the bandits were up to.

"Of course not. But you'd be amazed at what people will say in front of you when they think you're stupid. And me being a woman, in their minds, I'm a complete idiot."

Jasper let out a long sigh. "Emma Jane, they are not going to let us live. You know their plan, and I know where their hideout is."

"No, you don't." Emma Jane stared at him. "They knocked you out. You were unconscious the whole way here."

"But I'm sure, from our surroundings, I can figure it out pretty quickly. Once we find our way back to town, it will be easy enough for me to gather a posse and return."

Now who was the simple one? Emma Jane shook her head. "And how do you propose we get back to town?"

She pointed out the window. "Do you know how many men are out there? You've seen three. I've counted at least a dozen, and all of them are armed. They told me that if I cooperate, they'll let me live. But if I try to escape, I'm dead. Even with you here, what chance do the two of us have with a sick woman and a baby against that many men?"

"What do the sick woman and baby have to do with us getting out of here?"

The infant fussed slightly, bringing Emma Jane's attention to him rather than the incorrigible man sitting on the pallet. Otherwise, she might have lost her temper. But this gave her the opportunity to collect her thoughts, take a deep breath and look him in the eye.

"We can't leave them here."

Jasper let out an exasperated sigh. "I know you like to help others, but this woman and her baby are with the bandits. They…"

"You don't know that. She could have been kidnapped, just like me. Didn't you say this woman you were looking for, Daisy, was being held by the bandits?"

Light filled Jasper's eyes, but then it dimmed. "She didn't have a baby." Then he stopped and exhaled sharply. "But she was with child."

Jasper sat quietly for a moment, and Emma Jane thought it wise to just let him be. It was a lot to take in. Besides, the baby had started fussing again.

"I'm just going to give him some milk. You rest."

Who was this woman, bossing him around? Emma Jane had always been so meek and mild mannered. Maybe he'd been hit on the head harder than he'd thought.

His wife had only been partially right about him not knowing where the gang's hideout was. When the men were arguing about what to do with him, he pretended to be injured worse than he was. The kicks to his side they'd given him were well worth the pain, given he now knew exactly how to get here. And how to get back to town. Sure, he'd blacked out a few times, but he knew enough.

It now made sense why they kept losing the gang's trail. With the various creek crossings and doubling back the men did to hide their trail, it was no wonder the posse couldn't find them. Especially with the way the cabin was hidden among some rock outcroppings.

He watched as Emma Jane cooed at the baby and fed him from some weird contraption.

"Where'd you come up with that?" Jasper pointed to the bottle.

"Oh. One of the men helped me fix it up. They have bottles for babies in the mercantile, and when I explained to him what I wanted, he helped me put a few odds and ends together to do it."

Emma Jane acted like this was simply one of her mission projects rather than the cold-blooded killers they'd been pursuing.

"One of the men?"

"His name is Mack," Emma Jane said with a smile as she lifted the baby to her shoulder to burp. "He's quite nice, considering his profession. Calls me 'ma'am,' and is always offering to help me."

The name didn't sound familiar, but that didn't mean anything to Jasper. They'd still been trying to figure out the exact makeup of the gang. With the brothel fire, many of the men they'd thought were the leaders had been arrested and put in jail. But the remnant seemed to be just as strong and powerful without their leaders.

"He's not your friend," Jasper bit out, struggling to sit up straighter to get a better look around the place. His head pounded harder now, and spots danced in front of his eyes. Maybe he'd been hit harder than he'd thought.

"Maybe not," Emma Jane said, returning to her spot in the rocking chair. "But I've learned that when dealing with your enemies, you have to give them as little ammunition as possible. It seems to me, that in the case of men who are equally torn between killing you and keeping you alive, the best thing a person can do is be as useful as possible."

She smiled down at the baby and made a little cooing noise at him. "And that's what we're doing, isn't it, my sweet?"

He'd always known that Emma Jane was smart, but as he watched her bond with the baby as though her life wasn't in danger, he realized that she was a lot smarter than he'd given her credit for. Even without the infant and the sick woman who may or may not be Daisy, the odds of the two of them surviving an escape with a dozen men on guard were slim at best.

His stomach rumbled, and he remembered the broth Emma Jane had promised. "Could I have some of that soup you made?"

She smiled. "Of course. But broth only until we know your stomach can tolerate it."

Then she stood and tried to hand him the baby. "Take him so I can make the soup."

Jasper stared at the baby. "You want me to do what?"

"Hold him. Don't tell me you've never held a baby before."

He continued staring awkwardly at the child. "Actually, I haven't."

"Then let me show you. Babies are such a delight, and when you have your own…" Her face clouded. "Oh. I suppose… Well, that is… We never really talked about…"

Emma Jane turned away, clutching the baby to her chest before setting him in an old crate.

She didn't have to finish any of those sentences. After all, when a man promises a woman a marriage in name only, children aren't a likely outcome of the union.

As he watched her prepare the soup, taking longer than a simple task should have, he wondered how much she regretted their current circumstances, as well. Clearly, she loved babies, and with the marriage they agreed to, there would be none.

In this, they had both lost.

Jasper cleared his throat. "I would have liked children of my own. But I don't suppose that's possible now."

Her eyes glistened as she handed him the soup, but she didn't say anything. And he didn't ask.

They still had too many bridges to cross before they were in a place where such a conversation would be possible. Too many hurts stood in the way.

He supposed he shouldn't have said anything about his own desire for children when it seemed so out of reach right now. But the ache inside him, seeing Emma Jane with the baby and her seeming innocence on the subject, prevented him from keeping silent.

His silence often seemed like a willingness to be complicit in everyone else's plans for him. Maybe he should have spoken up sooner. Perhaps, if everyone had known that he wanted to fall in love, find a wife of his own choosing and have a home full of laughter and children, he wouldn't be in this mess.

Sipping his soup, Jasper watched Emma Jane go to the sleeping woman and bathe her face with a cloth. He couldn't hear the words she murmured, but the kindness and poise emanating from Emma Jane made him regret being so hard on her.

After a few sips, his stomach felt sour. He set the bowl aside.

Immediately, Emma Jane turned to him. "Are you all right?"

"Fine. You were right in saying I should take it slow."

"I just remembered what it was like from my own experience." Emma Jane stood and straightened her skirts. "I do wish I knew more about nursing the sick. All I know is that I should mop her face with a cool cloth and try to get her to drink some broth. But what if there is more I can do?"

The lines etched in her forehead spoke louder than anything she could have said. How could she be so deeply concerned for a stranger?

"You did just fine taking care of me."

She gave a half smile, but the lines didn't leave her forehead. "But I've had an injury to my head. I know what that feels like, and I know what helps. With this poor woman, I don't know what's wrong or what to do for her."

Seeing this side of Emma Jane made him question how she would be capable of the deceit leading to their marriage. Surely someone who cared this much about others wouldn't want to ruin someone else's life.

But would Emma Jane have seen it as ruining his life?

The door banged open, and Rex McGee, whose face

graced a number of wanted posters across the country, entered.

"I hear we got ourselves a special guest. Leadville royalty." Rex chortled at his own joke, then started toward Jasper. "What kind of ransom do you think you're worth?"

Emma Jane gasped, but Jasper looked at him as coldly as he could. "I think you know my father has a long-standing and vocal policy that he does not pay ransom."

Rex grinned. "So tell me why we shouldn't kill you, then. I don't run no charity cases, not like that pretty little wife of yours."

"I think you know. I die, and the ransom on your head would tempt even your most loyal guns to turn on you."

Jasper continued glaring at Rex, but Rex had turned his attention on Emma Jane.

"I hear you've been making yourself quite useful around here."

Demurely folding her hands in front of her, Emma Jane bobbed her head at him. "I like to be useful. This woman is sick, and she needs a doctor."

"We don't need anyone else sniffing around our business."

"So I've been told. Which is why I'm doing the best I can to ease her suffering. Do you know what's wrong with her?"

"Do I look like a doctor?"

Jasper clenched his jaw. What was Emma Jane thinking, going toe-to-toe with one of the country's most nefarious criminals?

She looked Rex in the eye, raised her chin and said, "I've learned not to judge people by their appearance."

He grinned. "Well, if that soup of yours is half as good as the other men are saying, I just might have to keep you around. Perhaps you'll earn the keep for that worthless husband of yours."

Jasper opened his mouth to speak, but Emma Jane shot him a look. Even if he could remember what he'd intended to say, he was too stunned at this mouse turned into a lioness to say anything.

Who *was* this woman?

"I'd be happy to get you some." Emma Jane smiled sweetly at Rex, then walked over to the fire, where she dished out the soup. "I don't suppose you'd be willing to tell me anything about the operation here? The other gentleman acted like he was in charge, but he wouldn't tell me anything."

She handed Rex a bowl of soup and beamed.

Clearly, Jasper had married a madwoman.

"You know I can't say anything." Rex nodded in Jasper's direction. "I hear tell that Leadville's newest deputy has a burr under his saddle about having my men in prison, so I'm not likely to help that cause."

"Actually," Emma Jane said quietly, "his main interest is finding and rescuing a woman named Daisy, so if you could just confirm our suspicions that the poor woman lying in the bed is she, then most of Jasper's motivation in pursuing your men would be gone."

Had he called her a madwoman yet?

"Emma Jane," he said through gritted teeth.

Rex waved a hand as if to tell Jasper to be quiet. "What would a married man want with Ben Perry's doxy?"

"Her sister saved Jasper's life. It was her dying wish that Jasper would save Daisy."

Rex had the gall to laugh. A full-out belly laugh that rang through the room, causing the baby to stir. Emma Jane immediately went to the infant and picked him up out of the crate.

"Shh…" She held the child close to her, then glared at Rex. "Do be mindful of the baby."

Jasper closed his eyes. She was going to get them all killed, that's what she was going to do. He'd heard tales of men being shot for looking at Rex wrong, and here was Emma Jane, chastising him as though he were an errant child.

Opening his eyes, he watched Rex give Emma Jane a little pat before coming to stand over Jasper. "You are one stupid man, you know that?"

As much as he hated to admit it, Jasper was starting to figure that out.

"A word of advice—chivalry only gets a man killed. You want Daisy, you found her. 'Course, you may not live much past this, but you can die with the satisfaction of honoring your promise."

He hated the bandit's condescending tone. But worse, he detested the knowledge that Rex was probably right.

Jasper's head was starting to throb again, and his stomach hadn't settled after the soup. With Emma Jane's clear lack of understanding of just how serious the situation was, there was no way he was going to get them all out alive.

He'd found Daisy, just as he'd promised. But the smirk on Rex's face told him that succeeding beyond this point was going to take a miracle.

Chapter Nine

Emma Jane had never hit a person in all her life, but if she could smack Jasper right about now, she would. He was glaring furiously, mouth set in a hard line, but didn't he realize that antagonizing this man was only going to get them all killed?

Holding the baby closer to her, Emma Jane gave the man her best smile. "I'm sure we will be most cooperative, and you will have no reason for hurting us."

The man slurped down the rest of his soup. "We'll see."

He turned to leave, but as his hand was on the door, Emma Jane spoke up again.

"I realize that I'm imposing on you... However, might I trouble you for the baby's name? I appreciate knowing that I'm caring for Daisy, and I'd sure like to know who this little guy is."

The man didn't turn around. "We all just refer to him as Ben's brat." Then he slammed the door behind him as he exited.

At least she'd tried. Obviously, she couldn't expect the bandits to warm up to her and have a friendly little chat over tea. But she was making progress, and soon enough, their ordeal would be over.

"What were you thinking, challenging a dangerous criminal like that?"

Jasper's scolding came as completely unexpected and, in Emma Jane's mind, completely inappropriate. Didn't he see that she was trying to keep them both alive?

"*Me?* You were the one who looked like you were trying to crucify him with your eyes. I was just trying to be sure he knew that we are not a threat."

"By telling him all about Daisy?"

"At least he confirmed her identity, which is more than any of the others have."

The baby started fussing again, so Emma Jane began rocking him slowly. Then she spoke in a soft voice.

"We can't quarrel. It upsets the baby. But you have to know that I am doing my very best to keep the peace to avoid any conflict with the bandits that would make them want to kill us. Is it so hard to try to be agreeable?"

The dark scowl on Jasper's face said that it was, indeed, a difficult task. In fact, he looked like he wanted to kill her almost as much as the bandits seemed to want to kill him.

"These men can't be reasoned with. They are cold-blooded murderers."

"So you keep saying." Emma Jane sat down in the rocking chair with the baby. "What proof do you have of this?"

"The man who was just in here? His name is Rex McGee. There are a number of wanted posters from several places with his name and face on it. Rumor has it that he's killed many a man just for giving him a cross look."

"I thought you didn't pay attention to rumors." Emma Jane couldn't help but glower at him. For all his talk about hating people saying bad things about him, he was awful quick to believe stories about the bandits.

"Wanted posters are not rumors." Jasper groaned and rubbed the sides of his head. "But you're right, I have no factual basis for the rest. I'm sorry."

And now Emma Jane was sorry. Clearly, Jasper's head was paining him, and here she was getting him all upset.

"You should rest. The men gave me some pain relieving powder to use on Daisy, but since I can't get her to take any of the broth, I could give it to you. I found it most helpful when my own head was hurting."

For a moment, she thought he'd refuse out of pure stubbornness.

But then he sighed. "Do you think it's safe?"

Emma Jane got up and showed him the packet. "It looks identical to the one I had when I was injured. I think you should try it."

Jasper nodded slowly and closed his eyes. "I suppose you're right."

She put the baby back in the crate, then mixed the powder. Part of her felt bad for using medicine intended for Daisy, but if the poor woman couldn't take it, then at least it was being put to good use.

Sitting next to Jasper, she handed him the concoction. "I would tell you to drink it slowly, but it tastes terrible, so you should drink quickly and get it over with."

He took the cup and did as she instructed. The lines

around his eyes seemed deeper as he released a ragged breath.

"Why don't you lie down and rest? I'm sure your head pains you more than you're letting on, and the rest will do you good."

Jasper examined her face, like he was seeing her for the first time. "I don't understand you."

"What's there to understand? You're in pain, and I'm trying to help you."

"And Daisy, a stranger."

He sounded so incredulous. Even after seeing her helping out with the pastor's mission, he seemed oblivious to the fact that helping others is what Emma Jane did.

"Why would I do any less?"

And then he looked at her with such intensity in his eyes. "But why haven't you ever helped yourself?"

His words thundered against her chest as she stood. How was she supposed to answer that question? Help herself? What did that even mean?

"I don't know what you're talking about."

She started to walk toward where she'd laid the baby down.

"Don't pick up that baby as an excuse to avoid the conversation."

Emma Jane turned to him. "What would you have me do instead?"

"I'm trying to figure you out. I have seen you take all kinds of abuse from others, but when it comes to taking care of someone else, you are like a tiger. No one gets in your way, and you stand up admirably to anyone who does. So why haven't you ever stood up for yourself?"

For a moment, it felt like Emma Jane couldn't

breathe. And then she did. She took a breath, and another.

"Because standing up for myself seemed like an exercise in futility. It never did any good."

Tears pricked the backs of her eyes as she remembered all the times she'd tried standing up for herself against people like Flora Montgomery.

"Who do you think you are?" Flora and her friends would taunt her and laugh.

But laughter wasn't the only thing Emma Jane remembered. Those darker memories, though, those she shoved down. No use in remembering when she could prevent them from happening again.

"If you're so brave in your defense of others, you should do the same for yourself."

Easy for him to say.

"I'll try." She started to go back to the baby, but once again, Jasper stopped her.

"Why are you so nice to the bandits?"

"Why shouldn't I be?"

"You don't owe them anything."

Emma Jane closed her eyes. Tried to shut down the thoughts of the past that had been threatening her ever since she was kidnapped.

"You're right. I don't. But I also know that the more cooperative I am, the less likely they are to harm me."

"Look at me."

She opened her eyes.

"You keep saying that, as if you know what it's like to be kidnapped. Have you been kidnapped before?"

Gentleness filled his voice, and compassion was in his brown eyes. They'd been at odds so much since his arrival at the cabin, and here was the reminder that underneath was a Jasper that she found she liked, quite a lot.

The truth was so far from his suspicions, and she found she couldn't give it voice. Yet how was she supposed to let him believe a lie?

"I've never been kidnapped."

Emma Jane swallowed, unable to tear her gaze from his. "But I know what it's like to live among people who make you afraid. Who will hurt you if you don't do as they ask."

"Who were you afraid of?"

She sighed, knowing that the only path out of this troubling conversation was the truth. Ignoring his previous request to not pick up the baby, she went to the baby and took him in her arms. Not as an excuse to avoid, but as comfort against the pain.

"My father got angry a lot. But I learned that if I just took care of things to make our household run smoothly, then he'd not be so angry."

Emma Jane sat in the rocking chair with the baby, snuggling him to her, and looking at him rather than Jasper's questioning eyes.

"Did he hurt you?"

The words pained her too much to come out. It somehow seemed disloyal to say such things about her father. He wasn't a bad man, not like these men.

Emma Jane didn't look up. "Everything was fine as long as I took care of everyone."

Then she brought her gaze to Jasper. "And that's what I'm doing here. Taking care of everyone so no one gets hurt."

"Your father..." A muscle pulsed in his jaw, and he rubbed his head again.

"I don't want to talk about it. Sometimes he drank too much. But everyone knows that. I learned to keep myself, and my sister, safe. And that's what I'm trying to do here. That's all that matters."

Standing, Emma Jane shifted the baby to another position as she grabbed a blanket from a nearby chair. "Now I must insist that you rest."

He looked at her, his eyes full of a fight, but his head clearly so weary that it was obvious what he needed. Fortunately, he lay down, and Emma Jane did her best to tuck the blanket around him.

"Thank you, Emma Jane," he said huskily, putting his hand over hers as she patted the blanket. "I appreciate what you've done, and I hope you get some rest, too."

"I will." She gave his hand a squeeze, noting the warmth that passed between them.

As cross as he'd been with her, he still had room in his heart for kind feelings toward her. For warmth. Perhaps even for friendship.

Then she got up and walked over to where Daisy lay. Her fever had gone down, and she seemed to be less restless than she'd been when Emma Jane had first arrived.

"Everything's going to be all right, Daisy," she told the sleeping woman. "Your baby is just fine, and I'm taking good care of him."

As if to confirm Emma Jane's words, the baby gurgled softly, a contented sound, giving her hope that things really were going to be okay.

Though she'd been firm in telling Jasper that being kind to the bandits was the best way to keep them alive, part of her feared that it wouldn't be enough. Because what she hadn't told Jasper was while her tactics worked to placate her father, nothing had ever seemed good enough for her mother. The only difference was that while her father used his hand, her mother always wounded Emma Jane with her words. And sometimes, Emma Jane thought she'd much rather have the bruises.

Marriage to Jasper hadn't been what she'd wanted. But in all her days as his wife, she hadn't once been afraid he was going to hurt her. His mother might not be the warmest woman in the world, and yes, her insults did sting, but Jasper and his father had shown her more kindness and consideration than her own family had.

Which again felt disloyal, since she was supposed to honor her father and mother. They did the best they could, she supposed, considering her father's battle with the drink and gambling. And her mother, being forced to live in a rough place like Leadville, when she'd been the belle of society before the war. Of course, Emma Jane had just been a baby during the war, and she didn't remember any of it.

All she knew was that her mother said the war had changed her father, changed their family, and nothing had been the same since. But at least with Emma Jane's marriage to Jasper, her family could have their finances restored. Maybe then they would find the happiness that had eluded them all these years.

As for Emma Jane, she'd learned not to pursue happiness for herself. But in taking care of others, she at least found a place where she could have contentment of sorts.

The smell of sizzling bacon woke Jasper. He tried to lift his head, but it felt heavy, like it was full of lead. When he opened his eyes, he could see Emma Jane, serving the bandits breakfast. He watched her, noting the same polite demeanor she'd had the previous day. But now, knowing what she'd said about her father, he noticed something more.

While Emma Jane appeared pleasant enough, the light didn't reach her eyes. How had he missed it before? She played the role of the servant beautifully, but her heart wasn't there.

He'd been wrong to chastise her. He still didn't like her being friendly with the bandits, but he could see where she was coming from. His heart weighed heavy in his chest as he realized how hard her life had been, and how he'd never noticed before.

"I fixed you some eggs," Emma Jane said softly as she knelt beside him. "If you're up to it, that is."

He tried reading her. Was the kindness because she cared for him, or because she feared him? The answer shouldn't matter, but he found it did—very much.

"Thank you." He struggled to sit up. "You don't have to wait on me, you know. You're not my servant."

She smiled, and her blue eyes warmed. "I know. But you're hurt, and it's important for you to get your strength up. So eat."

Emma Jane set a plate in front of him, then went to pick the baby up.

Efficient as always, and focused on the child. He thought again about their discussion last night regarding children. Rather, his avoidance of the discussion. As he watched her sing softly to the baby, he realized that she, too, had given up all dreams of having children.

Could they find a compromise? No, not a compromise. One didn't have a baby out of compromise. But could they find enough common ground that would allow them to have the sort of feelings a man and woman needed to bring a child into the world?

Emma Jane would make an excellent mother.

And the more he watched her, with the sun streaming into the room through cracks in the window, the more he had to admit that she was quite lovely. Even now, with her hair falling out of its bun, her dress dirty and a smudge of something on her cheek, he couldn't help but think everyone had been mistaken in mocking her for being unattractive.

"Is something amiss?" Emma Jane looked directly at him. She'd caught him staring.

"No." Swallowing hard, he had to remind himself that there was still a lot unsettled between them. Any admiration or attempts at expressing such admiration was best left for later.

One of the men entered the room, carrying Jasper's saddlebag. "Thought you might find something useful in here, miss."

A genuine smile lit up Emma Jane's face. "Oh, thank you, Mack. You've been so helpful."

"It was nothing, miss. You've sure brightened this place up, and while I do regret that we can't let you go, the least I can do is make sure you're comfortable."

Jasper tried not to groan. Unfortunately, he wasn't successful, because Emma Jane looked right at him. "Is your head paining you again? I could make you some more headache powder."

He sighed, then nodded. As much as he'd like to say he was completely recovered, he'd be a liar. And he'd need all his strength to plan their next move. Emma Jane might have faith that the gang would let them live after it was all over, but he knew better.

They might be under heavy guard, yet there *had* to be a way to escape.

She prepared the powder, then gave it to him. He drank it quickly, then, to ease the taste, ate some of the eggs Emma Jane had given him.

While he ate, she opened his saddlebags. He hadn't kept anything valuable in them, especially since he hadn't been preparing for a trip, but hopefully she'd happen upon something useful.

"Oh, my!" Emma Jane's eyes lit up. "You found my Bible!" Then she stopped and looked at him apologetically. "That is, *our* Bible. I was hoping you'd see it and realize I'd left you a clue."

Jasper couldn't help but grin back at her. "No, it's your Bible. I know it was a wedding gift to both of us, but it brings you such joy that I wouldn't dream of it being anything but yours."

He didn't have the heart to tell her that while the Bible was important to her, it was just a book to him. But it seemed to mean a lot to Emma Jane, and if it made her happy, then he was all for it.

"As for finding your Bible." He gave a shrug. "I may not know much about you, but I have noticed the way you always seem to have it with you."

Then he looked around—some of the bandits appeared to be huddled over some papers. Jasper could identify Rex, and he knew that several others remained outside. As he observed their interactions, it was becoming clearer how the gang's leadership had evolved with the arrest of Ben Perry and other key members of the gang. Of course, this meant that there was no way they were getting out alive.

No matter how optimistic Emma Jane sounded, the

gang wasn't going to be willing to risk being so exposed. Ultimately, if Jasper didn't find means of escape, they had but days to live. The only question was why the bandits were keeping them alive in the first place. Jasper didn't buy for a minute that they were afraid that killing him would bring about more attention. Surely they had to know, that even with Jasper having been kidnapped, there would be more people looking for them.

So what was their game?

As if he could sense the direction of Jasper's thoughts, Rex turned toward Jasper. "I need you to write me a letter."

"For...?" Even without looking at Emma Jane, he could tell she was glaring at him over his sullen tone.

"To your father. Letting him know you're alive, and where he can bring the ransom."

"I believe I mentioned that my father doesn't pay ransom."

Rex gave him a long, calculated look. "Doesn't matter. The sheriff will still send men to the drop-off point, giving us the perfect distraction to take care of stuff. We just need you to oblige us with a letter proving you're alive and that we mean business."

Jasper shook his head. At least he got the answer to his unspoken question. They wanted to keep him alive long enough to use him as bait.

Which meant as soon as the bandits had their plan in motion, Jasper and Emma Jane were dead. Well, he wasn't going to make it that easy for them.

"And what if I don't write that letter?"

Rex turned his attention to Emma Jane, who clutched her Bible to her chest and was observing their interactions with wide eyes.

"It'd be a shame if anything happened to that pretty little wife of yours."

Emma Jane's face screwed into an expression he couldn't read. For a moment, he thought she might start crying, but instead, she just stood there, looking like...

Like she did on their wedding day.

She hadn't wanted to marry him any more than he'd wanted to marry her. And now she was a pawn in some sick criminal's game, when all she'd wanted was to help others.

"What do you want me to write?"

He shouldn't have caved so easily, but as Emma Jane's posture relaxed, he knew it was the right decision, at least for her peace of mind.

Rex handed him a piece of paper. "And don't think I won't know if you're trying to trick me. I can read and write just as well as any of those uppity teachers in the school."

He gave Jasper pen and ink. "The only thing keeping you alive is your cooperation. That and Jimmy's squeamishness. He might not want to leave a trail of dead bodies, but make no mistake. I will shoot you dead if I have to. And if that means killing Jimmy, I'll do that, too." Rex's smile as he spoke verified the rumors Jasper had heard.

Rex liked killing. Chills pricked the back of Jasper's neck.

Did Emma Jane understand now how lethal these men were?

He looked at her for signs of having understood the import of Rex's words, but she was seemingly unaware, having opened her Bible and was now engrossed in its pages. Hands flexing at his sides, he strained to keep his temper in check. Maybe it wasn't right to be mad at her for it, but it seemed wrong that while he was trying to keep them alive, she seemed more interested in her Bible.

What was the Bible going to do for them? It wasn't as though God was going to reach down from Heaven to save them from these evil men. No, it was up to Jasper to find a way to get them out of this situation—before the gang decided they were no longer useful.

He picked up the pen and began writing the words Rex dictated. For now, he'd play the game and pretend to be just as agreeable as Emma Jane. But he'd be watching—and waiting. And he would find a way to save them both.

Chapter Ten

Emma Jane tried focusing on the words of the Psalms. David knew what it was like to be pursued by an enemy with greater might and power than his own. Surely God would give them a way out. If Jasper's stubbornness didn't get them killed first.

The baby started to cry. Again. Emma Jane sighed. If only Daisy would wake up and give her some idea as to how to take care of her son. At first, giving him the milk and some love had seemed to turn a baby who never stopped crying into a peaceful little thing. But now, all he seemed to do was cry, with a few moments of respite here and there.

She put her Bible down and went to pick up the baby. Fortunately, he always calmed down a little in her arms. His wails turned into whimpers, and she cradled him close as she went back to her chair to focus on her Bible again.

The bandits had gone outside, but the occasional shadows passing the window told Emma Jane that they were still standing guard. Jasper had tried the door once but found it locked tight.

Now he was pacing, walking the length of the cabin and back again. She should be grateful he didn't appear to have any ill effects from the injury to his head, but right now, he was making her crazy.

His pacing, the baby's whimpering and Daisy's ragged breathing—it was enough to send a woman to Bedlam.

"Please, Jasper. Can you sit and rest? You don't want to have a relapse."

Selfishly, she'd admit that any concern over his health was secondary to her own need for peace.

"I don't like being locked up like an animal."

"We don't have much of a choice in the matter, so you might as well make the best of it."

She didn't mean to sound so shrewish, but really…

"You're good at that, aren't you?"

Jerking her chin in his direction, she gave him a defiant look. Jasper's words sounded almost like an insult. But he didn't understand that, for most people, it was the only way to survive.

"Yes, I am. I've found that most of the circumstances of my life have been foisted upon me and are not of my choosing. But I can choose how I respond to them."

Emma Jane took a deep breath. "In the past, I haven't always done such a good job of that. Sometimes I am almost ashamed of how badly I've reacted in difficult situations. But I've learned that such behavior never makes things better."

The baby had started to drift off to sleep. She looked down at him and wondered what choices he would have in this world. Born of a notorious criminal and a woman of the night, he would never live the kind of respectable life Emma Jane had. And her level of respectability had been marginal at best. All she'd ever wanted was respectability, and yet here she held an infant whose chances of attaining it were much more miniscule than her own.

"But don't you want things to be different?" Jasper's voice sounded almost hoarse, like he was trying to contain emotions and not quite succeeding.

He was referring, of course, to their marriage. Contrary to popular belief, Emma Jane wasn't stupid. He didn't want their marriage any more than she had. All right. He'd wanted their marriage even less than she had. After all, Emma Jane had already accepted that her fate would not involve a love match.

Still, she had hoped that, in some way, the man she married would at least want her.

"Of course I want things to be different. But they are what they are, so why would I waste my time wishing for things that aren't possible?"

"Or you could make them what you want to be." His words were quiet as he sank into a chair by the fire.

What was he saying? How did you make a marriage what you wanted it to be when neither of you wanted the marriage? Or was he suggesting they end it?

"Or you make the best of what you have." She looked at him squarely, challenging him. Making lemonade out of lemons was something Emma Jane had become quite good at. Not just in her life circumstances, but even in turning someone else's cast-off dress into something beautiful. Everyone had said her sister, Gracie, was one of the finest dressed young ladies in town.

No one realized that it had been Emma Jane's skill that had accomplished that goal.

Even now, as she cared for this tiny baby with few

supplies, she'd made do, and while things weren't perfect, the baby seemed content enough.

She pulled her chair closer to Daisy. "Do you think she can hear us?"

"You're avoiding the conversation."

"What conversation?" Emma Jane didn't look at him, not wanting to see the expression on his face. Just as with the bandits, he seemed to be deliberately trying to bait her.

"About you."

"Me?" This time she did look at him. "Are you trying to provoke some sort of disagreement? I don't know what else you want to hear from me. I've told you that I believe in making the best of things. I'm not sure what else there is to discuss on the matter."

His eyes darkened, and his expression lay hidden by the shadows, which seemed to have deepened since he sat down.

"I'm trying to understand."

Though his words seemed to be in earnest, there seemed to be something else beneath the surface. Something Emma Jane wasn't sure she wanted to explore.

"Then please accept my need to make the best of things. We don't have a choice in being here. I could just as easily play the hysterical woman at being kidnapped. I've played that part before, and it did me no good. At least in this situation, I can feel like I'm doing something useful, and I have a distraction to keep my mind off the thing I fear the most."

"And what do you fear the most?"

Emma Jane swallowed. "Dying, of course. I have so much I want to do in my life, and I…"

She looked down at the baby. "I don't want to leave

this earth without having experienced some of the joys I've been longing for."

Truthfully, as the infant snuggled against her, she had to admit that caring for this child was one of those joys. She'd always hoped for a baby of her own, yet the longer she had this precious little boy with her, the more he seemed like her own.

What was she going to do when Daisy got better?

"What joys?" Jasper's stare felt so heavy on her she couldn't bear to look up.

She didn't have an answer for him. After all, most of the things she wanted seemed too impossible to even give voice. Love, happiness—those were ideas she had to find a way to let go of. But the warm bundle in her arms forced one word out of her mouth.

"Family."

"I want that, too," Jasper said gruffly.

Her head snapped up and she stared at him. "You said ours would be a marriage in name only."

"We could discuss…"

Jasper shifted as though the idea made him just as uncomfortable as it made her. No, worse. It seemed as though he was suggesting something completely intolerable to him, but he'd be willing to do it for the greater good.

"No. I'm perfectly aware of what having a family would take. And I can't do…that…without love."

Emma Jane could feel the heat on her face rise. Proper ladies didn't speak of such things. But a gentleman would never suggest them, either. She closed her eyes. Except, of course, if they were husband and wife. Which she and Jasper technically were.

"I'm sorry. I didn't mean to offend you. I just thought,

since we both wanted the same thing, we could find a way to compromise."

Finally finding the courage to look at him, Emma Jane opened her eyes. "I can't compromise on that."

She looked down at Daisy, whose breathing had grown more ragged. "It seems to me that a woman who compromises on those issues is no better than the women of her profession."

Smoothing Daisy's hair off her feverish brow, she examined the woman's features. Though probably younger than Emma Jane, Daisy's face was marked with years of rough living. "I mean no disrespect to Daisy, because I'm sure she did the best she could do."

Emma Jane brought her attention back to Jasper. "I've sacrificed enough in my life. There are some things I can cling to, and this is one of them. If you insist on fully being my husband, I won't fight you. But I hope you respect my desire to have at least that one choice belong to me."

"I would never force a woman in that regard. Like you, I believe such an act should be one of love." She couldn't read his expression in the firelight, but his tone was unmistakable. She'd offended him—deeply.

"I'm sorry… I didn't mean to suggest that you would. I was only trying…"

"Don't. I was wrong to bring it up," he said curtly. "We shouldn't be having this conversation. I'm sorry. Go back to your Bible, and I'll…" He shrugged. "Well, I'll do whatever I have to do. And we'll try not to infringe on each other's space too much."

Emma Jane didn't bother trying to respond. Jasper was right. It was the wrong conversation for them to be having, especially now in light of their current predicament. She sighed. Besides, talking about it only emphasized the fact that neither of them loved each other. Clearly, Jasper wasn't even attracted to her, given his penchant for kissing the other girls in town, and the fact that he hadn't even tried once with Emma Jane.

Oh, if only she hadn't had that silly dream of him kissing her in the mine. If only the feel of his lips against hers wasn't so deeply embedded in her memory.

But that wasn't love. Desire, maybe. Curiosity, certainly. But love? Love was an emotion she dared not even wish for, especially when it came to Jasper Jackson.

Daisy made a heaving sound, like she was struggling to breathe.

Her face was the color of day-old ashes, and as much as Emma Jane hated to admit it, there was little she could do for the other woman. She'd only seen one other person die, the Widow Sanders, who Emma Jane had briefly taken care of so her family could have extra money during one of her father's bad spells. Eugene Sanders had been a family friend, and he'd offered her father a goodly sum if only Emma Jane would sit with his elderly mother and make her last days peaceful.

Daisy had the look of Widow Sanders about her. So close to being claimed by death, yet desperately trying to cling to life. Fighting, not so much because she had it in her to live, but because she had so much unfinished business on earth.

Widow Sanders had been hanging on to the hope that her estranged daughter would come home. It was not until Emma Jane herself had whispered, "I love you. I forgive you," that she'd finally slipped into the beyond. Her words hadn't been a lie—she'd relied on the grace and peace of Christ to give a dying woman the comfort she'd needed. The daughter only came for the reading of the will, to take her thousand-dollar inheritance, then leave.

What comfort could Emma Jane give Daisy in these last hours? She'd been worshipping silently, but now, when she opened her Bible, she began to read aloud. Widow Sanders had taken great comfort in Emma Jane's Bible reading. During her brief awakenings, she'd told Emma Jane as such. She'd even confessed to Emma Jane her worries about God not wanting her after all she'd done in her life. But when Emma Jane spoke to her of God's forgiveness and love, Widow Sanders had appeared to take comfort.

Emma Jane read, noticing that the squeak of Jasper's footsteps against the floor had quieted. Even the baby had finally ceased fussing and had drifted off into a peaceful sleep.

She looked up at him, pausing in her recitation.

"Don't. I find your voice soothing." Jasper had settled into one of the chairs at the table and was watching her.

Emma Jane felt her face heat. "I'm not sure how to respond to that." She turned her attention back to her Bible.

"I was giving you a compliment. It's traditional to say thank-you when someone gives you a compliment."

His voice had taken on a teasing note, but Emma Jane found it unsettling. She'd seen him jest many a young lady, to be sure. He'd just never really done so with her. Why would he, when everyone knew that teasing was a form of flirting?

"Thank you," Emma Jane mumbled, not wanting to pursue the subject further.

She began to read again. Daisy's breathing caught, stopped, then just when Emma Jane thought it had been the other woman's last, she took another labored breath.

The poor woman was hanging on so tightly.

Lord, please, I've seen death before, and I know this woman is close. If it is Your will to save her, then save her. But if she is to pass, tell me what I need to ease her transition into the hereafter.

The baby gave a small whimper. Of course! What mother would willingly leave this earth with such a small child with no one to care for him?

"I'll care for your baby like he was my own," whispered Emma Jane, squeezing Daisy's hand. As she made the promise, she felt the love swell up in her heart for the baby. Oh, she already loved him, there was no question of that, but this was an additional measure, the kind a mother felt for a child. And, as she recalled, the love Pastor Lassiter spoke of as the kind that came from the Lord. She'd sought this love for her mother-in-law, but as the infant lay in Emma Jane's arms, she knew the Lord had reserved it for her to give to this innocent child.

Daisy gave one last shuddering breath, then was still. A tear rolled down Emma Jane's cheek as she realized the other woman was gone.

Emma Jane looked down at the baby. "I still don't know your name, little one. But it seems to me with no one left to tell me, I'm going to have to give you one myself."

The baby looked up at her, his dark blue eyes warm and trusting. As the son of a fallen woman, he had no hope, no future. But as the son of Emma Jane Jackson, wife of one of the wealthiest men in Leadville, he would have everything.

She recalled the story of Moses, how his mother had given him up to be raised by the pharaoh's daughter. Her sacrifice had given him a chance at life.

"Moses," she said softly, stroking the boy's hair. "I will call you Moses. Because, like your namesake, you are being given a great opportunity at life, and I pray you will do great things with that opportunity."

Jasper wasn't surprised when Emma Jane informed him of Daisy's passing. The woman's labored breathing had told him she didn't have much time left. He'd tried telling himself otherwise, but he'd known.

What good had his mission to save her done?

He'd failed Mel. The woman had died, taking a bullet for him, and all she'd wanted, her whole reason for living, had been to give Daisy a good life.

And now her sister was dead.

He didn't even know what illness had befallen Daisy, but surely, had he gotten to her sooner, maybe she wouldn't have needed to die. If only he'd been able to get her to a doctor.

Jasper looked over at Emma Jane, who sat in the rocking chair, quietly reading her Bible to the baby. She'd pulled the blanket over Daisy's face, but having a dead woman in the room with them still felt wrong.

Frustration knotted his gut.

All of it was wrong. Daisy dying. Being locked in this old cabin. A baby who'd started wailing again. Emma Jane, trying to console the poor child.

The door opened, and Ace Perry, Ben's older brother, walked in. Now the pieces of the puzzle fit together.

"I thought you said that milk you got would shut the brat up."

Mack, who'd followed him in, shrugged. "Maybe babies don't like goat milk. Was the best I could do, getting a goat from that farm. Don't reckon I've seen any cows around."

Emma Jane started to approach them, and Jasper bit back a groan. Was she ever going to learn? Why didn't she trust him to take care of things?

"I'm afraid I have bad news for you," she said quietly. "Daisy has passed away."

The mournful tone to his wife's voice almost made him want to cry. How could she be so tenderhearted toward a stranger she'd never really met? She truly sounded grieved over the loss.

"Well, that's one less problem we have to deal with." Ace grinned, then clapped Mack on the back. "See, now you won't have to worry about taking care of her."

"She was Ben's girl," Mack said, with an air of reverence that Jasper couldn't help but understand why Emma Jane liked him.

If you'd asked him why bandits were bad, he'd have just said because they were bad. But Mack had a sense of humanness, of gentility, that made Jasper wonder if there wasn't more to his original assumptions than he'd thought.

"And Ben's gone. Hanged by a bunch of vigilantes because he got sloppy."

There was no sadness in the other man's voice over the loss of his brother. Merely disgust at having been caught.

"Daisy was still a good woman, you know that." Mack walked over to the body. "We gotta do right by her."

Then Mack turned his attention to Emma Jane. "And the boy. He's your blood, Ace, you've got to…"

"I don't got to do anything. There's no proof, other than Daisy's word, that the brat was Ben's. Even Ben had his doubts."

"I'm going to take care of him," Emma Jane piped up. "I promised Daisy I'd love him like my own."

Ace grinned, his gold-capped teeth gleaming in the sunlight. "See there. It's already been settled."

Settled? Jasper shot a glance at Emma Jane, who stood proudly holding the baby. When had they discussed her taking care of the baby? Yes, while here in the cabin, it seemed like a reasonable thing to do. But moving forward? She hadn't even asked his opinion.

"If you've no objection, I'm calling him Moses." Again, Emma Jane looked at Ace for confirmation, completely ignoring Jasper. A baby wasn't like a stray puppy you could just bring home on a whim.

Ace snorted. "You can call him whatever you want. Like I said, not my problem."

Mack, though, turned to Emma Jane. "That sounds like a mighty nice name. The baby was born a couple of weeks before Ben was arrested, and Daisy wanted to wait until he could have a say in things before naming him. Now that the boy's daddy is gone, well…"

Ace walked over to Mack and smacked him on the side of the head. "What'd I say about being too free in your talk? Ben's big mouth and need to prove a point to that stupid lawman is what derailed our plans in the first place. We were this close to getting off to Mexico, and I'm not going to have it ruined a second time."

Jasper forced himself not to laugh at Ace's mistake. In chastising Mack, Ace confirmed what Emma Jane had already told him. They were planning something big, and then they were all headed to Mexico.

The question was, what was he plotting?

"Ain't no harm in being nice. This miss, here, she's been nothing but good to us," Mack said.

The door opened wider, and Ray and Jimmy strode in. "That's what I've been trying to tell Ray," Jimmy said. "She has no part in any of this, and with as much blood's on our hands, the last thing I want to do is take an innocent life."

Ray pulled out his gun and examined it. "I ain't got no problem with that." Then he pointed the gun at Jimmy. "I ain't got no problem with killing yellow-bellied cowards, either."

Jimmy slapped the gun away. "I'm not a coward, and you know it. Just ask Rex."

"Enough!" Ace's shout rang through the cabin. "No one is killing anyone."

Somehow, Jasper didn't find that comforting. He looked over at Emma Jane, who also didn't appear to be comforted by the bandit's words.

"Now." Ace turned his attention on Jimmy and Ray. "Did you or did you not go into town and deliver the letter, following my directions exactly?"

"Yes, sir," both men answered in unison.

"Good." Ace grinned at Jasper. "Your family has been informed of your status, as well as my demands. While it would be easier on my men to take care of business now, we may need to keep you around for a

while, just in case things don't go according to plan."
He spoke casually, but there was a dangerous glint in
his eye. "I know I said I was going to let you live, but
that depends on both your family's cooperation and
your compliance. Am I understood?"

Jasper didn't blink. "Yes." Ace might talk a good
game about possibly letting them live, but there was
no way.

Ace turned his attention back to his men. "Mack, go
dispose of the body."

"Dispose?" Emma Jane's voice squeaked as she in-
terrupted. "Aren't you going to have a funeral?"

A funeral? Jasper gaped as Ace laughed.

"We're not the sort of people a preacher is going to
visit."

Mack took a step forward. "That's a mighty fine
idea. We don't need the preacher. Ray can sing us some
songs on his guitar, and Jimmy can say a few words
since he used to…"

"Enough!" Ace glared at Mack. "We can discuss
this outside."

Jasper bit back his smile as the men left. The door
had stuck as Jimmy closed it, and Jasper could see that
it wasn't fully latched.

He crept toward the window and looked out. The
men had gathered near a barn and were arguing, gesturing wildly. Five more men rode in, joining them. No
one was watching the cabin.

At the door, Jasper noticed the simple lock mecha-
nism. Now that the door was open and he had a chance
to examine it, he could see how to disable it. This cabin
wasn't equipped for keeping prisoners. Which was prob-

ably why some of the men were eager to kill them and get it over with.

The arguing ceased, and Mack started walking back to the cabin. Jasper stepped away and toward Emma Jane.

"They're coming back. Pretend you and I have been busy talking."

Emma Jane stared at him.

"I hope you can make more of those biscuits for dinner," Jasper said a little more loudly than he'd been speaking. "I had no idea you could cook so well."

"I'll see what I can…" Emma Jane still looked puzzled as the door flew open.

"I'd be obliged if you'd make those biscuits, too," Mack said, grinning as he strode in.

Emma Jane nodded slowly. The baby began to fuss again, reminding Jasper of the promise Emma Jane had no right in making.

But he couldn't mention it now. Not when Mack, Emma Jane's biggest supporter, was in the cabin. Mack had begun wrapping Daisy in the blanket Emma Jane had covered her with.

"I'll be taking the body for burial now," Mack said solemnly, looking Emma Jane in the eye. "We'll be having a short service and digging her a grave. I know you think we're a bunch of animals, but some of us were raised to do the right thing, even when it doesn't seem like it."

Jasper's gut churned as he saw the sympathy flicker across his wife's face.

"Then why *do* you live like this?"

Mack picked Daisy up as though she weighed no more than the baby in Emma Jane's arms.

"A lot of reasons. Mostly, a man does something he's not proud of, then there's no going back. I may not like everything Ace does, but he's been good to me. Might be hard to believe, but out of all the men I've worked for, Ace is the best."

He tipped his hat at Emma Jane. "I don't expect you to understand. But I do hope that when you say those prayers of yours, you find it in your heart to say a few for me."

Emma Jane gave him a smile. "I'm sure you know by now that I'd be happy to. And if you ever want to pray with me, I'd be glad to do so."

Her words made Jasper's heart do a funny thing. He wasn't sure what it meant, because part of him still thought she had to be the most naive woman on the planet for thinking she could befriend a gang of notorious criminals. But part of him marveled at the kind of woman she was to even try.

Mack didn't respond to Emma Jane as he exited the cabin. With his arms full, he didn't quite get the door closed behind him again.

Were they testing Jasper? To see if he'd try to escape, then shoot him in the act?

Once again, Jasper crept to the window. The bandits were off to the side, talking among themselves as Mack approached, carrying Daisy's body.

He took stock of the land, noting the clouds moving in. They were in for a big storm. By the smell of the wind, it carried a heavy snow that would leave them trapped for days. With the bandits distracted, this might be their only chance at escape.

Chapter Eleven

Emma Jane stared at Jasper as he announced his plan to make a run for it. "That's madness."

"Right now, their attention is on burying Daisy. With the wind picking up, they're going to start noticing the weather blowing in." Jasper pointed in the direction of the field. "They have livestock grazing there that they'll want to get in the barn before the storm hits. They're going to be so occupied that it'll be a while before they notice we're gone."

Two riders came in from the direction of the canyon opening leading to where the cabin lay.

"I'm pretty sure those are the lookouts. Right now, this place is unguarded and might be the only chance we have."

"Pretty sure?" The baby fussed against her.

Jasper gave her a hard look. "As sure as I am that if we don't escape, we're dead, anyway. If I'm going to die, I'd rather die trying."

"All right," Emma Jane said, trying not to sound as resigned as she felt. "Let me gather the baby's things."

"What things?" Jasper shook his head. "The baby's not coming with us."

Jasper might as well have shot her himself. "Wh-what do you mean?"

"Look, you made a promise to keep the baby without even consulting me. I didn't agree to care for a baby."

"You promised to save Daisy without consulting me." She snuggled Moses closer to her. "I am all he has in this world. You heard Ace. He wants nothing to do with the baby, and I'm pretty sure none of the other men do, either. They all call this sweet little boy a brat."

"Saving a person is different from taking a child into your home. You always act without thinking. I'm telling you, we are not taking this baby with us."

Emma Jane went and sat in the rocking chair. She'd never seen Jasper so angry, with his arms folded across his chest, and his eyes set so firm. She missed the twinkle they usually held. They'd both said they wanted children, and they'd both agreed that they did not have the kind of relationship people had to have children. He was the one who mentioned compromise. Surely taking in a child who needed a home was a sort of compromise.

Besides, he'd made a promise, too. "What about your promise to Mel about taking care of Daisy? Shouldn't that extend to taking care of her child?"

Jasper let out an exasperated huff. "I don't have time to argue with you about this. We have to make a run for it while we can. And taking a baby, especially one who won't stop fussing, is going to slow us down. We're barely going to make it out as it is. Bringing him will make it impossible."

Emma Jane didn't move. "Then I guess you're going alone. I won't leave Moses."

"Stop calling him that name! He's not your baby."

The door opened, and Jimmy walked in. "What's all this fuss about?"

The weight of Jasper's glare on her stung. What exactly did he think she was going to do? Tell a bandit they were arguing over escape plans?

"My husband doesn't approve of my plans to raise poor Moses as my own."

Jimmy snorted. "Don't blame you there. I wouldn't raise some other fellow's git. It ain't natural. And I got the scars from my stepdaddy's belt to prove it."

He grabbed a book off one of the shelves. "They want me to read a few words from the Bible."

Shrugging, he looked at Emma Jane. "'Course, I don't really know what to read, so if you'd like to come say a few words, I'm sure it would be welcome. The good Lord may not shine His face upon us, but it doesn't mean we don't have a little respect for doing the right thing by our dead."

For a moment, Jimmy looked sorrowful. "You may not like the kind of woman Daisy was, but she was a good woman. And we all respected her, no matter what Ace might say."

Emma Jane nodded slowly. "I'm sure she was. I'd be happy to suggest some passages to read, and if you'd like me to say a few words, I can do that, too."

Jasper's glare on her was so hard she didn't need to look at him. They were clearly at an impasse on the escape plan, so what harm did it do for her to say a few words at Moses's mother's funeral?

"I'd be obliged." Jimmy started for the door, then stopped. "Let me check with Ace first. He may not like me bringing you out of the cabin."

As soon as Jimmy shut the door behind him, Jasper stormed over toward her.

"What do you think you're doing?" His whisper was harsh, biting, unlike the man she'd thought she'd gotten to know.

"Cooperating."

"How are we supposed to escape if you're presiding over a funeral?"

Emma Jane took a deep breath. "We are not escaping unless Moses comes with us."

She emphasized the *we* as she gave him her most obstinate look. She'd promised to raise Moses as her own, and as far as she was concerned, she'd die to save her own child. So if staying here to take care of Moses while Jasper escaped meant sacrificing her own life, then so be it.

"He's just an innocent baby," Emma Jane said, using her most pleading voice. "A child of God…just like all of us. You were the one who stayed in a burning brothel to make sure everyone got out safely. If you were thinking clearly, you'd be doing anything to save him, too." Looking at him desperately, she asked, "Why aren't you?"

Jasper's face crumpled. "Because I'm not even sure I can save us."

He turned and walked toward the fire. "Bringing along a colicky baby only makes it that much more impossible."

Then he spun around, eyes blazing. "Fine. Bring the baby. But you're not keeping him."

Jasper's face was unreadable, and though she was resolute about keeping Moses, now was not the time to challenge him. He was right about the difficulty in surviving an escape. Which was why part of her brain screamed that it was suicide to even try.

However, the practical side knew that they'd never survive if they stayed. She wasn't so naive as to believe anymore that the bandits intended to let them live. She'd seen too much of their bloodthirsty side. "I'll gather his things." Emma Jane filled Jasper's saddlebag with the makeshift bottles and scraps of cloth used to change the baby. It wasn't much, but hopefully they wouldn't need them long. As she recalled, it wasn't a very long trip back to town.

"Someone's coming."

Jasper moved back to the fire as Emma Jane set the saddlebag on the ground by the door. Near enough to grab easily, but not so near as to look suspicious.

Jimmy opened the door. "Sorry, miss. I appreciate your kind offer, but Ace isn't willing to take a chance on letting you out of the cabin. What do you suggest I read?"

He held out the Bible, and she turned it to the Twenty-third Psalm. "Try this one."

"Thank you." He tipped his hat at her and left.

Jasper immediately returned to his post by the window. "It looks like they're all gathered on the north side of the barn. I'm going out first. Look for me to the left, and when I signal, hurry out to meet me."

Emma Jane watched as Jasper fiddled with the door handle, then quietly slipped out, closing the door behind him. She watched as he ran to the side of the cabin, then stopped. The bandits still appeared to be oblivious to anything other than Daisy's services. Actually, they were still busy digging her grave, and it appeared the men watching were enjoying the spectacle of the other men digging.

She looked in the direction Jasper had gone, but he'd disappeared. Panic swept through her. Had the bandits gotten him?

Clutching Moses closer to her, she pulled a shawl she'd found tight against her, tying the baby against her body. The shawl probably belonged to Daisy, and Emma Jane liked to think that it would be good for Moses to have something of his mother's.

Then Jasper gave the signal. The tightness in her chest eased momentarily as she realized he was safe— for now. Emma Jane grabbed the saddlebag, then exited the cabin, pulling the door tightly closed as she left. Hopefully, none of the men would return to the cabin for a while, and they'd have some time before they realized that Jasper and Emma Jane had taken off.

The wind whipped fiercely at her as she made her way to the small shed Jasper hid behind. Tiny pellets of ice pelted her, a hint of the storm to come.

Was it wise to leave now, or one more reason they were doomed?

Moses started to fuss, and Emma Jane put her little finger in his mouth, hoping he'd suckle and be quiet. Fortunately, that was all the comfort the tiny baby needed, and he nestled more closely to her body.

"They left a horse saddled over there." Jasper pointed at a horse several yards away. "I'm going to bring him over here. We'll have to ride double. It's too risky to try for two horses."

As Jasper went to get the horse, Emma Jane surveyed their surroundings. The bandits had chosen a good location for their ranch, with the natural protection of the mountains around them, and several rock formations to act as sentinels where the men could guard the place.

Jasper brought the horse over. "Give me the saddlebag."

She handed it to him.

"Why is this so heavy? We can't take much."

"Moses needs his milk and change of diapers and clothes." Selfishly, she'd also packed her Bible. It had come too far to be left behind now.

Jasper didn't respond but took the saddlebag and secured it to the horse.

"You'll have to ride astride," he told her solemnly. "It's not proper, but it's the only way we're going to make good time."

Emma Jane nodded slowly. "I can do it."

He helped her onto the horse, then mounted. The horse reared. Emma Jane clung to Jasper as he got the horse under control.

"Well, I guess we know why he was standing all alone with a saddle on him. He's barely saddle broke."

"I don't know what that means," she said.

"It's going to be a rough ride. Hang on as tight as you can, and if I tell you to do something, do it quickly, without questioning or arguing."

"All right."

"Now stay quiet."

Jasper led the horse into the clearing. They had several dozen yards of open space where the bandits could see them before they would find the protection of the rocks.

Once they got to the rocks, and out of sight of the bandits, Jasper made a clicking sound, and his legs scraped against hers as he urged the horse on.

The horse took off—faster than anything Emma Jane had ever been on, even faster than when the bandits had kidnapped her.

After the initial jolt, the horse settled into a rhythm, and as she squeezed Jasper tight, she found the warmth of his body in front of hers comforting. Her arms wrapped around his large, solid frame made her feel more secure than she'd imagined. Even little Moses seemed to be lulled into sleep as they barreled down the mountainside.

It seemed almost impossible to feel so sheltered with so much at stake. The farther they got from the cabin, the safer Emma Jane felt. At least until she looked down. The ground whizzed past them at an alarming speed.

"Don't," Jasper commanded. "If you look at the ground, you'll lose your orientation. Look out or close your eyes."

"How did you know?"

"I can feel your weight shift. Keep steady."

She pressed her head against his back, keeping enough space at her midsection so Moses had plenty of room. The wind was blowing harder now, and the little ice pellets had begun to turn to snow. Without her legs fully covered by her skirts, the air seemed even colder. Emma Jane shivered. The wind howled in response.

As she looked around, their surroundings became increasingly white. Though it would be almost impossible for the bandits to come searching for them in this weather, Emma Jane couldn't help but think that their chances of survival were almost as slim.

Saying a quick prayer, Emma Jane huddled closer to Jasper, grateful that Moses had the body heat of the two of them to keep him warm. Still, she feared that if they didn't find shelter soon, they would all freeze to death.

Jasper blinked against the decreasing visibility. The snow was almost blinding now, and even though he'd pointed the horse in the right direction toward town, he still feared they might be lost.

Escaping with a blizzard approaching had been a good idea in theory. However, he hadn't anticipated the weather would move in this fast. The wind screeching at his ears mocked him for daring to think he could predict Mother Nature.

He glanced behind him once again to be sure the bandits hadn't followed. The good news about the fast-moving storm was that their tracks were being erased by the snow and wind.

As for the bad news, well, Jasper just had to keep hoping they were indeed headed in the right direction.

Emma Jane's head rested on his back, but her body was not pressed as firmly against his as he would have liked. If the horse slipped on the ice, she would be jolted and easily fall off. But a tiny bundle lay between them—the baby.

On one hand, his wife was right. He couldn't leave a child behind to die. On the other hand, why hadn't she at least talked to him? Why hadn't she asked his opinion? One more decision about his life that was made for him without his consent.

Worse, Emma Jane had to have known that he wouldn't have said no to rescuing the baby, even if it did make escaping more difficult. Which meant he shouldn't be mad, except he felt as though she was taking advantage of his good nature and making assumptions about what he wanted without discussing it first.

And yet…how could he resist the warmth of the woman pressed against him, who would stand up to anyone who would harm an innocent child? He was mad, yes, but how could he stay mad knowing that Emma Jane was only acting in accordance with her good nature?

The snow started falling harder. No, *falling* wasn't the right word. It was as though the snow was coming at them like a train barreling down the mountain with no brakes. Faster, faster and still faster, with no end in sight.

He could feel Emma Jane shiver against him.

"We've got to be close," he shouted back at her. A half truth, because he really didn't know how close they were, and traveling against the wind, he'd had to slow the horse's pace to a walk.

The truth was, they could be miles from town yet. Worse, with the whiteout conditions, they could have veered far off course.

Why had he been such a fool as to think he could outrun both a gang of bandits and a storm?

"I hope so," Emma Jane shouted back. "I can't feel my legs."

A quick glance behind him reminded Jasper that, riding astride, Emma Jane's legs were partially exposed. Her thin stockings would yield little protection against the cold.

He gritted his teeth. Why hadn't he thought this plan through? He'd thought he had, and yet, the farther they went, the more he realized that Emma Jane might have been right to be more cautious.

"Let's pray we find shelter soon."

God had never bothered with such trivialities in Jasper's life. Why would He? After all, he had pretty much everything a body could want. Then again, Jasper had never asked.

But it seemed like Emma Jane's faith was different. She talked to God about these things and seemed to believe that God was real in His actions toward her.

He couldn't hear her words, but the soft murmur of her words echoed against his back. It was like all the time she'd spent reading her Bible to Daisy in the cabin. Emma Jane had spoken quietly enough that Jasper couldn't hear the words, and yet he'd felt a greater peace than he imagined would be possible given the circumstances.

Even now, Emma Jane's hands around his waist felt warmer, even though he was pretty sure she was in danger of frostbite.

Frostbite.

One more thing he hadn't thought of in planning their escape. He could only hope that they'd both survive long enough for Emma Jane to forgive him for being so...

Wait. Were those lights in the distance?

At first it was hard to tell with the snow swirling around them, but then Emma Jane spoke.

"Is that what I think it is?"

Jasper nudged the horse to go faster. The animal also seemed to sense they were close to civilization as it lifted its head. Soon, he could smell smoke on the air, and the horse picked up its pace.

The lights weren't bright enough to be Leadville, or

even one of the small neighboring towns. More than likely, they'd come upon a ranch or some other outpost.

"What if we've just gone in a circle and returned to the bandits?" Emma Jane's query chilled him far more than the swirling ice and snow.

Had they come all this way for nothing?

"We'd have seen the rock formations." But as soon as the words came out of his mouth, he knew that with such low visibility, they could have easily missed them.

Surely the answer to Emma Jane's prayer wasn't to return them to the bandits?

But even so, at least they'd be warm.

A gust of wind sent the snow swirling past them, revealing a sign up ahead. There were no signs in front of the gang's cabin. Which meant they were safe.

As long as the owners of the building ahead were friendly.

They got closer to the sign.

"I know where we are," Emma Jane shouted just as Jasper was able to read what it said.

Spruce Lakes Resort.

If there was a place worse than arriving back at the bandits' hideout, this would be it. Not because it wasn't a nice place, or the owners weren't welcoming and friendly, but because he wasn't ready to deal with the memories associated with the place.

After he and Emma Jane had been trapped in the mine together, they'd been brought here. The resort was closer to the mine than town and had the advantage of having a doctor there, who could tend their injuries. Emma Jane had been unconscious, and Jasper had feared for her life.

At the time, Jasper had said that he'd be willing to

do anything, if only Emma Jane would survive. He'd made that promise before he knew that getting compromised by him had been Emma Jane's plan all along.

"It will be so good to see the Lewises again," Emma Jane said, her teeth chattering. "They were so helpful the last time we were here. I can't think of a better place to wait out a storm. I have so many pleasant memories of our time here."

Jasper swallowed the bile that rose up in his throat. He, too, had pleasant memories of their time here. At least until they'd been tainted by overhearing Emma Jane's mother congratulate her on finding such a masterful way of compromising herself.

Jasper snorted, then choked on the snow. Just how much of the friendship they'd developed while at the resort had been real?

He'd like to think that they were starting to become friends again, but could he trust those feelings? What emotions could he trust when it came to Emma Jane?

As if to echo his tumultuous thoughts, the baby let out a small cry. Weak, thready, almost as if he, too, was cold and weary.

"It's all right, Moses, we're almost there," Emma Jane said gently, the wind having shifted so that it carried each and every word straight to Jasper's heart. So gentle and loving, the tenderness made him yearn for some of that directed towards him.

But how could they ever hope to find common ground when Emma Jane seemed determined to do everything her way? She hadn't even asked him what he'd thought of the baby's name. Jasper shivered, forcing his hands to maintain their grip on the reins. He had so many reasons to be angry with her, yet as he felt

Emma Jane tremble against him, he found it easier to hold on to the icy reins than to count them.

They reached the hotel, and Jasper slid off the horse, his body half-frozen, then helped Emma Jane down. She landed, unsteady, but never losing her grip on the baby.

Jasper pounded on the door.

Stephen Lewis opened the door. "Jasper?"

"We got lost in the storm. Emma Jane is nearly frozen through."

Stephen ushered them in quickly as Mrs. Lewis came around the corner. "Olivia, put some water on."

"Oh, my!" Mrs. Lewis scurried off, and Stephen helped them get settled by the fire.

Emma Jane's lips had turned blue, and her normally pale skin had turned such a deathly pallor that Jasper feared they'd gotten her inside too late.

Stephen handed her a thick buffalo robe.

But Emma Jane, fool that she was, said, "Wait, we need to be sure the baby is all right first. Help me untie this shawl."

Another woman scurried over and quickly helped Emma Jane with the bundle.

"It's a baby."

"Yes," Emma Jane said, the exhaustion in her voice obvious. "I've done everything I could for poor Moses, but I'm afraid…"

As much as Jasper resented Emma Jane taking on the baby without his consent, it didn't mean Jasper wished him ill. Just as he started to say a prayer that the baby would be all right, the woman took Moses in her arms.

"Oh, the little dear. He is chilled to the bone. But he'll be fine. Nothing a little of his mother's milk and a good cuddle won't fix."

The woman held the baby out to Emma Jane, and she shook her head.

"His mother is dead. I've been taking care of him." She turned to Jasper. "His bottles and milk are in the saddlebags. Hopefully, it's not too frozen for him to drink."

"Don't worry about it," the woman said, pulling the baby closer to her. "I've a baby of my own and plenty of milk. I'll just take him in the other room and feed him."

"Could I..." Emma Jane's fatigue was more visible now, and she closed her eyes for a moment before continuing. "That is, I know you need your privacy, but I've been caring for him like my own, and I just need to be sure he'll be all right."

"Of course. We'll sit by the stove in the kitchen, where it's warm. Perhaps Mother will have some warm broth ready for you to drink."

Emma Jane seemed to gain more strength with the woman's words, and Jasper watched as the two women exited the room.

"Don't you worry none about the wee one. Abigail is my daughter, and a fine mother, if I do say so," Stephen said, smiling as his wife reentered the room, carrying a tray with a pot of tea and a bowl of steaming broth.

"Indeed she is." Mrs. Lewis smiled back at her husband. "I was thinking it was too early for the two of you to have a baby already, but knowing your generosity in taking in a foundling child, oh, how it does my heart good."

She handed Jasper the bowl. "This'll warm you right up. You're a good man, Jasper Jackson, and we are so pleased to once again be of service to you. The world needs more people like you."

He tried sipping the broth, but his throat was too clogged with emotion for it to go down. The Lewises might think he was a good man, but Jasper had his doubts. His desire to be a good man and bring justice to poor Mel was what had landed them in this situation. He'd nearly killed himself, Emma Jane and an innocent child.

As for his generosity in taking in the baby, how could it be considered generosity when it had been foisted upon him? He'd never agreed to raise the child, and despite what Emma Jane said on the matter, he wasn't sure he was going to. Jasper had done his duty by saving the baby, but now…now they could find the baby a real home, with a real family.

Chapter Twelve

The next morning, Emma Jane held Moses as the women sat near the fire, working on some embroidery. He hadn't fussed at all since coming to Spruce Lakes Resort. Abigail said that, most likely, the goat's milk had been upsetting the baby's stomach. She'd said she had plenty of milk for both her baby, who was nearly weaned, and Moses. And so, since their arrival, Abigail had been feeding the little boy.

"I declare, I haven't seen a baby fill out so fast in all my life," Olivia Lewis said with a smile as she handed Emma Jane an embroidered cloth. "Just look at those chubby cheeks."

"What's this?" She looked at the fine stitching and held it up to the light.

"Those rags you came with for him are disgraceful. I've made so many diapers for my babies and grandbabies that putting together a few things for little Moses was simple."

Emma Jane warmed at the older woman's generosity. For the second time, she felt so loved and well nurtured by this virtual stranger. And yet, Olivia felt dearer to her than her own mother.

"Thank you. Your kindness means the world to me. I know nothing about babies, just that they're darling little creatures. But I promised his mother I'd care for him as my own before she died, so I hope you'll teach me everything I need to know."

"You're a natural. Isn't she, Abigail?"

Abigail smiled as she reached forward and tickled Moses under his chin. "Indeed. You'd think he really was your own child. Had you not explained the circumstances of his birth, I wouldn't have known he wasn't yours."

The compliment gave Emma Jane more confidence than she thought it would. Until now, she hadn't realized her own fears in becoming a mother. Yes, she'd always loved babies, but her own mother had never done any of the motherly things she saw happening between Olivia and Abigail. The unmistakable affection between the two women sent a twinge to Emma Jane's heart.

Jasper and Stephen entered the room, flanked by Charles, Abigail's husband.

"Jasper!" Olivia smiled up at the men. "I was just telling Emma Jane what a fine boy you have. He'll be such a credit to you and your family."

A dark look crossed Jasper's face, and it pained Emma Jane to see that he was still resistant to the idea of taking in Moses.

"He's not my boy."

Stephen clapped him on the shoulder. "It's hard to form an attachment so soon, but mark my words, you'll love him like your own before you know it. Olivia and I have taken in more than our share of children needing homes—none as babies, mind you—but each and every one is as precious to us as if they were our own."

Jasper's scowl only deepened. Didn't he realize that this may be the solution to their problem? Both of them despaired of ever having children, so in taking in other children who needed homes, they could have a family of their own. Surely with all of Jasper's money, he could afford plenty. Perhaps he just needed a little time and the encouragement of how it had worked for the Lewises before he was sold on the idea.

Emma Jane turned to Olivia. "I had no idea that you'd done that. I'd love to hear more about how you were able to take in other children."

Jasper grunted, and the look he gave her made Emma Jane wonder if she'd made a mistake in asking the older woman to share her story. But the happy glow on Olivia's face was enough to convince Emma Jane that she'd made the right decision. After all, Olivia had been so good to them, it seemed only right to show support for Olivia's endeavors.

As Olivia talked about her joy in being able to give less fortunate children a home, Emma Jane couldn't help but watch the lines deepen between Jasper's brows. She hadn't meant to make him uncomfortable, but they also hadn't had much of a chance to speak privately since arriving. Last night, they'd both been so tired, and Emma Jane had fallen asleep as soon as her head hit the pillow. Since rising, they'd both been occupied by various members of the Lewis family.

Moses began to fuss, and before Emma Jane could ascertain what the problem was, Abigail reached for him. "I think this little one is due for another feeding." She gave Emma Jane a smile. "I am so glad to be able to help you with him. David is getting so big and independent that I miss these days of having a small one."

Abigail glanced fondly at the little boy who sat on his father's knee, tugging at his beard. Then she gave Charles such a deep look of love that it made Emma Jane's heart churn again. Oh, to have that for her own life. What would it be like to exchange such sweet, tender glances?

Emma Jane transferred the baby to Abigail's arms, then looked down at her own embroidery. Seeing her new initials stitched with her own neat hand seemed almost out of a dream or some other reality that couldn't possibly exist. Jasper glanced at her, then at her embroidery, then looked away.

Things were so different between them now. When they were last here, they'd built a friendship of sorts. During their time in the mine, they'd talked, really talked, and Emma Jane had thought they'd come to a level of mutual respect. Then here at the hotel, where Emma Jane recuperated from her injuries, they'd become even friendlier.

She looked out the window, covered by the swirling snow. The last time they'd been stuck here, they'd also been trapped by a snowstorm, but it was nothing like this one. Now that they were closer to winter, the snow lasted longer and was colder and thicker.

Spying the basket of yarn near Jasper's chair, Emma Jane smiled. Perhaps all Jasper needed was a reminder of their previous bond.

"Do you remember how I tried teaching you how to knit?"

When they were trapped here before, Emma Jane and Mary had tried showing Jasper and Will how to knit. The men's hands were clumsy with the needles and yarn, and while they did not get any real knitting accomplished, they'd had great fun. And, as Emma Jane remembered with a pang, she'd felt a connection between her and Jasper.

A hint of a smile twitched at his lips. But his voice remained dull. "As I recall, it was not a successful endeavor."

"Well, maybe we can play checkers instead," Emma Jane said brightly, hoping to engage him in some way.

"I don't like checkers." Jasper turned to Stephen. "You wouldn't happen to have any good books in that study of yours, would you?"

Emma Jane's heart sank as her husband stood.

"Oh, yes, yes, I do!" Stephen jumped up, and the two men exited the room, Charles joining them.

"Don't mind them," Olivia said, patting Emma Jane as she walked over to the teapot. "Stephen and Charles were arguing politics earlier, and they know I only allow it in the gentlemen's room. They've been itching to continue their discussion. Would you care for some more tea?"

Emma Jane nodded as she stared into the empty space Jasper left. If only it were as simple as Jasper wanting to discuss politics. Unfortunately, she knew for a fact that Jasper found the subject distasteful. No, he wanted to get away from her.

Being forced to marry someone was one thing. In the Jackson mansion, avoiding one another was easy enough. But here, trapped at the Spruce Lakes Resort, they were forced to be together. Except that Jasper seemed to be doing everything in his power to avoid it.

Was it so wrong to wish they would rekindle the

connection they'd once had? Emma Jane dreaded the thought of spending the rest of her life married to a man who was sullen whenever he was in her presence.

Friendship… It was all she wanted from him. The romance, yes, that would be nice, but clearly it wasn't going to happen. So why couldn't they at least settle on a good old-fashioned companionship?

Jasper groaned at the heated argument between the two men, wishing he could be anywhere else, yet because he couldn't handle the mix of emotions he felt being with Emma Jane, here he was. Stuck.

Stephen pointed to the bookcase. "Help yourself to anything that suits your fancy. You sure you don't want to share an opinion on the upcoming elections?"

Jasper shook his head. "Quite sure." He already knew how he'd be voting, and listening to the heated debates in his father's study had given him a distaste for participating in them himself.

He glanced at the book titles. Everything he'd already read, and nothing that struck his interest. Once again, his mind drifted to Emma Jane. She'd spent a lot of time reading her Bible, and it seemed to take the edge off the somber mood while they were in the bandits' cabin. In fact, it seemed to make even an unconscious Daisy more at peace.

"You wouldn't happen to have an extra Bible, would you?"

Stephen smiled. "Ah, a man of the Word. I am so pleased to see one of the pillars of society so dedicated, not only to doing good, but in immersing himself in the Bible."

Stephen's compliment, while sincerely meant, felt

like empty praise. Jasper didn't want to do the good he was credited with, and his Bible reading, well, he didn't really even know what it was about. He hadn't spent much time studying the Bible on his own. Even now, he couldn't understand why he felt drawn to it.

Jasper remained silent.

"As it so happens, my good man, when we emptied your saddlebag, I found your Bible. I set it on the dresser in your room."

Of course Emma Jane would bring the Bible. He hadn't given it any thought during their escape. Even though he'd warned her about carrying any extra weight, he found he couldn't fault her for bringing the Bible. After all, when she'd gone missing, he'd even brought it along.

"Thank you. If you'll excuse me…" Jasper nodded at both men and went up to the room he and Emma Jane had been given.

The Bible was not on the dresser but on the small table beside a chair that sat in front of the window. Emma Jane had probably already been reading it today.

He picked up the book and examined it. What treasure did it hold that kept Emma Jane so enthralled? And if it was really as useful in a person's life as the pastor seemed to think, then why wasn't she more… reasonable?

Sitting down, he thumbed through the pages. The Psalms seemed to be more creased and worn than the others, and he remembered Emma Jane reading from them at the cabin. Would this give him the peace he needed?

It hadn't seemed like he'd been reading long when he heard footsteps on the stairs. Jasper quickly closed the Bible and put it back on the table. He couldn't explain it, but he wasn't ready for Emma Jane to know that her Bible reading had inspired something in him. Maybe because he wasn't quite sure yet exactly what had been inspired.

"There you are." Emma Jane peered into the room. "Are you all right?"

"I'm fine." He gave what he hoped was an acceptable smile.

But he should have known that Emma Jane wasn't going to simply accept such a short answer and leave it at that.

"Things are different between us," she said slowly, hesitantly, like she was almost afraid to say it.

The trouble was, he wasn't sure he wanted to have the conversation. Not when he was still trying to figure out the puzzle of his life—the one that had been put together all without his consent.

"I don't like having so many choices taken from me." There. He said it. The thing that stood between them, that they could never find a way through.

"You're still upset that I'm keeping Moses."

There it was again. Her decision. Not his. Not even theirs.

"We didn't discuss it."

Emma Jane sighed. "There are a lot of things we don't discuss. But the right decision in this case should be obvious. Moses needs a home. We both want children, but aren't going to have any of our own."

The longing on her face was obvious. And her argument made sense. Especially after the conversation he'd avoided having with her about children.

"This isn't what I meant by compromise."

"You don't want to adopt?" Emma Jane looked at him like she didn't understand what he was trying to say. And clearly, she didn't.

"Compromise means both people talking about a subject and coming to a decision together. Everything in our relationship has been about you making a decision without me."

His throat felt raw as the words came out. Burned. Oozed with the emotion he'd been holding in. He took a deep breath. Closed his eyes. Tried to steady himself.

But, of course, Emma Jane wouldn't allow him that space to even find a steady place.

"Me, making decisions without you?" she huffed. "Who skipped out on our wedding without telling me? Who made a promise to a dying woman to save her sister? Who signed up to be a deputy? I'm not sure if you think you're the pot or the kettle, but either way, you are not entitled to be angry with me for making a decision without you."

He opened his eyes, and she stood before him—head held high, cheeks flushed, chest heaving. Looking like an Amazon ready for battle. Funny how he'd chastised her for not standing up for herself, and now that she was doing it, Emma Jane was every bit as glorious as he'd imagined. Only he'd never thought it would be used against him.

"You started it," he said, knowing the words were childish but unable to help himself. If Emma Jane wanted to have this out, they were going to have it all out.

"I have done everything you have asked." Tears streamed down her face. "What more do you want from me?"

"You didn't trust me to find a solution for your family that didn't involve marriage," he said quietly. "You didn't trust me when I told you not to get involved with the bandits. I asked you to please trust me, and I told you that the very foundation of our marriage depended on it, but every time I turn around, you are doing what you think is best, without regard to what I may want."

He shook his head slowly. "I thought we could build something. But the longer I'm with you, the more I realize that I can't trust you, because you don't trust me."

Jasper knew what it looked like when a woman was shot. He'd seen the look on Mel's face when she died. The expression on Emma Jane's face was no different. He'd hurt her. Part of him was deeply sorry.

But the other part of him felt free. For the first time since he'd married her, he felt like everything he'd been stuffing inside finally came out.

Except that only made him hurt more.

Because he knew that what he'd said was true. He didn't trust Emma Jane, and she didn't trust him.

So what exactly did they have?

"I do trust you." Her voice shook slightly, echoes of the tears she'd been shedding. "But I don't know how to get you to understand that."

"When we leave, leave the baby here."

Her face registered shock, but she didn't say anything, so he continued. "Abigail loves him and has the ability to take care of him in ways you can't. The Lewises have said that they believe God brings them children who need homes. We've done our duty by the baby. We've found him a home with people who love him and will care for him like their own, which is what Daisy wanted."

"But I promised Daisy I would…"

"No." The word caught in his throat. "Every time I see that baby, I think about how you didn't trust me enough to talk to me about your decision. How every other important decision in my life was taken from me. And rather than working together as a couple to figure out what was best for the baby, you did what you wanted."

Even now, he could hear the baby fussing downstairs and saw that Emma Jane's attention was immediately drawn to the sound.

"We can't even talk about our marriage without that baby taking your attention away."

He regarded her solemnly, hating how cold he sounded but not knowing how else to get Emma Jane to understand. "I need my feelings to matter, too."

"Ordering me to leave the baby here doesn't sound like my feelings matter to you."

There it was again. The strong Emma Jane with a ferocity he couldn't help but admire. But as much as he admired it, he also couldn't live with the way she continually disregarded his feelings.

"You're right," he rasped. "Right now, it feels like no matter what we do, one of us has to lose. The very foundation of our relationship is broken, and I don't know how to fix it."

A knock sounded at the door, and Stephen poked his head in. "Sorry to disturb you, but Abigail was wanting Emma Jane."

He turned his attention to Emma Jane. "She was going to give the wee one his first bath and thought you'd enjoy being a part of it."

"Thank you." Emma Jane didn't spare Jasper a glance as she hurried from the room.

He should have expected it, given that he'd been so hard on her. Even now, his gut churned, and he wished he could have taken back some of his words. But which ones? Did he continue walking on eggshells and avoiding what was really bothering him? He'd been completely honest about his feelings, and yet…it felt wrong.

"Marriage is harder than it looks, isn't it?" Stephen said quietly.

Jasper didn't look at him. "How much did you hear?"

"You were talking pretty loud."

"I'm sorry, I didn't realize…"

Stephen stepped in and put a hand on Jasper's shoulder. "Seems to me you've been holding a lot in. Sometimes, when it comes out, the explosion is bigger than any dynamite could create."

The older man's touch was warm in a way Jasper hadn't expected. Like he could almost feel the love flowing into him.

"I just don't know what to do. I know my words hurt Emma Jane, but I can't keep pretending that everything is fine. How do I be honest about my feelings when it's going to hurt hers?"

Stephen didn't answer, but he stood there, looking at Jasper as if Jasper was supposed to know what to do. Keep bottling it up and pretending that he didn't mind having his life stolen?

Jasper closed his eyes for a moment. "I suppose what's done is done. No matter what I do, I'm not going to get my old life back."

"Once a man marries, his life isn't his own."

Jasper opened his eyes to stare at the other man. His father had told him the same thing.

"So I just let her make all of these decisions without me?"

Stephen shrugged. "You'll find a way to make decisions that you both can live with. It takes time, son. But that can only happen if you move on past your anger."

"How do you move on when you feel like you can't trust the other person? When everything you dreamed of has been taken from you?"

"Well," Stephen said slowly. "You can keep looking back on shaky ground, expecting it to change when you can't change the past. Or you can look forward, finding something new and stable to build on."

"Again…*how*?" From Jasper's vantage point, it seemed impossible.

"Pretend you just met her. How would you court a woman, who, for all intents and purposes, you've just met?"

Court Emma Jane? "You want me to court my wife? Doesn't that end when a couple gets married?"

Stephen grinned, shaking his head. "Once a couple gets married, that's the most important time for folks to court. Otherwise, you run the risk of taking each other for granted and missing out on the really beautiful parts of being husband and wife."

There had been no beautiful parts about being married to Emma Jane. And with the way he'd just talked to her, he imagined there probably weren't any beautiful parts about being married to him.

Maybe he had set an impossible standard, asking her to trust him before they even knew each other.

Could he do as Stephen advised and court Emma

Jane? Would a courtship help them find common ground?

At this point, Jasper wasn't sure he had anything else to lose. Stuck in the hotel, with nowhere to go and nothing else to do, he could at least try.

Otherwise, he might as well resign himself to a lifetime of marital misery.

Chapter Thirteen

Emma Jane smiled as Moses cooed up at her from the bucket they were using to wash him. She was beginning to see signs of dimples in his cheeks, and now that his dark hair was clean, it laid on his head in tiny little curls.

Abigail handed her a warm towel. "Usually I wouldn't give anyone a bath in this weather, but he seemed particularly grimy, and I wanted you to have Mother and me here for the first one in case you had questions."

Moses fussed as she lifted him out of the water, but once she had him securely wrapped in the towel, he quieted, staring up at her with his dark eyes.

"I appreciate having your assistance. So much. I didn't know anything about taking care of babies. How do women manage with their own?"

Abigail smiled at Olivia, and the two women exchanged the kind of loving glance that made Emma Jane wish once again that she'd had that sort of relationship with her own mother. Even her mother-in-law would never possess that level of warmth toward her.

"They have wonderful mothers who take care of them." Abigail gave her mother a squeeze as she passed.

"Speaking of mothers, I need to check on my own brood. Charles tries, bless him, but I'm sure they're driving him crazy about now."

As Emma Jane dried Moses, Olivia came beside her and rested her hand on Emma Jane's shoulder. "I know you must be thinking how hard it is, given that your mother isn't the warmest of women."

Emma Jane glanced up at her. She'd forgotten that Olivia had met her mother. Emma Jane's stay here last time had ended when her parents arrived, full of fire over their daughter being "compromised" by Jasper. Her mother had *not* been kind.

"But don't worry." Olivia reached for Moses. "May I?"

Emma Jane handed her the baby, smiling as the older woman made baby noises at him.

"Becoming a grandmother changes a woman. I can't explain it, but I am convinced that a grandchild makes a woman's heart grow even bigger. I love my children, but my grandchildren…" She looked up at Emma Jane and smiled. "That love is so much deeper."

Olivia planted a kiss on top of Moses's head and handed him back to Emma Jane. "And this little one is so darling I can't imagine not falling in love with him. You'll see."

"My mother went back east," Emma Jane said, adjusting Moses in her arms. "She's not likely to return."

Actually, it had been a condition of Jasper's father paying off her father's gambling debts. The family was sent back to Charleston to live with relatives. Jasper's father had some connections there, and her father was given a job. The Jacksons had made it clear that the Logans were not to return to Leadville or cause any scandal that would reflect back on them.

Emma Jane didn't miss her parents much—at all, really—but she often thought about her sister, Gracie. How would Gracie do without Emma Jane to protect her? The only reason Emma Jane had chosen this life, marrying Jasper, was to protect Gracie. Would someone be willing to teach Gracie the way Olivia was her?

"Well," Emma Jane said, looking down at the baby. "I think someone has fallen asleep. I'm going to put him down for his nap."

Olivia touched Emma Jane's arm as she passed. "You know, just because your mother wasn't warm, it doesn't mean you won't be a good mother. You're doing an excellent job of taking care of Moses."

Funny, that idea had never occurred to Emma Jane. As she carried Moses to the cradle the Lewises had so thoughtfully put in her room, she realized that caring for the baby had brought out a strength in her she hadn't realized she possessed. Defending her sister against her parents was one thing, but something about this innocent child made Emma Jane feel even more empowered.

Still, deep down she knew she shouldn't have said all those things to Jasper. But he'd just made her so mad! She was tired of him acting like he was the victim of all the bad circumstances of his life. Didn't he realize how lucky he was? Emma Jane had to make a life out of so much worse.

She smoothed Moses's hair as she set him in the cradle. People shouldn't fear their parents the way Emma Jane and Gracie had.

The only reason Emma Jane had agreed to Gracie leaving as well was that Mrs. Jackson had enrolled Gracie in a private girls' boarding school, where Gracie could get an education and be away from their parents.

"Hello," Jasper said, causing her to jump.

Emma Jane didn't turn around. "If you're here to continue our argument, I'd prefer you just leave. Moses is sleeping."

"No. I came to apologize. I shouldn't have taken all of my anger and hurt out on you."

She stood and whirled around to face him. "So what's the truth, Jasper? Do you resent me for taking away your choices, or is it something else?"

His Adam's apple bobbed. His broad shoulders rose and fell, then he spoke. "It's the truth. I am hurt. I imagined my life different than this. But I can either stay stuck in the past, angry that I didn't get my way, or I can find a way to make my life good in spite of those things."

Then his lips turned up slightly. "Like you did in the bandits' cabin. That's what you were trying to tell me back there, isn't it? We didn't have a choice in being there, but you were making the best of it."

"Yes."

He crossed the room to sit on the bed, then patted the spot next to him. "I don't know how deep your role in trapping me into marriage was, but I'm choosing to forgive you. The past hurts, and we need time to heal from that. But rather than dwelling in it, I'd like to start over."

His words tumbled around in her head. Even now, Jasper still believed that Emma Jane was complicit in her family's plan to force a marriage between them. She'd been honest with him and told him of their plan and that she didn't want to go through with it. Yet he still blamed her.

But he was right. There was no sense in dwelling on it. She could proclaim her innocence until the day she died, and he still wasn't going to believe it. So what did arguing about it accomplish?

"All right," she said, sitting beside him. "I'm willing to start over."

Moses made a noise in his sleep, and Emma Jane looked at him briefly, reminded that this was about more than just their marriage, but a little boy relying on her for his care.

"But you have to understand that I refuse to give up Moses. I love him, and somehow you're going to have to find a way to accept him."

Jasper followed her gaze to the sleeping baby. "What if I can't love him?"

Squaring her shoulders, Emma Jane lifted her chin and gave him a no-nonsense look. "You will be kind to him. I've lived with unkindness from a parent, and my son will not have that same existence."

In the silence, Emma Jane could hear Jasper swallow. "I've never been unkind to a child."

"I wouldn't know that." She looked at the ground. Had she been wrong to make the comparison between Jasper and her father? Jasper had been angry with her, but he hadn't been cruel. And while his words hurt, he hadn't made her feel worthless. Rather, in their argument, while they had disagreed, she realized that he'd done his best to treat her with respect.

"No. I don't suppose you know me well enough."

Jasper stood and held out his hand. "Ordinarily, I'd ask you to go for a ride with me in my carriage, but since the wind is still howling, I don't suppose you'd be willing to head down with me to the kitchen to see if Olivia has any cookies."

An olive branch. Jasper wanted to make peace, and that gave Emma Jane hope. Perhaps they could find a way to make a life together, after all.

She glanced over at Moses.

"He's asleep. He'll be fine." Then Jasper paused. "If you leave the door open, you'll hear him if he cries."

It wasn't a declaration that he would care for Moses as his own, but the fact that he was giving consideration to Emma Jane's feelings for Moses, well, it was a start.

Emma Jane smiled. "Then I'd be delighted."

She took Jasper's hand, and they walked down to the kitchen, where Olivia was pulling a batch of cookies out of the oven.

"You knew she was baking cookies," Emma Jane teased.

"I am motivated by many things," Jasper said with a grin. "And freshly baked cookies are one of them. Mother was always harping on me for being in the kitchen when Cook was trying to bake."

Emma Jane rolled her eyes. "I can imagine. And I can't imagine that Cook was put out at all by your presence."

"No. She even let me eat some of the unbaked cookie dough, which is my favorite."

He grabbed a cookie from the pan. "Ouch!"

"Patience," Olivia admonished with a smile. "Let them cool for a few minutes. I'll leave you two alone, but please, save some of the cookies for the others. Stephen and Charles went to go check on the livestock, and they'll be mighty disappointed if you ate them all."

The kitchen door opened, and Molly, one of Abigail's daughters, entered. "Grammy? Is dem cookies ready?"

Jasper handed her the cookie that had been cooling in his hand. "Here's one for you, sweetheart." He patted her light blond hair and gave her a smile.

Molly grinned, then scampered away.

"Well, I did hear you have a reputation for the ladies," Olivia said with a grin, putting some cookies on a plate.

"What can I say? I can't resist a pretty face."

Jasper winked at her, but Emma Jane turned away. Why did he have to rub in the fact that she was so plain and unattractive? Especially now, dressed in a dress borrowed from Abigail that was too loose and slightly too long. Her hair had been pulled back into a serviceable braid, and she hardly looked the picture of any of the society debutantes Jasper had courted.

He reached for her hand. "Hey. I'm married to one of the prettiest faces in all of Leadville, so no need to be hurt that I'd admire someone so sweet."

"Please don't." Emma Jane pulled her hand away.

"I'm just going to bring some of these cookies in to the others, so we don't have any more cookie thieves in the kitchen," Olivia said, excusing herself.

"Don't what?" Jasper asked with a furrowed brow, pivoting around to face her. "I was trying to pay you a compliment."

"I don't want your charming lies. Flattery may work on the other girls in town, but I won't be trifled with. I know I'm not the prettiest girl in Leadville, so why perjure yourself?"

Jasper's face fell. "I wasn't lying."

Then he reached for the pan of cookies. "Do you want one?"

"No, thank you," Emma Jane said, wishing she could take her words back and wondering why it was so hard to get along with Jasper. Even if he had been lying, he was just trying to be nice.

"Well," he said, biting into a cookie. "We can't talk about the past, and I can't compliment your looks, so what would you like to talk about?"

Emma Jane shook her head in exasperation. "You mean to tell me that when you take a girl for a ride in your carriage, all you talk about is how pretty she is?"

Jasper shrugged. "And the weather, but…" He pointed to the window, where the snow still swirled. "I think that says it all."

"So, looks and the weather. That's all you have to say, and you're the town's most eligible bachelor?"

"Was." Jasper finished the cookie. "They prattled on about the goings-on around town, but truthfully, I don't think I paid any of it much mind. I couldn't care less about who was having what dance, and what they planned on wearing. I'm not sure we ever talked about things that mattered."

He grabbed another cookie. "You sure you don't want one?"

Emma Jane shook her head. She'd seen signs of this Jasper in some of their earlier conversations. Thoughtful, charming and well…enjoyable to be around. Especially during their time in the mine, and then when they were here, recuperating and waiting out the storm.

The truth was, she liked this Jasper. And that scared her. They'd become friends, and yet, once they were married, he seemed to have forgotten all about that friendship.

"So what do you think we should talk about, then?" A dangerous question, and Emma Jane almost regretted asking it. But Jasper was right. They couldn't keep fearing the future based on their turbulent past.

"Um…" He stared at his cookie. "What do you like to do for fun? Besides read the Bible, of course."

"I like to knit, and sew, and do needlepoint." Emma Jane frowned. Those were all hobbies of women who needed the results of those hobbies to keep her family clothed. How would Mrs. Jackson feel about Emma Jane continuing those passions?

"Your attempts at teaching me to knit the last time we were here didn't work out so well." Jasper grinned. "I was all thumbs."

Then he looked at Emma Jane. "You know, my mother likes to do those things. She's made a number of blankets for the church. I know she hasn't warmed up to you, so perhaps that might be a way for you to find common ground."

Emma Jane shook her head. "I'm not sure she'd want to find common ground with the woman who stole her precious son."

She didn't mean for her words to sound so harsh, especially when Jasper frowned.

"You have to understand. My mother means well. According to my father, she tried for years to have a baby. Before I was born, they had a little girl. But she died as a baby. When they finally had me, my mother was so protective. So fierce. She was just so scared of losing me, too."

He smiled wryly. "It wasn't until Will came into our

lives that she let me do anything she didn't think was too dangerous."

"I remember you telling me how Will taught you about defending yourself and all the things involved with being a lawman."

The small connection warmed Emma Jane's heart. Somehow it made Jasper seem all the more human to her.

"Anyway, Mother likes having control more than I do. You think I'm upset at losing control of my life? I think, for her, it's even worse."

Then he regarded her in a way Emma Jane didn't understand. Like he was puzzling her out.

"I know it bothers you to see the way my father and I defend her. But deep down, she's a good person. She's just lost so much, and being in control is the only thing that's kept her going over the years."

Emma Jane reached out and took his hand. "Thank you for telling me. It makes her seem more human. I was praying about my relationship with her the other day and that God would give me a way to love her. Your words are an answered prayer."

And indeed they were. Even now, for as little time as Emma Jane had Moses, she couldn't imagine the heartbreak of losing him. That was the hard part about Jasper's lack of compassion for her wanting to raise the boy. He didn't understand how deeply she already loved him.

What would it have been like for Mrs. Jackson to have lost a child?

It didn't excuse her behavior toward Emma Jane, but she did find that knowing the depths of Mrs. Jackson's pain gave her compassion for the other woman.

"You talk a lot about answered prayers," Jasper said slowly. "I know the pastor talks about it, but I don't understand. We're just ordinary people—not pastors. We have no special connection to God. Why does He listen to you?"

Those words gave Emma Jane more compassion for Jasper. He'd made a lot of comments, here and there, that made her wonder how deep his relationship with the Lord was, and now she understood.

He didn't have one. Jasper Jackson, pillar of society, and one of the leading members of their church, didn't know the Lord.

"God listens to all of us," Emma Jane said, squeezing his hand. "We don't need anyone to speak for us. No qualifications, no special learning. He just wants us to talk to Him. To read His Word, and to seek His voice."

"But why would He listen to me?"

"Why would He listen to *me*?" Emma Jane smiled gently. "That's the wonderful thing about the Lord. He doesn't distinguish people between social standing, ability, goodness, any of that. He loves us, each and every one of us, just as we are."

She could tell that Jasper was struggling to process her words. How had he gone to church all these years and not realized this about the Lord? Then she thought about the other girls in church and her own family. Not all of them seemed to be living in the truth they'd been taught. And, if she was honest with herself, it was only her recent friendship with Mary that taught her that the Lord loved her just as she was. Emma Jane had always tried to be good enough to win the Lord's approval.

"I struggled with that idea myself," Emma Jane confessed, noting that Jasper still appeared to be befuddled by what she was saying. "I used to try my best to be good and follow all the rules, thinking that if I were good enough, I would be worthy. But Mary loved me in my darkest moment, when I was probably the least worthy of love. If a person could do that for me, how much more so could God?"

Jasper nodded slowly, but his furrowed brow and pursed lips told her that he still didn't fully comprehend her words. It would be easy to wonder why, but instead, she focused on her gratitude that her husband was finally trying to understand.

With the Lord's help, perhaps they could find their way.

"Well," Emma Jane said, giving Jasper's hand a final squeeze before going over to the cookies. "I suppose I should try one of these cookies before you eat them all."

She gave him a soft smile, hoping he understood that she was giving him space to work out his own relationship with God. When she first began helping Pastor Lassiter with his mission to the less fortunate in Leadville, he'd cautioned her not to push too hard in encouraging others to follow Christ. If a person pushed too hard, it had the opposite effect.

"They're good cookies," Jasper said, reaching for another as Emma Jane sat down next to him.

Emma Jane took a bite, then gave him a sly look. "Not as good as mine."

Jasper snatched the cookie out of her hand. "You don't deserve it if you can't appreciate it."

"Hey!" She gave him a stern look and retrieved her prize. "Just because mine are better doesn't mean I can't eat someone else's."

A wide grin filled Jasper's face, and the jovial man

everyone liked, the one she wished would make an appearance more often, returned.

"I suppose. But you know this means you're going to have to bake me some when we get home."

She gave him a look of what she hoped to be mock horror. "And intrude on the servants' domain?"

"I'll distract Mother." Jasper winked, but something in his eyes dimmed.

He looked away from her, and she followed his gaze to the snow pelting the window.

"You're worried about getting home, aren't you?" Emma Jane said quietly, reaching for his free hand.

He let her take it, though his fingers remained limp, not participating in the gesture.

For a few moments, the only sounds in the room were the crackling fire and the wind's mournful cry.

Then Jasper spoke. "Getting home isn't the problem. Making sure the bandits don't get there first is."

Jasper wished he could have taken back his words to Emma Jane the second he noticed the lines furrowing her forehead.

"I'm sorry, I shouldn't have said that," Jasper said, staring at the cookie still in his hand. Suddenly, it seemed as unpalatable as a rock.

"Why?" Emma Jane lowered her gaze to meet his, drawing him away from his cookie and into the swirling blue depths, the brown flecks mesmerizing him.

Jasper shook his head. "I don't want you to be worried about what's going to happen to us."

He was doing enough worrying for both of them. And now that the baby was in the picture, he had one more life counting on him to get them through safely.

Which made this situation even more difficult. Trapped in this place, there was nothing he could do to keep them safe but hope the bandits would remain snowed in longer than they were. Emma Jane would probably say that he should pray, but he wasn't sure what good it would do.

Once again, Emma Jane squeezed his hand, the one he'd left carelessly on the table, not realizing how easy it would be for Emma Jane to touch him. And how desperately he wanted her to.

One more distraction he hoped wouldn't interfere with his ability to keep them safe.

"Everything will be all right." Her voice was low and gentle, and if there weren't so many facts that said otherwise, he might have believed her.

Jasper gave a noncommittal murmur, wishing he had something to say that wouldn't provoke an argument.

"It will be," Emma Jane said, her voice filled with a passion he'd never seen in her before. "You mustn't lose hope. Think of all the hopeless situations we've been in together over the past few weeks—being trapped in the mine, kidnapped by bandits… And here we are, safe."

He looked over at her, unable to fathom the optimism coming from her. "I seem to remember a girl sobbing her eyes out at the church picnic because her life seemed so hopeless."

And then she did a remarkable thing. Emma Jane smiled. "That's true. I did. And Mary encouraged me, telling me not to lose hope because it would be all right. And it has been. Which is why I can have hope now."

They had one of the most notorious gangs in the region wanting them dead. Emma Jane might believe that the bandits wouldn't hurt them, but at this point, they knew too much for the bandits to be willing to keep them alive.

As much as Jasper wanted to believe that everything would be all right, he wouldn't put much stock in that belief until justice had been done.

He had valuable information about the gang, and when he returned to town, he'd be able to get the others in the sheriff's office to bring them to justice. Regardless of Daisy's outcome, the gang was still dangerous to the citizens of Leadville. Even if the gang made good on their plans to go to Mexico after their last job, not apprehending them would send a message to all of the other criminals in the country that Leadville was a place where they could get away with a life of crime.

He looked over at Emma Jane, who was staring at the remains of her cookie absently.

"Is everything all right? You're not upset, are you?" Jasper asked, looking for signs that he'd broken the fragile peace between them.

She shook her head. "No. I was just thinking about how my mother used to always spin her fantasies about what life must be like living in the Jackson mansion, having all the things you have and being at the pinnacle of society."

Jasper's stomach knotted. Everyone had their ideas of what his life must be like. Ladies used to beg for rides in their gold-leafed carriage. Jasper himself had never seen a need for such frippery, but his parents always thought it was good fun.

Then she let out a long, plaintive sigh. "But I wish I could go back and tell her that all those things are not what's important. It seems to me that no matter who you are, even with a life as wonderful as what people think yours must be, people wish their lives could have been different."

He couldn't speak. Couldn't feel his own heart beating in his chest. Everything he'd revealed to her, even the things that he'd only hinted at, she'd understood.

All this time, he'd been so angry at everyone not caring about his needs, his desires, and here she was, speaking to the fact that he felt so out of control. Not in so many words, perhaps, but at least she understood that the Jasper Jackson everyone so deeply admired was not the Jasper Jackson he wanted to be.

He took her hand as he moved closer to her. "Thank you. You've given me hope that you really do see me. You hear me. And I appreciate it."

Then he looked into her eyes. Those deep, mystifying blue eyes whose flecks of brown made it impossible for him to decipher what was going on inside her.

"I know our marriage started out rocky, but I promise you, I'll do my best to improve upon it."

"Thank you." She smiled and it lit up her whole face. A beautiful sight he hoped to see more of over the years. He truly hadn't understood the value of such a simple thing until now.

Then Emma Jane shifted her weight. "Does that mean you're more open to accepting Moses in your life, as well?"

His stomach dropped. Was that what all of this was about? Their connection? The seeming moments of hope in finding their way?

Every woman in his acquaintance was gifted at the pretty words, the lovely looks and the subtle manipulation used to get what they want. He hadn't seen it coming with Emma Jane—not when the words she'd used were all so…deep. So profound. She'd figured him out, all right. She'd known that he was tired of all the fluff and had been searching for substance.

Jasper coughed. "I'd hoped our conversation would be more about us. Without involving the child."

"I…I…I'm sorry." She looked away, but then turned her gaze back at him. "I didn't mean to offend you."

Then her shoulders rose and fell before she squared off with him. "But you must know that I'm different now. Emma Jane Logan did everything she could to please others and be as little trouble as possible. Emma Jane Jackson, she stands up for what she believes in, even if that's inconvenient to others."

She stood, her petite frame towering over him. "Moses is my son. He needs a mother, and I promised to be that mother. If you're looking to improve our relationship, then you need to accept that fact."

Perhaps she hadn't done such a good job of figuring him out, after all. No one backed Jasper Jackson into a corner. And clearly, she'd failed to understand that the one miserable thing in his life was his lack of choices. Because, yet again, she'd made it clear that she didn't care about what he wanted.

Telling her that meant rehashing the same argument they'd already been around. Clearly, she didn't respect his point of view in this matter. What other matters in their marriage would she fail to respect his wishes?

Jasper met her gaze with a steely look of his own. "And you need to accept that, in a marriage, a husband and wife make decisions like that *together*."

He didn't want to talk to her anymore. Couldn't, really. Taking care of an orphaned child, it was a noble decision. Daisy's child, yes, it made taking in the baby even more so. But he hadn't even been given the opportunity to think it through.

"You'll have to excuse me." He rose to his feet and exited the kitchen. Not his finest manners, he'd admit, but what was a man to do?

Jasper took the steps to their bedroom two at a time. Their bedroom. Ha! The Lewises had given them a room together, but the previous night, Jasper had slept in the chair while Emma Jane sprawled out on the bed. Not that he wanted to share the bed with her, but she'd been comfortable where he had not.

Childish of him to think that way now, because of course sleeping in the chair was the right thing to do. Just as raising Daisy's baby was the right thing to do. And eventually, he would tell Emma Jane that. But was it too much to ask for Emma Jane to... Jasper flopped on the bed. Pointless. He'd asked himself this question, asked Emma Jane that question, dozens of times with no answer.

It wasn't even that he wanted to say no. He just wanted to feel like he had some say in a life he felt like he had no control over.

He closed his eyes for a moment, thinking this might be a good time to catch up on the sleep he hadn't gotten the night before. While the chair by the window was pretty enough, it definitely wasn't suited for a man to spend the night in.

But immediately, Emma Jane's words about God, and how He was available to anyone who asked, came to mind. Did God care about Jasper? Would God be willing to help him see through the darkness of the situation?

He opened his eyes and looked over at the table where the Bible sat. Just a few pages. He could read a few pages, and maybe somewhere in there he could find an understanding like what Emma Jane had. Like what Pastor Lassiter taught. Perhaps then he could pray to God, and He would hear him.

And then maybe, just maybe, he could see a way to a future where he and Emma Jane could peaceably spend their lives together.

Chapter Fourteen

Jasper had barely spoken to her at supper. In fact, the only thing he'd said to her was, "Could you please pass the peas?"

Why had she brought up Moses when they'd been getting along so well? Why couldn't he understand how important taking care of Moses was to her?

Emma Jane blew out a breath and set down the knitting project she'd began.

Abigail looked at her sympathetically. "That wool is a mess to work with. I think I should have spun it differently. At the time, I thought it would be good for socks."

"It's not the wool." Emma Jane sighed as she looked over at Jasper, who was reading the same newspaper he'd been reading since they'd arrived at the hotel.

"Marriage is hard, I'll give you that."

Abigail glanced in the direction of the men's study, where her husband and father were closeted. "Sometimes," she said in a low voice, "Charles makes me so angry I can hardly stand it. But as Mother always says, marriage is for better or for worse. Most of the time, I'm pretty content with him, but, oh, how I wish he'd spend more time with the children and less time with his horses!"

Emma Jane couldn't help but smile at the other woman's expression. If only her marital woes were as simple as Jasper spending too much time with his horses. She understood that marriage was about the good times and the bad, but when would she and Jasper ever get to the good?

Though he was clearly trying to make an effort, his disdain for her was just as clear. He didn't want to be married to her, and no matter how hard she tried to make things better between them, they always ended up fighting. Or worse.

If Jasper had heard Abigail's comment, he gave no indication. Apparently, the same article he must have read several times over was far more interesting than anything the ladies were talking about. His brow was furrowed, as though that same article contained such monumental information that all of his careful rereads concerned him deeply. Emma Jane sighed yet again. It wasn't her place to judge his reading habits, but if the story was so important, why did he not attempt to discuss it with her?

He'd said he wanted to start over, to get to know each other as they should have done in the first place. Well, perhaps it was time they did so now. Emma Jane cleared her throat.

"Whatever is it in that article that has you so enthralled?" she asked.

Jasper didn't look up but he kept reading the newspaper. Was he deliberately ignoring her? Was he merely so engrossed in his reading that he simply didn't hear her?

"Jasper!"

Finally he glanced over at her. "Did you want something?"

"Why, yes, I did. I was wondering what you found so interesting in that paper that you keep reading?"

"This? You wouldn't be interested."

"Of course I would," she retorted. "Isn't the point of our time together that I learn about you? Even if you don't think I would be interested, I still would like to know what is engaging you."

Jasper sighed and put the paper down. Emma Jane noticed that he set it awkwardly under the table, as though he wasn't quite ready to put the paper away.

"I suppose you're right," he said. "It was an article on a boxing match coming to town. I was thinking about how very much I would enjoy taking Will to see it at the Tabor Opera House. However, with the bandits on the loose, I'm not sure it's wise to make plans."

Then his frown deepened. "It's so frustrating being stuck here knowing what I know about the bandits while everyone else is back in town coming up with a plan that probably won't work."

Immediately, Emma Jane felt guilty for pressing the issue. After all, it was selfish of her to focus on their relationship when very dangerous men were on the loose. But there was nothing they could do now. They were trapped until the snow let up. Since they were stuck here, why couldn't they make the most of their time?

"I can understand that," Emma Jane said, softening her tone. "However, it seems to me that worrying over something you can't change isn't going to make the situation better. So let's focus on what we can change."

He quirked a brow. "Is this more of your wisdom on making the best of things?"

"Yes, I suppose it is."

"Well," he said. "There you have it. There are many things I enjoy in life, but I'm finding that more pressing matters keep distracting me."

"Even though you can't do anything about them?"

A hint of a smile teased the corners of Jasper's lips. "Seems to me we just had this conversation."

"Then why are we having it again?" She kept her voice light at first but then looked at him with enough seriousness that she hoped he'd understand. "Why aren't you letting God take control of your worries?"

"I suppose you're right," he said slowly, his brows furrowing back into the expression he'd worn while reading the paper. "I'd like to think that God is in control, but if that indeed is the case, how can He let these bandits continue plaguing our town?"

"Have you tried asking Him? Have you prayed about the direction to take in pursuing the bandits?"

Abigail gave an approving murmur, and while it felt good to have her support, Emma Jane was grateful she stayed out of the conversation. This matter was something that needed to be settled between Emma Jane and Jasper, and while it wasn't ideal to have this talk among other people, Jasper needed to know the importance of trusting God.

Jasper looked at her as though she were daft. "What good does that do? God doesn't give a person a battle plan."

Emma Jane frowned. "Maybe not literally, but it's amazing how God is present if only you just look."

Jasper didn't appear to hear her words, staring sullenly off into space, as though he wasn't even seeing her despite his face being turned toward her. "I've spent my whole life ignorant of the plight of others around me, and now that it's been brought to my attention, all of my attempts to do something about it seem to fail. I look, and I see nothing but problems."

Finally his gaze fixed on her. "I know you want me to make the best of being trapped here in the hotel, but I can't."

He gave Abigail a halfhearted smile. "No disrespect to you, ma'am. Your family's hospitality has been among the best I've ever experienced."

Once again, he frowned. "But what good is being a Jackson when I can't make a difference? What good is having all this information about the bandits when I'm stuck here and can't use it?"

"At least you can take heart in knowing that the bandits are also trapped in the storm. As for making a difference, you've made a difference to me," Emma Jane said softly. "Because of you, I have a home. My sister isn't married to Amos Burdette. And I'm able to do things that matter."

She should have known that Jasper's expression wouldn't lighten. Not when she knew what a burden she was to him.

"What kind of things?" A start. At least in that his curiosity was piqued. He wanted to see the impact his actions had for the good.

Emma Jane smiled. "Like helping with Pastor Lassiter's ministry. I'd always wanted to do more, but Mother was constantly harping on me for the time I spent at church. I'd have to sneak away, and then I felt guilty for disobeying her. Mary says I've been a great help to the ministry and that she has no idea how they'd have managed after the brothel fire without me."

Even now, with everyone else in town thinking Emma Jane worthless, she couldn't help the feeling of satisfaction in knowing her contribution to the community. She'd have also liked to have mentioned how Jasper's wealth would enable her to care for Moses, but given that they were finally communicating, it seemed wrong to bring up a topic that would only make him shut down again.

Jasper nodded slowly, like he was considering her words. And, if Emma Jane were to be so bold as to read his thoughts, like he was seeing her in a new light.

"Will said that Mary counts on you tremendously. You two weren't friends before?"

Emma Jane shook her head. "I would have never imagined I could be friends with someone as good as Mary. But when she reached out to me, and was kind to me, even when I least deserved it, something in me changed. I can't explain it. Because of Mary's kindness, I realized that all of the words in the Bible that I so cherished…they weren't just God's promises to the worthy. They were meant for someone like me."

"That is so beautiful," Abigail said, looking up from her knitting. "I don't mean to intrude on a somewhat-private conversation, but I cannot help but be thankful for what a marvelous work the Lord is doing in you."

Emma Jane smiled at her. "I'm thankful, too. I had no idea how miserable my life was, and while I knew how to bear through all things, I had no peace in my heart. Now I have nothing but joy, knowing that I can bear all things through the love of God."

Even as she spoke the words, all of her frustrations over her marriage to Jasper disappeared. The Lord had been with her through everything, and now, even with the future so uncertain, He would be with her still.

Moses gave a small cry, and Emma Jane started to get up to get him. She'd left him sleeping in the other room. Had she been wrong to leave him alone?

Abigail set a hand on her knee. "Give him a few moments. He needs to learn patience."

Patience? But he was just a baby. Moses began to wail.

"The baby's crying," Jasper said in the same dull voice he always used when mentioning Moses.

"Why don't you see what he needs, Jasper," Abigail suggested in a singsong voice.

The look on Jasper's face was almost worth all the trouble he'd been giving her. You'd have thought she'd asked him to pet a snake.

"Uh, I don't know anything about babies." He looked imploringly at Emma Jane, but Abigail set a hand on her knee.

"Sounds like the perfect time to learn," Abigail said in a matter-of-fact tone. "Every man needs to know how to take care of his children."

The weight of everyone's stares hung heavily on Emma Jane. She knew Jasper didn't want to have anything to do with Moses, and he certainly didn't consider the baby to be his son.

But maybe, if Jasper could just get to know Moses, he'd fall in love with him, just as Emma Jane had.

She'd just been praising God for taking care of her even when things looked bleak. Right now, Jasper's lack of interest in taking care of Moses was perhaps the most difficult thing she faced.

"It's all right, Jasper, he won't break." Emma Jane

gave an encouraging smile. "Just pick him up and bring him in here. He might stop crying just because someone is holding him. But if he has other needs, we can help you figure them out."

"Just be mindful of his head," Abigail said. "You'll need to support it with your hand because he's not strong enough to hold it up himself."

Emma Jane was tempted to give him a few other cautions. After all, Jasper wouldn't know how Moses always managed to wiggle out of his blanket but preferred to be wrapped snugly. But too many instructions might be overwhelming for him, and it would give him an excuse not to try.

"Fine." Jasper turned and stalked out of the room.

Abigail patted Emma Jane's knee. "It will be all right. Every man needs to learn how to take care of a baby, and since Jasper has had no inclination to learn, this will be a good way for his feet to get wet."

Olivia entered the room from the kitchen, smiling as she said, "So true. Stephen was terrified of holding our children when they were babies. But a man has to get comfortable taking care of the little ones. There will come a time when you can't do it all yourself and he's going to need to help."

If only Jasper's hesitation at taking care of Moses was so simple. Were it his own child, Emma Jane had a feeling that Jasper would be much more hands-on and willing to take care of the baby. But Moses?

"What if he doesn't want the baby in the first place?"

The words slipped out of Emma Jane's mouth before she could take them back.

Olivia gave her a strange look. "I'm not sure what

that has to do with anything. Babies come whether you want them or not."

Emma Jane sighed. "Not Moses."

"Who wouldn't want a sweet boy like Moses?" Abigail picked up her knitting and motioned for Emma Jane to do the same. "Why, if I thought Charles would let me, I'd be tempted to take him myself. He is such a dear boy. But Charles is upset because we already have too many mouths to feed, and he does so hate that we are dependent on my family providing work for him."

Abigail's long-suffering sigh made Emma Jane wonder if this wasn't part of the marital problems Abigail had alluded to earlier.

"Let's not vex poor Charles further," Olivia murmured. "We wouldn't want to give him one more thing to take responsibility for."

"Mother!" Abigail threw down her knitting. "Why must you make such remarks? You can't imagine how intimidating it is for a man to marry a woman whose parents can give her far more than he can. And then, to have to work for his father-in-law because there are no other jobs available to him."

Emma Jane thought she heard Olivia mutter something about him being too lazy, but she couldn't be certain. Regardless, it wasn't her fight, but clearly she wasn't the only one whose marriage made things awkward for the family.

Perhaps she'd expected too much out of her marriage so soon. When they returned to town, Emma Jane would make more of an effort with her mother-in-law.

Abigail looked over at Emma Jane. "You're never going to get anything accomplished if you don't pick up your needles. Now, show me what you're doing, so I can see where you've gone wrong."

Emma Jane complied, staring more at the door than at her work. Moses had stopped crying, but Jasper hadn't returned.

"Well, that's where half of your mistake is. You're paying more attention to the door than you are to your knitting. Jasper and the baby are fine."

Emma Jane couldn't manage to find a way to take her eyes off the door to focus on her project. The wool would have ordinarily been a comfort to her, its softness a balm on her fingertips. Even the cheery yellow would have ordinarily brightened her mood, but she found that her thoughts of Jasper seemed to give everything a grayish hue.

"That's how I knew she was meant to be Moses's mother," Olivia said, her smile evident in her words. "She worries about him just as she would her own."

The words didn't comfort her, not when Jasper didn't want to accept that fact. How could others see it when he couldn't?

Abigail nudged Emma Jane again. "Now, let's get focused."

"How?" She looked down at the tangle of yarn and needles, and sighed. "How do you focus on something when the only thing on your mind is wondering if your baby is all right?"

"He's not crying anymore, is he?"

Acknowledging the silence was almost embarrassing, especially with the knowing look Abigail gave her.

"Oh, now." Olivia gave her daughter a sharp look. "As I recall, you were just as bad when Molly was born.

You would hardly use the outhouse for fear something might happen to her."

"Mother!" Despite Abigail's rebuke, Emma Jane could hear the affection in the other girl's voice.

This was the sort of family life she'd always wished to have for herself. Was it too much to hope that it was still possible?

Jasper tried telling himself that this all had to be some crazy nightmare. Why would they want him to get the baby? Probably some bizarre test.

He entered the room where they baby lay in a small basket. The infant's hands were balled up at his red little face as big tears ran down his cheeks. If it weren't for all the trouble the little thing was causing in his life, he'd almost feel sorry for him.

Leaning over the basket, he muttered, "Don't cry."

The baby continued to wail.

"Look, baby," Jasper said as gently as he could. "I don't know anything about babies. They all seem to think I'm just going to pick you up and suddenly be able to take care of you, but listen…"

The baby had ceased his wailing and was looking up at him with dark eyes. Watching. Like he really was listening.

"I don't want to break you, all right? So if you could just stay settled down, then I won't have to pick you up and then I won't drop you. Because as mad as I am at Emma Jane for getting us into this situation, I don't want any harm to come to you."

The baby reached a hand toward Jasper, and Jasper couldn't help but reach in to touch the hand. So tiny. Fragile.

No, he couldn't possibly pick up the baby.

"Were you just lonely, little fella?"

The baby blinked up at him.

"You're probably missing all the pretty ladies fussing over you, aren't you?"

Jasper shifted his position slightly, so he was kneeling beside the cradle, and the baby's head seemed to move in the same direction, as if to follow him.

"I suppose they're taking good care of you. Emma Jane sure has taken a shine to you."

Jasper frowned. He had to admit, the baby was pretty cute, if you liked wrinkly faces, dark hair that didn't seem to go in any particular direction and big dark eyes that didn't seem able to stay focused on anything.

"What do I do about her, little guy?"

"You could try talking to her and working through the uncomfortable moments, instead of shutting down or walking away."

Jasper jumped at the sound of Emma Jane's sweet voice.

"I didn't hear you come in."

"Perhaps I should leave, so you could keep talking to Moses and I can hear more of what's in your heart." She knelt beside him. "He likes you."

Her words warmed him. They shouldn't have. After all, she'd gone and taken in this baby without his consent. Worse, he was starting to find that despite all of his frustrations in her lack of respect for his wishes, somehow Emma Jane was finding a way into his heart.

"Why do you want to know more of what's in my heart?" he asked, his voice catching as he spoke.

Emma Jane looked at him, the dark specks in her

blue eyes mesmerizing him, as though they were a puzzle waiting for him to solve.

"You were the one who suggested we start over and get to know each other."

If she had been any other woman, he'd have complimented the beautiful smile lighting her face far better than the fire burning gently in the fireplace. But every time he told her of her beauty, it made her uncomfortable. She'd probably heard him compliment all the other ladies in town, and now it was probably difficult for her to ascertain his sincerity.

In truth, any compliment he'd want to pay her far outshone any he'd ever given. Emma Jane had a quiet loveliness, like an unexpected flower in... Jasper shook his head. He was known for that sort of compliment, and it clearly wouldn't work on Emma Jane. He'd need to think of another way to think about her.

"You're right," he said slowly. "Thank you. I appreciate you making the effort."

"Why did it take you so long to answer me?" Her words were gentle, not an accusation. But a deeper probing into the recesses of his heart.

He hadn't meant for their courtship to enter such troubled waters. Jasper was quite adept at maneuvering through all the small talk that occurred when courting a young lady. But Emma Jane... It was like diving into a place he'd never been.

"Because I don't know what to say."

"Whatever's in your heart." Her expression was guileless, and he hated how it immediately made him suspicious. Everyone always wanted something from him, and since Emma Jane knew his weakness, it almost made it harder to open up.

"I don't know how to do this." The words were hard to say, burning in his throat as they came out.

"It's all right." Emma Jane patted his knee and reached into the cradle, picking up the baby. "Just put your arm out, like mine, and I'm going to set his head in the crook of your elbow."

Jasper hadn't been talking about the baby. But as Emma Jane's soft hands placed the downy head against his arm, he had to wonder if it would have been safer to simply confess the longings and confusion in his heart. Having the baby in his arms, it made him feel…

"Please, Emma Jane, I know you mean well, but…"

"Look at him. He likes you."

Her voice was so soft and tender he couldn't help but obey. How could this baby look at him with so much… was it love?

"I don't understand." Jasper turned his gaze to Emma Jane. "He doesn't know me. Why would he?"

She looked down at the baby and smoothed the hairs on his head. "Because that's what babies do. All they ask is for someone to care for them and give them a loving touch."

Then she turned her face back up to Jasper, her eyes looking deep into his. "That's all any of us needs, really. But somehow we get it all mixed up as adults. Babies love automatically and unconditionally. We turn love into this complicated thing that seems to be unattainable. But it's not. We just have to be willing to trust as blindly as a baby."

Trust. He'd asked that from her, and she seemed to be asking that from him. Except Emma Jane was asking for trust on a different level. To jump into completely unknown territory and give her his heart, not just his fortune. Fortunes were easily gained and lost. But his heart…?

He'd never risked that before. Never even offered it.

Which was why, when he leaned in to kiss her, it wasn't with the teasing look, flirtatious comments or flattery he'd given every other girl in town. He pressed his lips to hers with the gentle question, asking her to let him in. But more than that, it was an offering.

Every kiss he'd given had merely been to taste, to take, and had all been for pure amusement. As Emma Jane's lips moved against his, he knew that this kiss sealed something special between them. For Jasper, kissing Emma Jane was offering his first kiss, or at least the first sharing of all of him, asking for all of her.

When he pulled her closer to him, deepening the embrace, he felt the bundle in his other arm pressing between them. Emma Jane must have felt it, too, because she jerked away.

"What was that?" She sounded angry as she pressed her fingers to her lips.

"I'm sorry, I got caught in the moment."

Emma Jane backed away. "That wasn't supposed to happen."

No, it wasn't. "I'm sorry," he said simply. "I…"

He'd tried giving her a part of his heart and she'd…

She kept her fingers on her lips, like they were tingling the way his still were. Their kiss might not have been what was supposed to happen, but she'd felt it, too. Something intense had passed between them, and while he was trying to acknowledge it, Emma Jane seemed too afraid.

"I think I might be developing feelings for you," he said, hoping that his admission would put her at ease.

Emma Jane removed her fingertips from her lips. "You might?"

Then she shook her head. "I should have known. You know, at first I was offended that you hadn't tried to kiss me. I even imagined at one point that when we were trapped in the mine together, just before it caved in, you *had* kissed me. And now you've kissed me for real, and all you can say is that you *might* have feelings for me?"

She took the baby out of his arms and stood. "I am not one of your playthings to toy with."

Jasper quickly scrambled to his feet. "I know. And I wasn't. There is something between us, and I'm trying to make sense of it."

Then he stopped. Stared at her. Examined her flushed face, her flashing eyes and her heaving chest. She was angry. Truly angry. Confused. And hurt.

"Wait. You thought you imagined our kiss in the mine?"

Emma Jane nodded slowly.

"Why would you think you imagined it?"

A tear trickled down her cheek. "Who would want to kiss me? Why would you, a handsome, well-bred man who could have any girl he wanted, want to kiss me?"

So many reasons, and as they crossed his mind, he remembered all the compliments he'd paid her, and all the arguments she'd had against him. How could he tell her how very lovely she was? How desirable she was to him? How could he make her believe him?

All he had was the truth.

"That night, in the mine, I was attracted to you. When you approached me earlier in the barn and told me what was happening to your family and how you wanted me to help, I admired you."

Jasper took a deep breath as he remembered how he'd noticed her eyes and the way the dark flecks danced back then, just as they were doing now.

"I barely knew you, and I didn't want to marry anyone, let alone you, but I was so impressed that you came right out and told me that's what you wanted. No one had ever been honest with their intentions like that before."

She continued looking at him with that accusatory expression.

"Beauty isn't just about a person's outward appearance, you know." He returned her glare. "Your dress was the most awful thing I'd ever seen on a person, but I admired your honesty and courage. I'm sorry if you don't believe me, but I found that very attractive. And when we were stuck in the mine, and we were talking about real things, I felt a real connection to you. So I kissed you."

Jasper shrugged. "I'm sorry if that offends you, Emma Jane. It was wrong, I know. I shouldn't have taken the liberty. I acted impulsively in the moment, and I'm sorry if it caused you pain."

He'd tried to be sorry for kissing her, but even now, having kissed her a second time, he couldn't regret it.

"Why didn't you mention the kiss before?" Her eyes were still watery from her tears, but at least they were no longer trickling down her cheeks.

"Why didn't you?"

Emma Jane looked at the ground. "I told you. Why would anyone want to kiss me? I figured I must have imagined it."

He reached forward and lifted her chin, looking into her eyes. "No. But I felt like I'd taken advantage of your weakened state, and the honorable thing was to pretend like it had never happened."

"Is that why you so readily gave in to my family's demands that you marry me?"

"In a way," he admitted with a brusque nod. "I knew you'd been compromised, and the honorable thing to do was marry you. Plus, you'd saved my life. I felt like I owed it to you."

"And now?"

"Now what?" he murmured.

"Why did you kiss me?"

Jasper closed his eyes. Tried to come up with the right words when he had no explanation other than the one he'd already given.

He finally opened his eyes and looked down at her. "Things are changing inside me. My feelings for you are changing."

His answer didn't appear to be what she wanted to hear. Tears streamed down her cheeks. "You have told me over and over how much you do not want to be married to me. You've said that you don't believe me when I say that I did not trap you on purpose. You keep telling me that you don't trust me and that I have to earn your trust."

His own words hurt more when used against him. Especially because even though he'd tried offering himself to her, part of him knew they were still true. Yet they weren't. How could it be both?

"I can't explain it." He didn't even know what to tell himself. He wanted her, but he was still afraid. Something inside him had shifted, but he didn't know what or how. Was it the Bible reading he'd been doing when he thought Emma Jane wasn't looking? Or the wisdom from the Lewises? Or was it Emma Jane herself?

She stared at him, as if he owed her something more.

"It's like what you told me with Mary. How something inside you was different. I don't know why, but it's the same for me."

Her shoulders seemed to relax, and her posture seemed less tense. "I understand." Then she frowned. "And I suppose I also understand why you were hesitant to believe in me. Because I don't know if I believe you."

How quickly the tables turned. Jasper felt a new sympathy for Emma Jane and how his disbelief in her must have hurt. Yet this wound seemed to sting a little deeper. After all, he'd offered her something he'd offered no other—his heart—and she needed more proof.

"What do you want from me?"

Emma Jane held the baby out to him. "I want you to accept Moses as your son."

He looked at the baby, then he looked at her. "I've already held the baby."

"The baby." Emma Jane made a derisive noise. "You've not once mentioned him by name."

Jasper swallowed. He'd barely begun to accept the child, and now she wanted him to acknowledge a name he hadn't chosen and wasn't even sure he liked?

"I thought maybe we could discuss the baby's name."

"His name is Moses." She set her jaw stubbornly as she brought the baby back closer to her body.

"Moses," Jasper said slowly, feeling the word on his lips. He looked at the baby, then he looked back at her. "I'm really trying to make this work. But I give you all I have to offer, and you ask for more."

Emma Jane looked down at the baby and stroked his head. "A few days ago, that would have been enough. But now I have a child to think about, and I have to do what's best for him."

As he watched her retreat, Jasper suddenly felt weary. The room seemed emptier without her and the baby, but he didn't know how to make her stay. And if she stayed, would they continue hurting each other with their words?

The life he'd planned for himself was so much simpler. Chasing bandits was easy enough. No, not easy, but at least he didn't have to sort through feelings only to find his effort had been for naught.

He'd offered a piece of himself to Emma Jane that he'd never offered anyone else. But she acted like he'd insulted her instead.

Exhaling wearily, Jasper shoved his hand through his hair. Obviously, he'd been wrong in following his heart and attempting to connect with her on a romantic level. He'd promised her a marriage of convenience, and tonight's kiss had violated that promise.

Emma Jane might have thought herself foolish to have imagined their kiss in the mine, but Jasper had been more foolish. He'd repeated what was clearly a mistake. One that wouldn't happen again.

Chapter Fifteen

Emma Jane slept poorly that night. Sometime around dawn, she gave up the fight for sleep and wandered into the kitchen. Jasper had never come to bed, not that they were sharing a bed, of course, but he hadn't even come to their room to keep up the appearance of being a married couple.

She heated a kettle of water and looked out the window, noticing that the snow had finally stopped falling. Moonlight glittered on the surface of the ground, blanketed in white. The drifts were almost to the base of the window, so that if she opened the window, she could touch the top of the snowbank.

Jasper would want to leave as soon as he realized the worst of the weather was over. How they'd make it to town through the deep snow, she didn't know, but knowing Jasper, he'd find a way.

As she'd found herself doing multiple times throughout the night, Emma Jane touched her fingertips to her lips again.

Why had he kissed her like that?

Jasper had said he'd been attracted to her. Which

hardly seemed possible, considering how unattractive Emma Jane was. Everyone said so. Her mother used to tell her that only a blind man would be able to overlook her lack of beauty. Certainly all of the young ladies had far more to recommend them than Emma Jane.

Why then would he find *her* attractive?

Though Jasper had mentioned admiring pieces of her character, Emma Jane could hardly fathom such things would make up for her lack of looks.

Her eyes filled with tears. Why would he toy with her like that?

All this time, she'd been curious about what it would be like to kiss him, hurt because he'd kissed every girl in town except her, and now, she found it only to be more confusing than anything else.

She'd liked his kiss. Liked the way his big, strong arms felt around her. As if she was safe. And she could count on him.

For a moment, she even thought she might have felt a spark between them.

But for Jasper, he'd only thought he might be developing feelings. So what had the kiss been? A game? Just one more of his experiments in curiosity, like he'd had with every other girl in town?

He'd said it was different, but Emma Jane wasn't sure she could trust him. If he'd really changed, why was he still being so obstinate about Moses?

The water was finally ready, and Emma Jane began making her tea. Soon the sun would be up, and Olivia would be in to prepare breakfast. Emma Jane glanced at the closed door to the rooms off the kitchen. Abigail and her family occupied those rooms, and it was hard not to peek in and check on Moses. Because the baby was still too young to sleep through the night, Abigail had said it would be easier to keep him with her for his midnight feedings.

How was it possible to love someone so completely in such a short period of time? If only Jasper could understand that love and be more accepting of Moses.

Emma Jane sighed.

One more reason why it seemed hard to accept that Jasper's feelings were anything more than one of his passing fancies. His moods seemed to be up-and-down, not at all the steady emotion she felt for Moses.

Jasper's driving passion to find Daisy had been stronger than any of the emotion he'd expressed toward Emma Jane. And if she was to be completely honest about Jasper, well…

She sighed again.

The last time they'd been stuck here, she'd thought the two of them had developed a strong friendship. They'd talked and laughed, and Emma Jane was certain they'd have a good relationship once they returned to town. When her parents demanded they marry, she believed it wouldn't be so bad, considering she and Jasper had already bonded.

But this? The constant up-and-down and never knowing if Jasper was going to be friendly or antagonistic?

Which Jasper would she return home to?

The door creaked open, and Emma Jane turned, expecting to see Olivia but instead found Jasper, hair mussed and rubbing his eyes, walking through the door.

"I'm making tea," she told him, realizing that she'd oversteeped the leaves, but not sure she cared. Perhaps the stronger drink would help her gather her thoughts.

"I thought you'd still be asleep." He walked to the table and accepted the cup she offered him. "Thank you."

"What are you doing up so early?"

"I woke up when the wind stopped howling. Couldn't get back to sleep. Too much on my mind. I'm hoping to beat the bandits back to town."

That was the kind of devotion she'd hoped for him to feel toward her. The kind of devotion that should have backed up his kiss.

"I've been thinking," Emma Jane said slowly, even though the idea was just coming to her. "I'm going to stay here. You need to get back to deal with the bandits, but I need Abigail to feed Moses, so I'm going to stay with them."

Time seemed to stand still for a few moments as Jasper watched her. He had to know that she was right. Without Abigail, Moses wouldn't be able to eat. Why she hadn't thought of it sooner, she didn't know, but here, in the stillness of the morning with Jasper preparing to leave, it was all too clear. He'd have to go without her.

"Why do you think I asked you to leave Moses here?" His words were gentle, and while she'd expected some level of argument from him, she hadn't expected him to sound so…reasonable.

"I need to stay with my son."

"People will talk if I come home without you," he rasped.

"I thought you didn't care about what people said."

She watched as he flattened his lips, his jaw tightening. He didn't have an argument she couldn't counter, and she found, as he appeared to weigh her words, that she no longer cared.

What if people talked? She had done everything to avoid people talking. And yet, it hadn't changed a thing. In fact, all the painstaking measures she'd taken to silence her critics had only made her miserable.

Well, she was done with that way of thinking. If people wanted to talk because she was doing what was best for her son, then so be it.

Jasper looked at her long and slow. "I don't like it, but that's the way of things. People talk, and while I try to ignore it, I know how it hurts people."

His expression softened. "Like you." He sighed and ran his fingers through his hair. "I know I haven't done my best by you to keep the talk down, but once this business with the bandits is done, I'll do what I can."

Yet again, Jasper was putting her off. Now that he was heading back to town, Emma Jane was no longer a priority. Just as she'd suspected, her husband had no interest in her other than being a passing fancy. He'd kissed her because she was convenient to him, not because he'd developed any special feelings for her.

She'd almost been fooled. For a moment, she'd almost thought that he'd developed a level of tenderness toward her. But no. He'd merely sought his amusement with her because there'd been little else to do.

Worse, Emma Jane had been the one to incite the action. Had she not taunted him into holding Moses, they'd have both remained content in their own worlds. The attachment she'd been forming to Jasper would never have happened, and then her brain wouldn't be so muddled by the kiss.

Spending time with Jasper was simply too dangerous to her heart. So prickly on the outside, he wasn't a man she wanted to know. But when he lowered his defenses...

Emma Jane sighed. Now that was a Jasper she liked. Could perhaps feel something more for. Except that just as quickly as he let his guard down, the prickles came back up, and that was a man she couldn't live with.

Their marriage vows had been for better or for worse, but as Emma Jane watched her husband calmly sip his tea, she had to wonder if they really had a marriage at all. Technically, with their marriage not consummated, they weren't married. Emma Jane had heard that some people in those circumstances were able to get an annulment.

It seemed their reasons for getting married were no longer valid, at least not to Emma Jane. And after spending all this time trying to make things work with Jasper, to even establish a friendship, they'd gained no ground. He was still the same Jasper who refused to see anything other than his own interests.

Emma Jane cleared her throat. "All the same, I'd prefer to remain here. The talk doesn't bother me so much as the worry over what might happen to Moses."

Irritation flashed across Jasper's face. "And you don't think I care about what happens to the child? I'm not without feeling, you know. I can understand that you want what's best for the baby, but you seem to be forgetting that you lack the ability to feed him." Nostrils flaring, he drew several deep breaths, then bit out, "He was sick before we came here, Emma Jane, and now that he's well, it seems selfish to take him away."

Selfish? She glared at him. "It seems to me that, yet again, you're putting your motives right back on me.

But you refuse to see any possibility other than my leaving him behind."

"And you refuse to see the fact that you may not be the best person to take care of that baby right now." Jasper's eyes flashed as his jaw tightened. "We're married, Emma Jane. And while I'm trying to get to know you so we can find common ground, you keep hiding behind that baby and using him as an excuse to keep me at arm's length."

Every cell in Emma Jane's body heated. "I am merely doing what's right. Something I thought you would support, considering this is Daisy's child. You have just as many excuses keeping me at bay. As for using the baby as an excuse, you're the one who runs away every time the subject comes up."

Jasper took another swallow, then set his teacup down slowly. "Of course I do. Because no matter what I say or do, you refuse to see my side of things. So what's the point in sticking around and having the same argument over and over? Even now, what are we accomplishing?"

Emma Jane smoothed her skirts and straightened her shoulders as she gave him a long, steady look. "Precisely. Which is why it's time we both admit that what we hoped to accomplish with our marriage has failed. No matter what we do, people are going to talk. And you and I are never going to see eye to eye. So why would we spend the rest of our lives making each other miserable?"

"What are you saying?" Jasper's eyes narrowed.

She'd seen that expression on his face before. Her suggestion would have wounded the pride of any man, but since Jasper took such stock in his ability to help her, this wound probably cut deeper.

"You shouldn't have to give up your dreams because of my parents' greed. Because of my simple mistake. You deserve to have the life you want for yourself." She released a trembling breath. "So I'm setting you free, Jasper. Go back to town. Be a lawman. Find someone to fall in love with."

Emma Jane's throat tightened. Something in her heart constricted at the thought of him finding someone else. But it was clear that she wasn't the one for him.

"Do you know the scandal a divorce would cause?" Jasper's voice was hoarse.

His response gave Emma Jane all the assurance she needed that ending their sham of a marriage was the right decision. If all he cared about was the gossip, well, that would blow over soon enough.

"I'm not asking for a divorce," she said quietly. "We have enough grounds for an annulment, given that we never had a real marriage to begin with. People might talk at first, but soon enough the Jackson fortune will be enough to smooth things over."

Even in the dim light, Emma Jane could see Jasper's face pale. He probably hadn't realized the extent to which she'd thought her idea through. There were still some details she hadn't figured out, like how she was going to support herself and her son, but she would find a way.

"I can't leave you with nothing. You're right, my reputation would be easily repaired, but you wouldn't fare so well. The only option available to you would be the same lifestyle as the women you're working so hard to help."

His blunt words were like being dumped into one of the snowbanks.

"Pastor Lassiter…" Emma Jane began, but the expression on Jasper's face told her all she needed to know.

The older man had been working so hard to help their marriage that he'd feel betrayed at Emma Jane giving up so quickly. He'd meant the words when he married the couple, and he'd expected them to mean something to them, as well. If there was anything to feel guilty about, it was the fact that she'd be breaking faith with the only person who'd truly believed in her.

"I could leave Leadville. Tell people I'm a widow. No one would question…"

"You'd make a liar of yourself?" His voice was quiet, but the accusation stung worse than it would have had he slapped her.

"I don't know. I hadn't thought…" Tears clogged her throat. Ending their marriage had seemed so simple, but Jasper's questions made it look more and more impossible.

But he was right. Of all the things Emma Jane valued most, it was her own integrity. She could sleep at night knowing she'd done nothing wrong, but how would she sleep if she built her future on a lie?

"Is being married to me truly that bad?" Jasper asked hoarsely.

"We want different things."

The expression on his face was tortured. "Is it because I kissed you?" His Adam's apple bobbed. "I am so sorry, Emma Jane. I acted without thinking. You were promised a marriage of convenience, and I crossed a line. I was wrong to have kissed you. I promise, I won't seek to impose on you ever again."

Tears escaped her eyes and rolled down her cheeks. "Don't you understand? That's precisely what I don't want. Being kissed was wonderful, and I can't imagine spending the rest of my life never having that again. You deserve a woman who will love you, just as much as I deserve a man who will do the same for me."

She took a breath, strengthened by finally being able to express the feelings deep in her heart. "I want to be kissed with the passion of a man who loves me. I want to be a man's choice, not a decision he was forced into."

Wiping the tears from her cheeks, Emma Jane looked at him. "Isn't this what you told me you wanted for your own life? I care enough about you to want that for you, just as I hope you want that for me. Our happiness is between the two of us. So let's give that to each other as a final gift." She drew a bolstering breath, then went on. "I'll figure out what to do about caring for Moses, but I can't spend the rest of my life making us both miserable simply for the sake of living the good life."

Silence echoed through the room. She could almost hear Jasper's heart beating—or was that her own?

"All right," he finally gritted out. "If that's what you truly want, I'll see about getting an annulment. As for how you'll support yourself, I won't let you do without. My family won't like it, but I'll see that you get a house and a small amount of money to get you by each month." He rubbed a hand over his eyes. "I suppose I bear my own share of the blame for this mess, and I won't have you suffer for it."

His acquiescence should have been a victory, but the heaviness tearing at her heart felt like she'd just lost everything.

* * *

The words were harder to say than Jasper thought they'd be. But he'd been up all night, reading Emma Jane's Bible, unable to sleep. He'd been trying to figure out what to do about her and his growing feelings for the wife he hadn't been sure he wanted.

One section in particular, 1 Corinthians, talked about love. Had he shown patience to Emma Jane? Kindness? Long-suffering?

The desperation with which she made her arguments made it clear that Emma Jane found no joy in her marriage to him. And why would she? He'd never shown her any of the things the Bible said about love. Foolishly, he'd believed that giving her his name would be all she needed, but he could see now how he'd sold her short.

Miserable. That was the word she'd used to describe their marriage.

"Are you sure?" Emma Jane looked at him as though she wasn't confident she'd heard him right.

"Yes. I never meant you any harm, I hope you know that."

"I never meant you any harm, either," she whispered.

He knew that now, deep down in his soul, and he wished he'd been able to see it sooner, rather than thinking the worst of her. Of course her falling into the mine had been an accident. He didn't even need to ask to know.

"I know," he said thickly, watching her expression for any sign that she might believe him. "I'm sorry if I conveyed otherwise."

Emma Jane sat on a chair, her skirts whooshing with the movement. "For two people who never meant to hurt each other, we've sure caused a lot of damage, haven't we?"

He pulled up the chair next to her and sat beside her. "Nothing that can't be repaired. I'd still like us to be friends."

Friends. Actually, he wanted more. Much, much more. The memory of her kiss burned in his brain, and he knew he'd never again have the like. At least not from anyone but her. But for now, he knew what he had to do. Start over. Just like Stephen said. Court her. Be her friend.

"I'd like that, too." She smiled at him, one of the same smiles that had stirred something deep inside him, telling him that Emma Jane was a treasure he couldn't let go of.

The door on the side of the kitchen opened, and Abigail entered, carrying the baby.

"I thought I heard voices in here." She smiled, then yawned. "This happy little fellow has been up for a while now. He's fed, changed and gurgling happily."

Abigail handed the baby to Emma Jane, whose mood seemed to immediately lift just by having the baby in her arms.

Jasper should have paid more attention to the effect the baby had on her. He'd already known, he supposed, but he'd been too busy fighting the battle to really acknowledge how good Emma Jane was with the little guy.

"You look like you could go back to bed," Emma Jane said to Abigail, cuddling the baby. "Why don't you get some rest and I can help your mother prepare breakfast?"

"I couldn't do that." Abigail frowned. "I need to earn my keep."

"You've been doing that, and more. After all, without you, I don't know what I would have done for Moses."

The two women exchanged smiles that spoke of their bond shared over the baby.

"You know I'm delighted to care for him." Abigail looked at Emma Jane, then over at Jasper. "In fact, that's something I'd like to talk to you both about."

Jasper's stomach knotted. He'd known Emma Jane and Abigail had become close over the past couple of days, but this felt like an ambush. Had Emma Jane already been making plans to leave him?

"As you know, Charles and I have been living here with my parents, and as much as I love my family, it's not the best situation for Charles. I was hoping that we could return to town with you, and I could..." She hesitated, twisting her hands in front of her.

"That is, it's a pleasure to help with Moses, but if you could give me employment as his wet nurse, then Charles would have the opportunity to find a job in town and we could eventually have a home of our own."

The woman's unease only served to make the knots in Jasper's gut tighten. Why was his automatic response to question Emma Jane's integrity? Especially when he knew better.

He looked over at Emma Jane, whose face was downcast at Abigail's request. To say yes to Abigail meant that Emma Jane couldn't stay here. But to say no would be cruel to her friend, even if it gave Emma Jane what she wanted.

But at least it would help with Jasper's quest.

"We would be delighted to have you," he said

smoothly, looking over at Emma Jane. "In fact, I would be willing to arrange an interview for Charles at my father's bank. Your husband is an amiable fellow, and if there's a position available, I'm sure he'd get on just fine."

Abigail's face lit up. "You would do that for us?"

"Of course I would. This is the second time your family has taken us in, and I can't tell you what it's meant to me."

Then he looked at Emma Jane, who was most likely put out that he'd spoiled her plans without discussing them with her first. Even now, that was still the trouble. They both acted, thinking it was in everyone's best interests, but never talked about it.

Which was where everything always went wrong.

"As far as helping Emma Jane with the baby, I have no objection, but I'm sure that's something she'll want to work out with you." He stole a glance at Emma Jane, whose attention remained fixed on the baby rather than the conversation.

Yes, she was angry. Using the baby as something to hide behind while she gathered her thoughts. Again.

"Although I will say, in case Emma Jane has any concern over finances, that she is fully authorized to pay whatever she feels is best. I trust her completely, and you have my word that I will pay whatever sum the two of you settle on."

He watched Emma Jane for any sign of acknowledgment that he was trying his best to give her what she wanted. That he would provide for her needs as well as the baby's.

Finally, Emma Jane looked up. Slowly. Her face

shadowed, but not so much as to hide the tears forming in her eyes.

"I had hoped to remain here for a while longer."

"I'm afraid that isn't a good idea," Stephen's voice
boomed across the kitchen. "I've been thinking a lot
about your situation, and based on Jasper's description
of the gang's hideout, it's not far from here. I wouldn't
be surprised if they come here, looking for you."

The knot that had formed in Jasper's gut clenched,
nearly ripping him in two. Why hadn't he considered
the danger he might be putting others in?

"I am so sorry," he said slowly. "I hadn't thought
of the fact that your family might be in danger. Please
forgive me."

Stephen waved his arm. "Nonsense. Of course we
would help you. But if the bandits come here looking for you and find Emma Jane here, there's no telling what danger she'd be in. I think the best move is to
head back to town, where you can alert the sheriff, and
everyone will be safe."

The older man's words made sense, if only they
didn't cause such a look of despair on his wife's face.

His wife.

Jasper had finally gotten used to the word, and now
it seemed, if Emma Jane had her way, it wouldn't be
applicable at all.

But he would find a way to change her mind and win
her back. Well, maybe not back, since he'd never had
her to begin with.

"You're right," Jasper answered smoothly, then
turned to look at Emma Jane, hoping to reassure her
that he'd been on her side this whole time. "I'm sure
the bandits are mighty angry that we got away, and if

they manage to catch my wife alone, I don't even want to think about what they'd do."

He reached out and took her hand. "I'm sorry, Emma Jane, but you're going to have to come back to town with me."

Then Jasper looked back up at Stephen. "We'd just been talking to Abigail about the possibility of bringing her and her family with us to town. We still need a wet nurse, and I'm sure we can find a position for Charles. Would you be able to spare them?"

The older man nodded slowly.

But when Emma Jane squeezed Jasper's hand back, he had hope that things wouldn't be as bad as he feared.

"Please say yes," Emma Jane said, her voice steadier than it had been earlier. "I don't know what I would do without Abigail's help."

"They're both adults. If they want to go, they can go."

"Oh, thank you," Abigail said, tears filling her eyes as she looked from her father to Emma Jane, then her gaze landing on Jasper.

"You have no idea how much this means to me." Then she looked up, past Jasper. "To us."

Jasper turned his head to see Charles standing in the doorway. The poor fellow had just had his entire life rearranged, and he hadn't been part of the conversation. Having been resentful of that type of managing his whole life, Jasper felt guilty.

"That is," Jasper said, removing his hand from Emma Jane's, then standing to face the other man. "If you're in agreement. I wouldn't want to force a man into a life he didn't want."

Emma Jane made a noise, and while Jasper didn't know for sure what it meant, once again he feared having said the wrong thing. While it was true he'd felt that way about his own life, this wasn't about him and Emma Jane.

"I appreciate it." Charles held out his hand to Jasper. "And I'm right honored that you'd be willing to help Abigail and me. I'd rather live in town, so this is an answer to prayer. So long as we're not putting you out, we gladly accept."

Jasper shook on their deal, grateful that, at least in this, he wasn't ruining someone else's life for his own convenience. It seemed as though all of the noble deeds he'd hoped to accomplish lately only turned out sour.

He glanced back at Emma Jane, who'd once again turned her attention back to the baby. Would his efforts to make amends actually work? Or was it too late?

Chapter Sixteen

As town loomed ahead, Emma Jane's uneasiness grew. Jasper had agreed to an annulment, but what would happen once they returned? He seemed to be just as eager as she to move on with his life. But would that change once they arrived at the Jackson mansion and Jasper faced pressure from his parents? Their biggest fear had been the scandal, which is why they'd sent her family away.

How would they react when they found out that Emma Jane was seeking an annulment?

The sleigh jostled as it hit another snowbank. Thankfully Stephen had a sleigh and had been willing to drive them back to town. Jasper had said that the roads were still impassable, which was one more advantage they'd have over the bandits.

Another bump sent Emma Jane closer into Jasper.

"Easy now," he said, putting an arm around her.

Jasper held her close, and though she'd steadied herself, it felt good to have his arm around her. She'd have liked to have said that it was because he offered more protection from the cold, but Emma Jane knew it was more than that.

She liked being in Jasper's arms. Their kiss might not have meant anything to him, since he so readily agreed to the annulment, but to Emma Jane, it had opened her eyes to a world where she could no longer exist.

No wonder all of the girls were crazy about Jasper. His kiss had been something like that out of a dream. And if all of them felt that way about his kisses, it was no surprise that every girl in town mooned over him.

Emma Jane had never thought that she'd be among the ones to succumb to his charm.

Even now, as her mind kept telling her she should pull away, she found herself snuggling closer. Despite all of her warnings to her heart that Jasper was not safe, a piece of her felt as though here was the safest place to be.

Nonsense. All of it. He'd agreed to the annulment, and even very generously agreed to provide support for her and Moses. Those weren't the words of a man who cared for her, but of a man who wanted to move on with his life as painlessly as possible.

Straightening her posture, blinking back a sudden stinging in her eyes, Emma Jane moved out of his embrace.

"I don't want to go back to your parents' house," she said, looking at him but avoiding his eyes.

His gaze landed firmly on her. "We've been over this. You're safer in town."

"I'd like to stay at a hotel."

The old Emma Jane would have never made such a bold suggestion. But she found, the more her ideas were accepted, the more it seemed like she was doing herself a disservice not to at least try.

Jasper didn't answer at first. Instead, his dark eyes bore into her like he was trying to puzzle her out.

"Father has a suite at the Rafferty. As long as it's not in use, I see no reason why you can't stay there."

The Rafferty. Leadville's finest hotel. She'd had tea there once, a prize for all the young ladies finishing school with top marks. Flora had been beastly to her about it, making snide remarks about it being the only way the likes of Emma Jane would be able to take tea in such a fine place.

She had vowed that, one day, she would have tea there again, and not one person would make fun of her for it.

Of course now, with her pending annulment and being a mother to Moses, there would be no stopping the talk. And yet, Emma Jane found that she didn't mind so much. In her heart, she knew she was doing the right thing, which was far better than nasty people like Flora Montgomery, who always seemed to do the wrong thing.

"Thank you," Emma Jane told Jasper, giving him a tremulous smile. "I appreciate how good you're being about all of this."

"It's the least I could do." He shrugged. "Plus, Father's suite will allow you to have more space than a regular hotel room. There's a sitting room and two bedrooms—one for you, and another for Abigail and Charles."

He sounded like he'd thought of everything. Worse, he sounded so accepting of the decision. Emma Jane sighed. She was right not to let her heart lead in this situation.

Jasper leaned forward and tapped Charles on the shoulder. "We'll be going to the Rafferty instead."

She couldn't hear Charles's response, but Abigail turned and gave Emma Jane a quizzical look. Emma Jane merely smiled tightly in response. With the wind, it was nearly impossible to hold a conversation with the occupants of the front seat. Besides, she hadn't told Abigail of her plans to have her marriage annulled.

As much as Emma Jane had told herself she didn't care what people thought anymore, people like Abigail were different. What if her friends disagreed with her decision? Worse, what if they refused to stand by her?

Abigail smiled back, then turned to face front again. She snuggled in closer to Charles, and for a moment, Emma Jane envied her. Even though Abigail hinted that things weren't perfect between her and Charles, they seemed happy. Abigail seemed to genuinely love her husband. Even their children, who'd stayed behind with Olivia until the weather cleared, since there wasn't enough room in the sleigh, were a part of that deep, abiding love.

Would Emma Jane have that for herself? The annulment would free her to marry again, but would a man be willing to love both her and Moses? She adjusted the blanket around the baby, cradling him closer to her. If only Jasper had been willing to accept the boy as his own.

She sighed. That wasn't their entire problem, but it sure had complicated matters.

"None of that," Jasper said, putting his arm around her again. "We're almost to town, and I've promised that I'll take care of everything. So have a little faith. Everything will work out all right."

For him, perhaps. He still had the Jackson fortune as inducement for someone to marry him.

Emma Jane's breath caught. Could she stand to see another marrying Jasper? She stole a glance at him. Would he be so easily trapped into marriage again? Or would he finally find someone to love?

Part of her wanted to see Jasper happy. Part of her... Emma Jane told her aching heart to be quiet. The Jasper she loved was the Jasper who only seemed to be present part of the time. Too many parts, and not enough to make a whole.

"Are you cold?" Jasper rubbed her arm gently. "It's not far now. We're almost to Harrison Avenue."

"I'll be fine," she told him, wishing she had the strength to move out of his embrace but feeling proud that she hadn't snuggled any closer. At least it was progress.

As they pulled up in front of the hotel, Emma Jane's confidence sagged. Too many people were there, watching. Waiting to see who had arrived in such a spiffy sleigh.

Jasper alighted first, ignoring the crowd, and held a hand out for Emma Jane. She took it, careful to hold Moses against her as she stepped down.

As soon as she set foot on the sidewalk, she heard the familiar screech.

"Jasper, darling! Is that you? Everyone has been so worried since your disappearance after your unfortunate wife ran off on you."

Emma Jane took a deep breath, telling herself it didn't matter, yet straining to hear Jasper's response.

"Hello, Flora. My wife did not run off on me, as you can see by her standing beside me. I'm sure you're very eager to spread gossip about our return, and I won't waste your time with the truth. If you'll excuse us…"

He took Emma Jane by the arm and bustled her into the hotel.

"Is that a baby?" The words echoed behind Emma Jane, but Jasper did not stop to answer the question. He'd have to at some point, but she appreciated that they didn't have to deal with the confrontation so immediately.

He continued on to the front desk, where a brief discussion with the clerk confirmed that the Jackson suite was empty and Jasper was given a key.

"I'm sorry Flora was so ugly to you when we arrived," he said as they made their way to the room.

"It's not your fault. I'm glad you didn't turn it into a long conversation."

He stopped and looked at her. "Why would I? I thought you'd understand by now that I can't stand the woman. I owe her nothing, and given her penchant for gossip, I'm not telling her anything that would get to my parents before I have a chance to talk to them." Blowing out a sharp breath, he went on to say, "As it is, I can only hope the messenger I had the clerk send over gets to the house before she does."

He continued down the hall and stopped at a door, which he opened. "Here it is. Home sweet home."

The room, far larger than any of the modest rooms at the Spruce Lakes Resort, was a sitting room, as finely appointed as anything at the Jackson mansion. Emma Jane recognized the furniture as carved by the same hand that had done the intricate pieces she'd seen in Jasper's home. A crystal vase sat on a table, filled with delicate silk flowers. Even the wealthiest families couldn't get fresh flowers this time of year in Leadville, but the reproduction astounded her.

Abigail and Charles entered behind them.

"Oh, my," Abigail breathed, stepping inside.

"Mother decorated it," Jasper said with a sigh. "Father helped finance the hotel, and Mother asked that she be allowed to decorate our suite. It's not very practical, but it made her happy."

As Emma Jane's eyes swept the room, she couldn't help but feel pity for her mother-in-law. Imported lace was draped over every surface, and she was certain that the crystal chandelier hanging from the center of the room had to have come from a far-off place.

But had any of this stuff really made the other woman happy?

They quickly sorted out the rooms, and Emma Jane insisted that Abigail and Charles take the larger of the two bedrooms. Jasper had thoughtfully gone to find a basket for Moses to sleep in, and when he returned, Emma Jane quite happily began filling it with the blankets Olivia had sent her home with.

"He's going to grow up well loved, isn't he?" Jasper's deep, masculine voice came from the doorway.

"I'd like to think so." Emma Jane stood and stretched out her back, stepping away from him. Even at a distance, he was too close.

Jasper stepped into the room, looking around. "I hope you have everything that will make you comfortable."

"It's far more than I would have expected." Emma

Jane smiled at him. "I hope you know how much I appreciate all of this…"

He seemed to not hear her words, taking a step toward her, then reaching out and touching her cheek. "You are so beautiful when you smile. I know it makes you uncomfortable when I say it, but I wish you could accept how much I love your smile."

Emma Jane's face warmed. "I…I don't know what to say."

"*Thank you* would be a good start." He gave an impish grin, and for a moment, Emma Jane thought he might lean down to kiss her. Her heart fluttered at the prospect. Instead, he straightened, then took a step back.

A knock sounded at the main door, but before either of them could answer it, the door opened and Mrs. Jackson walked into the suite.

"I believe you owe me some answers."

Jasper winced. He should have known it wouldn't be enough to send a message to his father informing him of the circumstances. His father would wait, just as Jasper had requested. But his mother was an entirely different matter.

"Hello, Mother." He stepped forward and kissed her on the cheek. "I assume you read the note I sent Father."

"Note? What note?" She glared at him with enough ferocity to melt all of the snow in Leadville. "I was just at the dressmaker's, where I heard the most awful story from Flora Montgomery."

Jasper groaned. "Every story from Flora Montgomery is awful."

"How dare you speak of such a fine young lady in that manner? Her family is…"

"I don't want to hear it." Jasper shook his head, trying not to say exactly what he thought of Flora and her family. But he also wasn't going to allow the woman to continue maligning him and his wife. "Flora Montgomery has done nothing but spread vicious lies about me and Emma Jane, and I won't have it. And if you would ask me the truth rather than take her word on everything, you'd understand things a lot better."

The wounded expression on his mother's face gave him pause. "Sit. We'll order tea, and Emma Jane and I will tell you about everything that's transpired." He used a gentler tone with his request, and he was pleased to see that Emma Jane had already rang for service.

He'd asked her to try harder with his mother, and despite the fact that they were going to end their marriage, Emma Jane was still being kind to the difficult woman.

His mother sat on one of the gilt chairs, and Emma Jane sat across from her on the sofa. He took a seat next to his wife, then placed his hand over hers.

Then, calmly, as though being kidnapped by bandits and escaping through a snowstorm was an everyday occurrence, he relayed their story. Fortunately, his mother was too busy sniffling through her handkerchief to interrupt.

The tea service arrived, and Emma Jane immediately rose to serve them all tea. His hand grew cold without her warmth, and he found himself hoping she'd hurry so she could join him again.

Abigail entered the room carrying Moses. "He's been fed and changed, and I'm sure you're eager to have him back in your arms."

He watched as Emma Jane rushed over to her and immediately brought the baby against her. How could he have even suggested that she not raise this child? Her face glowed every time she held him.

"What is the meaning of this?" his mother demanded, looking at him rather than Emma Jane. "I know plenty of orphanages that can take the child. There's no sense in getting attached."

"Emma Jane is going to raise Moses," Jasper said quietly, looking at Emma Jane rather than his mother.

Did she understand what he was trying to say? What he couldn't say in front of his mother? He finally understood how Emma Jane felt about the baby, and hopefully, it wasn't too late.

"Why would she do such a foolish thing? Do you have any idea what people will say?"

He hated how his mother sounded, especially when he saw the way Emma Jane cringed.

"I would hope that they would say what I believe to be true. That Emma Jane is a fine woman, with a good heart and that she's doing a very noble thing by loving a child who needs a mother."

Continuing to keep his gaze on Emma Jane, he said quietly, "And I wish I'd realized that sooner, before pushing her away."

Then he looked at his mother. Taking a deep breath, he braced himself for his mother's reaction. "During our time away, we realized that our marriage was a mistake. Once things are settled with the bandits, I'll be speaking to Father's lawyers about getting an annulment. Emma Jane did nothing wrong, and she shouldn't be forced to marry me because of others' mistakes."

His mother turned a shade of scarlet that matched the lamp shade on the desk. "What kind of nonsense are you speaking? Have you any idea of the scandal it will cause?"

Jasper took a deep breath, then nodded. "I won't have Emma Jane be miserable for the rest of her life. Scandal will blow over. But…"

"Miserable?" His mother rose, turning her ire at Emma Jane. "You were taken from a low station in life, brought into my home and given everything a girl could have possibly wanted, yet you've somehow convinced my son that it makes you miserable?"

"How could it not? When you speak to her like that and treat her as though she were lower than a servant?"

Jasper moved to stand next to his wife. "Emma Jane is the kindest woman I have ever known, and she's tried so hard to do the right thing by all of us, yet none of us have given her the respect she deserves."

Then he turned to her, blocking his mother from her view. "I am sorry. I've been blind to a lot of things concerning you, and selfishly only cared about how I was affected by it all. I have been the worst of husbands to you, and I deeply regret that I didn't do more to make our marriage work."

Tears rolled down Emma Jane's face, and he reached out to gently wipe them away. "I'm sorry for all the times I've made you cry. I do not deserve a wife of your character."

"A wife of her character?" His mother's voice clawed at his back.

Stepping so that Emma Jane was by his side, he regarded his mother coldly. "If you had taken the time to get to know her, you would have realized that for yourself."

"She is nothing but a gold digger. Need I remind

you how much money your father spent to pay off her
father's debt, send them away and put her sister in that
fancy boarding school? There's nothing we can do about
what we already spent, but if she thinks we'll continue
supporting them…"

"Then she is absolutely right," he said smoothly.
"I've already promised her as much, as well as a house
and future support for her and Moses."

Jasper held out a hand to Emma Jane, and she took
it. "Even if it means giving up everything I have, I will
keep my promise to you."

More tears flowed down Emma Jane's cheeks. He
hated putting her in the middle of his fight with his
mother, because none of this was about her. No, this was
about Constance's need to control everything. When he
told Emma Jane about his mother's losses, he realized
just how much of his world she controlled. He'd done
so much to please his mother, but just like Emma Jane
working tirelessly to please everyone else, he'd only
made himself miserable.

He regretted the fact that this decision hurt his
mother, but this was his life, and by continuing to fall
in line with what she wanted, he was hurting someone
even dearer to him—Emma Jane.

"You clearly are not right in the head. I'll be speaking to your father about this, and when you come home
tonight, we'll discuss matters further."

"I'm not coming home." Actually, in his note to his
father, he'd said he'd be home, but at his mother's words,
he realized the Jackson mansion was no longer home
to him.

Home was where Emma Jane was, and while he'd

have to come to terms with her absence once they filed for the annulment, for now, he knew where he belonged.

"I'll send my apologies to Father. I know he was expecting me."

"You can't be serious," his mother said indignantly, looking from him to Emma Jane.

"I am. I won't stay anywhere where Emma Jane is not welcomed with open arms."

"Why have you turned him against me?" Tears filled the older woman's eyes as she looked at Emma Jane.

Before his wife had a chance to respond, Jasper did it for her. "She did nothing other than try to be agreeable in a place where everyone was unkind to her. I would suggest that you search your heart and find a way to make sure that Emma Jane is offered every kindness among those in your circle. I will not be kind to those who are not kind to her."

His words shamed him. They should have been uttered so long ago, and he should have done more to stand up for Emma Jane before they were even married.

Once again, he turned to her. "I'm sorry for not taking a stronger stand in your favor sooner."

"I…" Her lower lip quivered. "You don't need to do this. I've made my share of mistakes, and I can't bear…"

"We can talk about it later," he said, squeezing her hand, then releasing it.

Bringing his attention back to his mother, he said coolly, "You should leave now. I need to report in with the sheriff about everything that's happened, and I won't have you upsetting Emma Jane while I'm gone. When you feel that you are able to be kind, you may send us an invitation to dinner."

Her face turned as white as the scenery around them

when they'd been lost in the blizzard. The anger replaced with the knowledge that Jasper was serious. She would probably go home and cry, and as much as he'd always hated making her cry, maybe her tears would serve a purpose.

Jasper walked her to the door and closed it gently behind her. His father would be angry, but hopefully once they sat down and talked, he would understand.

When Jasper returned to Emma Jane's side, she looked as though she was trying to find her way in that same blizzard.

"I don't understand what just happened."

"A lot of things you said to me finally sunk in. I'm sorry it took so long to see reason."

Then he looked around the room. "I hope it's all right that I stay here. I can sleep on the sofa, and I'll try not to get in your way. We can settle things more firmly once the bandits are apprehended."

"Of course." Emma Jane frowned. She opened her mouth to say something, but then Moses began to fuss. After adjusting his blankets, she looked back at Jasper.

"I'm sorry. He needs to be changed."

"It's all right. I need to go talk to the sheriff, anyway."

Jasper turned toward the door, then paused. "I know it frustrates you that I've put you off in favor of pursuing this case. But I hope you understand the urgency of the situation."

"Yes." Emma Jane shifted the baby in her arms. "I suppose I owe you some apologies over that, as well. But as you've said, we can talk about everything later."

"Thank you for understanding." Jasper nodded goodbye, then left, torn between his duty to see the case through and his desire to make things right with Emma Jane.

Did she see enough sincerity in his words to his mother that she'd listen to what he had to say to her? Would she give him time to court her, to show her the true emotions in his heart?

Was there even room in her heart for him?

Chapter Seventeen

Jasper's absence created a void in the room that Emma Jane hadn't been prepared for. As much as she'd tried not to get attached to him, already the emptiness seemed as if it would swallow her whole.

What had he meant with all of his apologies and promises of talking later? Didn't he know it was only going to make their annulment that much harder? Leaving thoughtless Jasper was so much easier than leaving a man who seemed to genuinely care about her.

Moses had fallen asleep, and she'd laid him in his bed. Part of her yearned to pick him up and cuddle him close to have something to do, but Abigail had admonished her that if she held Moses too much, he'd be spoiled, and then when she needed to lay him down, he wouldn't let her.

At least she had her Bible. Since Moses had come into her life, she hadn't had as much time to read it as she'd have liked. The silence, with Abigail and Charles gone to bed and Moses asleep, was the perfect time to catch up.

Rummaging through her bag, she realized her Bible

was missing. Emma Jane sighed. In her hurry to gather their things for their return to town, she must have left it at the resort.

She walked down to the front desk to see if they had one she could borrow, but as she neared the entrance to the saloon, she heard voices.

"Stupid rich boy. Thought he was so smart, telling them about the hideout. Little does he know the trap we've got rigged."

The man's cohort chuckled. "Thanks to you letting us know when the posse was leaving. Some of the men have doubted your loyalty, but they'll be mighty glad we have you after tonight."

"I'm just happy to be sitting here in the saloon, enjoying a drink and getting an alibi, instead of being near Mack and his explosives. I don't care what he says, he gets it wrong more often than not."

Emma Jane's heart seized. Of course Jasper would be with the posse. But for it to all be a trap? How had the bandits been able to put everything together so quickly? They'd only been back in town for a few hours.

Glasses clinked. "You're telling me. I was there when he blew up the outhouse. How'd you get out of posse duty?"

"At least one deputy has to stay behind in case there's trouble in town."

Deputy. Emma Jane could feel her pulse racing as she closed her eyes and leaned against the wall. Jasper had been saying that he suspected someone inside the sheriff's office had ties to the bandits. Now she knew for sure.

But that wasn't any help to her husband, who was walking blindly into a trap.

The men discussed the plan a few moments longer, but then their conversation moved to admiring one of the serving women. Hopefully, they'd given enough away for Emma Jane to be able to warn Jasper.

Slowly, quietly, Emma Jane made her way back to her room. After leaving a note for Abigail explaining her whereabouts, she went out the back door and ran down the road to the livery.

"Hello, I'm…"

"Mrs. Jackson. What a pleasure to have you here. It's a little late for a ride, isn't it?"

"It's an emergency," she told him breathlessly, looking about to be sure no one else was around. "I need your fastest horse."

Wes, the proprietor, scratched his chin. "Well, now. Most of my horses went out with the posse. What's the trouble? Maybe I can help."

Emma Jane hesitated, not sure who she could trust. If one of the town's deputies could be bought, who else might be on the bandits' side?

"I need to speak to Jasper. It won't wait. *Please.* It's a matter of life and death."

She hated sounding so melodramatic, but the posse already had a head start on her.

Wes frowned. "Will told me that Mary might try something like this, and I have strict orders not to let her have a mount."

His desire to protect Mary gave Emma Jane hope that this man could be trusted. "I overheard some of the bandits talking just now. The men are riding into an ambush!"

A long sigh escaped Wes's lips. "I knew it sounded too good to be true. All the best men went with the posse, but Deputy Jenks said that he'd remain behind. I figured the threat was to the town, not to the posse. We should let him know."

The back of Emma Jane's neck tingled. "I don't know the man's name, but he said that he was a deputy and deliberately stayed behind so he had an alibi."

"I should have known." Wes spat on the ground. "He always was too rough on his horse. Not so much as to hurt him, but just enough for me to question the man's character."

He straightened, then looked at Emma Jane. "I'll come with you. You can ride PB. He's one of my own, and he's fast."

"Thank you." Emma Jane watched as he got the horses ready, glad that he moved much more swiftly than she would have. Selfishly, she was also glad he'd volunteered to come along.

Will had been right to warn Wes that Mary might try to follow them and right in that Mary had no business being there. Though Emma Jane's time with the bandits had taught her that some of them were not so bad, their leaders possessed a ruthlessness and cunning that made any dealings with them dangerous.

One more thing Jasper had been right about. She'd acted much more bravely when she'd been in their cabin than she ordinarily would have. Mostly because she was so angry that he seemed to be so... She sighed. He'd been trying to protect her in his own way. But she'd wanted Jasper's love and protection on her own terms. She could see that now.

Wes helped her onto her horse, and she was too busy focusing on staying on the horse to continue thinking about all her missteps with Jasper. Fortunately, Wes knew what the posse's plan was, and he also knew a shortcut.

"We can head them off if we cut through Stumptown. The posse didn't want to go that way in case folks saw them ride through and suspected something was up."

Emma Jane couldn't answer for fear of losing her concentration and falling off. Once again, she couldn't help but be thankful for Wes's presence.

They rode hard, or at least as hard as the snow on the ground would allow. They finally rounded a bend, and Emma Jane could see the entrance to the canyon that had led to the bandits' hideout. The posse was gathered there, and from the looks of things, they were too late.

The bandits were in front of the canyon entrance, and the posse appeared to be surrounded.

Wes slowed their horses, but someone had caught sight of their movement. A shout came from the bandits, and some of them turned in Emma Jane's direction.

The momentary distraction seemed to give the posse the edge they needed, and before Emma Jane knew it, shots rang out. She started to put her hands over her ears, but as soon as she loosened her grip on the reins, PB took off toward the shooting.

Emma Jane grabbed the reins and pulled as hard as she could. Behind her, she could hear Wes yelling instructions, but she couldn't hear them.

Ahead of her, Emma Jane spied Jasper. He seemed to recognize her instantly, his eyes widening. If there was any cause for his disappointment, it was that she'd promised him not to get involved with the case. He'd told her that was the very foundation of trust in their relationship, and she'd gone and broken it.

Just when he'd finally started standing up for her, she'd ruined everything.

But there was nothing to be done. Hopefully, he'd be willing to listen to her explanation afterward. She hadn't had a choice once she'd overheard the bandits talking about an ambush. Until they'd arrived, the posse had been surrounded, but Emma Jane and Wes had caused enough of a distraction to allow the posse to act.

Please, Emma Jane prayed. Let Jasper see it that way. But mostly, just let him come out of this alive.

He turned toward her, then a shot rang out. Jasper gave her a funny look as he fell off his horse.

"No!" Emma Jane screamed as she jumped off her horse, not waiting for it to slow down or stop. The force of hitting the ground jarred her, and she stumbled, then got back up. She ran toward Jasper, her heart thundering in her chest.

Why wasn't anyone else going to help him?

A bullet whizzed past her, and Emma Jane realized the bandits were shooting wildly at the posse now.

She reached Jasper, who lay on the ground at an odd angle.

"Jasper!"

He coughed. "I'm fine." His voice was raspy. "Just got the wind knocked out of me. Help me up."

Once he was sitting upright again, Jasper tugged at his great overcoat, fumbling with the buttons.

"Let me." Emma Jane brushed his hands aside and worked them open. Her Bible fell out of his coat.

She picked it up and examined it. A bullet was stuck right in the middle.

"Well, I'll be," he said, a smile teasing his lips. "I've

been saying that a Bible couldn't save a man's life, but I guess I was wrong."

He took the Bible and kissed it, then he turned to Emma Jane and kissed her.

The kiss happened so fast Emma Jane didn't have time to react. She simply kissed him back. When it was over, she pressed her fingers to her lips and stared at Jasper. "I don't understand."

"I've been reading your Bible in secret. Things were happening inside me, and I needed to know. I wasn't ready to talk about it."

A bullet zinged the ground next to them. Emma Jane jumped, clinging tighter to him. Her heart thundered in her chest so loudly, she almost didn't hear his next words. "When I left today, I just had a feeling that I should bring the Bible with me. I'm not sure why, but I'm glad."

Then Jasper quickly scanned the area around them. "I need to get you someplace safe." Setting his gaze on her once again, he gave her a stern look. "What were you thinking, riding into the middle of this?"

"I was trying to warn you," she said. "I overheard one of the deputies telling someone in the saloon that it was a trap. They have explosives."

Emma Jane glanced around, trying to see how and where they'd use them, but Jasper pulled her close to him. "I should wring your neck for taking a chance like that. But I'm just so grateful that you're all right."

He kissed the top of her head, and once again, Emma Jane found his warmth coursing through her. For a moment, she couldn't even tell there was snow on the ground.

Had she made a mistake in giving up on her marriage so soon?

"Stay close." Jasper took her hand and, crouching low to the ground, moved toward a group of nearby boulders.

Another bullet whizzed past them.

Emma Jane looked behind them, noticing one of the bandits headed their way. "Jasper, watch out!"

He turned, and Emma Jane watched in horror as the bandit raised his pistol in their direction.

"Rich boy or no, I'm gonna git you. You done messed with the wrong man."

With all of her strength, Emma Jane shoved Jasper to the ground. Then a searing pain radiated through her back, like she was on fire. Which made no sense, since everyone knew you couldn't light a fire in the snow.

Which is when she hit Jasper as she fell to the ground.

The weight of Emma Jane's body slamming against him felt wrong. "Emma Jane? Are you all right?"

She didn't answer, and as he shifted his weight, he felt something sticky on her back. When he pulled his hand away, he saw blood.

"Emma Jane!"

She blinked. Mumbled something incoherent about a fire in the snow, then her eyelids closed and she went limp. Jasper held her tight against his chest so she wouldn't fall in the snow.

The crunch of boots on snow made him look up to see Will standing beside him.

"Emma Jane was shot." The words burned as they

came out of his mouth. They were the correct words, but they felt so wrong.

Will's brow furrowed as he came closer. "Let me take a look at her. I saw the man take aim at you, but I thought I hit him before he managed to get a shot off. I'm sorry." The lines on his forehead deepend for a moment but relaxed as he squatted on the ground beside them, examining Emma Jane. "Fortunately, she appears to be breathing all right.

"I think we've finally got the upper hand against the bandits. They won't be bothering anyone else, that's for certain. Emma Jane and Wes coming when they did provided us the opening we needed. Let's see what we can do for her, and then we'll get her back to town."

Jasper watched as Will prodded at her wound. This was one area where Jasper had no idea what he was doing. A feeling of helplessness washed over him. The woman he loved had been shot, and he could do *nothing* to help her.

At least the moon gave off enough light that he could see the rise and fall of her chest.

"She's still unconscious," Jasper said, looking at Will for some reassurance.

"Her breathing's fine. She's had a shock, and it's probably best she's out. It won't be an easy trip back home."

One of the lawmen, Cam Higgins, joined them. "We got most of 'em, but we're sending a group of men to get the rest." Then he looked Jasper up and down. "You're the best rider we've got. Can you come with us?"

He glanced at Emma Jane, who murmured something incoherent as her eyelids fluttered. The old Jasper wouldn't have hesitated to go with Cam and the others. After all, what did he know about treating gunshot wounds? He'd be more useful chasing down the rest of the bandits.

Yet now, things were different. Leaving Emma Jane seemed almost inconceivable.

He turned to Cam. "My wife's been shot. I need to stay with her."

Shadows crossed the man's face. "Oh, no. I'm sorry. I didn't realize… Is she going to be all right?"

The question tore at Jasper's insides, biting in places so sensitive he wouldn't have known they existed otherwise.

"She'll be fine," Will said. "I just need something to press against the wound to stop the bleeding. My handkerchief and scarf are about soaked through."

Cam unwound the scarf from his neck. "Use this. Ugliest thing on earth, but it's made from good wool. A little blood can't make it any uglier."

Will took the scarf and pressed it to Emma Jane's back. Jasper adjusted Emma Jane's position to make it easier for Will to tend to her injury. If only he could do more than keep her out of the snow.

"I appreciate your help," Jasper told Cam. "I know you'll want to be with the posse going after the remaining bandits, but can you spare a rider to head to town to get a doctor?"

"Sure thing. You want him to meet you at your place?"

His place. Was there such a thing anymore? He couldn't imagine going back to his family home without Emma Jane, and she'd made it clear that it wasn't home to her.

"We're staying at the Rafferty."

If Jasper's change of address surprised Cam, he gave

no indication. The other man gave a nod. "I'll get on it. That wife of yours saved a lot of men from being killed tonight. Wes told us about the trap with the explosives. Had she not come when she did, providing a distraction, we'd have all been slaughtered."

Jasper shivered at the thought. For a moment there, he'd honestly believed that there was no hope. But then he'd thought of Emma Jane and asked what she would do. Immediately, he had the instinct to say a prayer. All he'd said was, *"Lord, help us,"* and then Emma Jane had showed up.

Was she an answer to all of his prayers? He'd asked her about how God spoke to her and answered prayers, and she'd said it all happened in the way he'd just described. God didn't literally step out and give him an answer or do something for him, but it always seemed like He had exactly what he needed when he needed it.

Jasper stroked Emma Jane's silky blond hair. He'd been so blind about so many things, including how simple it was to follow God. And how God had brought them together.

Will said she'd be fine, but Jasper couldn't help but send up another prayer for Emma Jane's survival.

And when she was better, could they find a way to heal the rift between them? Now, more than ever, Jasper wanted to make their marriage work. He'd hoped to court her and get her to come around to seeing things his way. But maybe there wasn't time for that. Maybe he just needed to be honest with his feelings, exposing the rawest places of his heart, and risk being rejected.

"I love you, Emma Jane," he whispered hoarsely.

She murmured something incoherent, and Jasper hoped that, somehow, she'd understood.

"Don't worry," Will said, catching Jasper's eye. "You'll be able to tell her that when she's awake. Like I said, she's going to be fine."

Then Will stood. "Now, I'm going to get on my horse, and you're going to put Emma Jane in my arms. You need to keep pressure on the wound. She's still bleeding, and from what I can tell, the bullet's still lodged inside her. We need to get her to the doctor and get the bullet out right away."

"I want to carry her." Jasper adjusted Emma Jane in his arms and stood. She was so light in his arms. How had he not noticed what a frail creature she was?

Probably because she was the strongest woman he knew.

Will looked at him like he wanted to argue, but then he shook his head. "Fine. But you need to keep her steady. Too much jostling is going to make the bullet move, and it could travel to her vital organs and kill her."

Jasper gave a quick nod. He'd already known what was at stake, but Will's reminder made it all the more important to be the one to carry Emma Jane into town. If these were to be her last moments, then he had so much he wanted to tell her.

Then Jasper stopped himself. No. He wouldn't let this be the end. Not for Emma Jane, not for them.

"You're going to live, Emma Jane," he rasped, kissing her on top of the head once more. "You're going to live and be my wife in all ways, and we're going to raise Moses…and whatever other children we may have."

Will and some of the other men helped Jasper mount his horse, and then helped get Emma Jane settled comfortably in his arms. Some of the posse had already ridden out in pursuit of the remaining bandits, while the rest were either gathering up the injured or keeping the ones they were apprehending together to send to jail.

They rode back to town, and Jasper was grateful for the buckskin's easy lope. When he'd bought the horse, he'd wondered if he was paying too much. But if it meant Emma Jane's survival, the gelding was worth every penny.

Doc Wallace was just getting off his horse when they arrived at the hotel. He helped Jasper get Emma Jane up to their room and settled in the bed.

"You did a good job of stopping the bleeding," the doc said as he examined her. "But I'm going to need to get the bullet out."

Emma Jane moaned, and her face was paler than he'd ever seen it. Too pale.

"It's going to be all right, sweetheart," Jasper told her. He looked at the doc for confirmation, and he nodded.

"I'm pretty sure the bullet didn't hit any vital organs. But she looks pretty torn up. It wasn't a clean shot."

Jasper closed his eyes. This was the second time a woman had taken a bullet for him. When they were in the brothel, Mel had died stepping in front of a bullet meant for Jasper. It had been that lifesaving action that had brought about Jasper's quest to find and rescue Daisy.

He'd failed to save Daisy, but the cry of a baby in the next room reminded him that he still had a promise to keep. Though he'd told Emma Jane finding a family for Moses would be enough, she'd been right in insisting on keeping him.

Seeing Emma Jane lying on the bed, wounded and

in pain, he knew the debt he owed both women was far greater than he could ever repay.

In truth, this was the second time Emma Jane had kept Jasper from harm. When they were trapped in the mine, she'd shoved him out of the way of a rock slide, injuring herself in the process. Typical Emma Jane. Always thinking of helping others before herself.

How could he ever be a man worthy of such a woman?

The doctor's assistant arrived. A young man who barely looked old enough to be shaving, let alone taking care of patients.

"This is my nephew, Augustus. He'll be assisting me in the surgery. I'm going to have to ask you to leave the room while we get out the bullet, as you'll only be in the way."

"Of course." Jasper pressed a gentle kiss to her forehead. "I'll be back soon," he said softly as he shut the door behind him and went into the sitting room to wait.

Abigail was already in there, rocking a fussy Moses and cooing to him softly.

"I think he knows something's happened to his mama," she said softly.

"Probably," Jasper said gruffly, reaching for the baby. "Let me try."

The knowing smile Abigail gave him made Jasper wonder why he'd spent so much time fighting the inevitable. He held Moses in his arms and gazed down at the little boy.

"Your mama is going to be just fine. But it doesn't hurt to ask God to make sure."

Jasper cradled Moses and began to pray.

Chapter Eighteen

Everything in Emma Jane's body ached. Well, not everything. But what didn't ache burned, and she felt like her entire head was stuffed with cotton. Nausea rolled in her stomach as she struggled to breathe normally. The best she could do was take a few shallow breaths, and even they hurt.

"Emma Jane?" Jasper's voice was soft, gentle and as welcoming as a fire after being out in the cold all day.

No, all night. The last thing she remembered was being cold. So cold. Yet her back had been on fire.

She opened her eyes and turned her head to look at him. Dark circles rimmed his eyes, and he was clearly in need of a shave, but she'd never seen a more welcome sight.

"Good. You're awake. The doctor gave you something for the pain, and he said it would help you sleep, but I'm glad to see you're all right."

Then his eyes examined her face in a funny way. "You *are* all right, aren't you?"

She closed her eyes. Then she remembered. After

taking a deep breath, she looked at Jasper again. "I was shot."

The few words took so much effort it felt like she'd already done a day's work, even though she'd just woken up.

"But you're going to be fine," he assured her. "The doctor got the bullet out, and he said it didn't hit anything serious. Just tore up the muscles in your back and shoulder. You've lost a lot of blood, so you'll need to take it easy for a while, but you'll be fine."

Fine. He kept using that word, almost as though he didn't believe it. Emma Jane looked around the room.

"If you're looking for Moses, he's in with Abigail. He and I have been sitting here, waiting for you to wake up, but he was starting to get fussy and I didn't want him to disturb you."

Emma Jane blinked. Moses? Jasper had never willingly used the baby's name before.

"I can get him if you want." He jumped up before she could answer. Then, just as quickly as he left, he returned, carrying Moses as if holding the baby was the most natural thing in the world.

"There she is," Jasper said in a voice so sweet and tender, and clearly aimed at the baby, that Emma Jane hardly knew him. "See? I told you that your mama would be fine."

Her eyes filled with tears. Not only was Jasper calling her son by his name, but he referred to her as Moses's mama.

"Emma Jane? Are you all right? What's wrong? Is your shoulder paining you?"

The worry scattered across Jasper's face made her stomach flip-flop. Who *was* this man?

"I'm fine," she said, her throat scratchy. "I could use some water, though."

Keeping Moses cradled in one arm, Jasper poured her a glass of water. "You're supposed to sip it slowly. Doc Wallace says you may not tolerate much for a while, but it's good for you to drink as much as you can."

She sipped the water, marveling at how comfortable Jasper seemed to be with the baby. When she was finished, he took the glass. She'd only managed a few small sips, but at least her throat wasn't so dry.

"So you remember being shot?" Jasper studied her face intently, making her feel ill at ease. She'd never seen such concern in him before.

"Yes." Emma Jane took a breath. If only it didn't hurt so much to breathe, let alone talk. But so much needed to be said. "I'd gone to warn you that it was an ambush, but I got there too late. And then…they were shooting, and I pushed you, but something struck me. It must have been the bullet."

"It was," Jasper said, his voice solemn. "You saved my life."

Of course. Emma Jane closed her eyes. That's what all of this was about. Jasper had felt guilty when they were trapped in the mine and she'd saved him, which was one of the reasons why he'd married her. Then, when Mel saved him, he'd felt guilty again, thus propelling him on his quest to save Daisy.

Well, this was one act of gratitude Emma Jane wasn't about to accept.

She opened her eyes and stared at Jasper, drawing from all of her strength. "And now you can get on with it. I know you mean well, but living your life shouldn't be about repaying someone else."

Taking another breath hurt more than she'd expected it would. But this wasn't the pain of her wound. No, this was something deeper, and she didn't expect it to heal as quickly as the gunshot would.

"I want you to be happy," she choked out. "I know you feel responsible for what happened to me, and I'm telling you right now that this was my own choice. So go live the life you choose for yourself. You're not allowed to be beholden to me."

Jasper looked at her like she'd gone mad. And maybe she had. Who wouldn't want the town's handsomest, wealthiest man beholden to her?

Emma Jane Jackson, that's who. She deserved better than a man who felt only gratitude for her.

She wanted a man who loved her.

"I will be beholden to you for the rest of my life," Jasper said, looking at her with enough intensity that, if she'd been a block of ice, she'd have melted.

"But not for the reasons you think."

Then he looked down at Moses with such a loving expression, Emma Jane's heart felt like it was about to burst.

"You've taught me a lot of things. About God. About family. About selflessly giving to others."

Then he turned that same loving look on her. *Loving?* Emma Jane blinked. Surely...

"I had hoped that by agreeing to an annulment, it would soften your heart toward me, and eventually I would be able to court you and to convince you to share your life, your heart, with me."

His Adam's apple bobbed. "But that isn't what I want. If you want an annulment, I will give it to you because I love you. The Bible says that when you love someone, you are not selfish. You are not proud. You put the other person first."

Tears glimmered in his eyes. "The night I kissed you by the fire, I was too proud to say that I loved you, because I wasn't sure if you loved me back. And I was afraid I was giving my heart away to someone who would reject it."

Memories of that night flooded her mind, and her eyes also filled with tears. She'd wanted to say the same thing, but her fear of rejection, her comparison to others, it had been too strong, as well.

"I love you, Emma Jane Logan, and I hope will remain Jackson. I want a real marriage. I want to raise Moses together. And I want to raise whatever other children the Lord sees fit to give us—together—as a family."

His hand shook as he reached for her hand. "I said all these things when I thought I was going to lose you, and I don't know if you heard me or not. But I want you to hear me now. And I want you to understand."

Then he brought her hand to his lips, sending a tingle all the way down to her toes. "I'm asking you to be my wife in all ways. To share my life. I will give you everything you need to care for Moses, regardless of whether or not you accept my offer. I want you to say yes, not because of any of the reasons we were together before, but because you love me, too."

Her throat tightened, and she couldn't speak. Was this a dream brought on by her injury? She reached for Jasper with her other arm, ignoring the searing pain in her shoulder and chest.

"Is this real?"

Jasper leaned into her. "Yes."

"You love me?"

"Yes." And then he kissed her, gently pressing his lips to hers, spreading warmth throughout her body.

He was much more careful in this kiss, Emma Jane noted as she kissed him back. But when she tried bringing her arms around him, she understood why.

Pain ripped through her shoulder, and she couldn't help but wince.

"Careful," Jasper warned, pulling away. "I am convinced that you can do just about anything you set your mind to, but I won't have you tearing apart Doc Wallace's careful stitches when we have the rest of our lives for this."

Emma Jane let out a long, contented sigh. Despite the burning sensation in her shoulder, she'd never felt so light. Could she trust Jasper's words? Or were they merely a result of his concern over her condition?

So much in him had changed. He seemed to be every bit the Jasper she liked. *Loved.* When she'd found him last night, he'd told her that he'd been reading her Bible. He'd stood up for her against his mother.

"What happened with the bandits?" she asked carefully.

Jasper shrugged. "I was too busy taking care of you to pay much attention. From what I hear, though, most are either dead or in jail. Deputy Jenks had no idea you'd heard him and gone out to warn us, so they managed to capture him, too. They sent a posse after the couple who got away, but I haven't heard if they got them or not."

Emma Jane closed her eyes for a brief moment before opening them again. If only she didn't feel so weak. But she had to know.

"Why didn't you go with them?"

Jasper looked at her like she'd gone daft. "Why

would I leave my wife when she needed me the most? Why would I leave Moses when his mama is so ill?"

"But you've always wanted to be a lawman," she said quietly.

He shook his head. "No. I've always wanted to make a difference. I thought that meant being brave and being a lawman, but I'm learning that it also means being brave in the sense of standing up for what's right and taking care of those who need it the most."

Adjusting Moses in his arms, he set the baby at Emma Jane's side. She'd been longing to hold him but had been afraid that, with her lack of strength, she wouldn't be able to bear his weight. Having him lay at her side was a good compromise, and she wrapped her good arm around the baby as Jasper continued.

"There is so much good I can do with my money. Not just by donating it, as my family has always done, but also in the ways the Lord has shown me. Because of you, I know there are people in this world who need love and compassion, and that I need to keep my eyes open, serving where I am led."

Then Jasper smoothed Moses's hair. "Right now, that means being here for you and Moses and loving you the best I know how."

The door opened, and Emma Jane lifted her head to see Mrs. Jackson entering her room. She closed her eyes, not wanting another confrontation with the woman.

What would she blame Emma Jane for this time? She'd been the one shot, not Jasper. Surely no one had told the older woman of the near-misses Jasper had.

"I thought I heard voices," she said in a gentle tone that Emma Jane hadn't known the other woman was capable of. "Jasper, I'd like a moment with your wife, if that's all right. Perhaps you could go tell the doctor she's awake."

Emma Jane opened her eyes and gave Jasper a pleading look. She wouldn't ask him not to leave her alone with his mother, not in front of her, but surely he'd not set her to the wolf when she was so weak.

"Of course." Jasper stood. "I can't believe I didn't think of that."

Then he looked down at Emma Jane. "You'll be all right for a few minutes."

He exchanged a glance with his mother, one Emma Jane couldn't read. Mrs. Jackson took Jasper's place as he closed the door behind him.

"I realize this seems peculiar to you," Mrs. Jackson began, her brow furrowed. "I have never been in this situation before, and I hardly know what to say."

Emma Jane didn't respond and instead focused her attention on tucking the blanket around Moses.

"I don't know if you recall, but we had a rather difficult disagreement yesterday." Mrs. Jackson's voice shook, and her eyes were filled with tears.

"I do." Emma Jane kept her response short, not knowing where this conversation was going. She didn't have the strength to continue that argument or defend her choices.

"My son's words hurt me deeply," she said, a tear streaking down her cheek. "I was angry, and I'd thought for sure that I'd lost him to some gold digger."

The words didn't sting as much as Emma Jane thought they would. She'd heard them enough that they'd lost their power over her.

"But I spoke to my husband, and we prayed and

I took a deeper look at everything Jasper said." Mrs. Jackson shook her head. "How was I so blind to everything? To the truth?"

She looked down at Emma Jane. "I misjudged you. I'm sorry." Jasper's mother reached down and took Emma Jane's hand. "I know that I have acted unforgivably toward you, but Jasper is all I have. I was scared, and I thought his life was ruined."

Emma Jane squeezed Mrs. Jackson's hand. "It's all right."

"No, it's not," the older woman said. "Jasper was right. Your behavior was without reproach, and I acted inexcusably."

Mrs. Jackson pulled a handkerchief out of her sleeve and dabbed at her eyes. "I pride myself on being a good Christian woman, and I denied you basic kindness. When Jasper read to me from 1 Corinthians about love and asked me if I'd displayed those characteristics of love, I've never been so ashamed of myself."

Emma Jane closed her eyes as she recalled Jasper's words to her about his treatment of her. Of not being selfish or proud. He'd mentioned reading the Bible, and now she understood. Jasper had changed. He'd allowed God into his heart.

Warmth surged through her as she turned to look at Mrs. Jackson. "I understand. I don't know why, but for some reason, we hear the words all our lives and we don't live them out. It took me a long time to learn that lesson."

She squeezed Mrs. Jackson's hand again. "I forgive you. So now you need to forgive yourself and move forward in the new knowledge God has given you."

At Emma Jane's movement, Moses started to fuss.

She tried adjusting him, but it only seemed to make him angrier.

"Let me." Mrs. Jackson picked up the baby and cradled him in her arms. "There now, it's all right. I've got you now."

She adjusted his blankets. "You are a handsome little fellow, aren't you?"

If Emma Jane hadn't seen it for herself, she'd have never believed it. The stiff, formal woman who presided over Leadville society with a hawk-like expression had softened. She sat there, holding Moses, making cooing noises at him.

Then Mrs. Jackson turned her expression to Emma Jane. "I understand you call the boy Moses. I was wondering if you'd decided on a middle name."

Emma Jane looked at her blankly.

"Jasper says I'm not to interfere, but I was hoping you wouldn't mind if I made a suggestion. You see, we named Jasper after my father, who hated his given name, but I loved it, so we called him Jasper. My father, who went by his middle name, James, always thought we were trying to insult him. Even though my father has long passed, I thought perhaps you might consider James as a middle name."

The door opened, and Jasper walked in, carrying a tray. "Mother, I thought we'd agreed that you wouldn't interfere."

"It's all right," Emma Jane said, smiling at her mother-in-law. "The truth is, I didn't consider Jasper's wishes in naming Moses, and I know my lack of consideration hurt him deeply. I think we've all been guilty of not living out 1 Corinthians, and that's something I'm going to do better at, as well."

Then she turned her head toward Jasper. "I was hoping you'd be the one to give Moses a middle name." Then she hesitated. Was this enough of a compromise? Of working together. "That is, if you're agreeable to naming him Moses."

The sides of Jasper's lips twitched into a smile. "Does that mean you've accepted my proposal?"

"Oh, my! I didn't, did I?"

A grin so wide she thought it would split her face in two filled her. "Yes! I do love you, Jasper. So very much. And I want to be your wife and have children and spend the rest of our lives together."

Jasper set the tray on the table beside the bed. "Good." Then he set a hand on his mother's shoulder. "I'm sure my mother will rest easier knowing that the woman I love happens to love me back."

Mrs. Jackson smiled. "Indeed. I can't imagine wanting anything different for my son." Then she looked down at Moses. "Or my grandson."

If it were possible for a person's heart to burst from joy, surely Emma Jane's would. But it was the expression on Jasper's face that made Emma Jane's joy complete. She had never seen him looking so content, smiling down at his mother, holding his son, then catching her eye as if to say, "This is everything I always dreamed of."

Perhaps it was just fancy on her part, since in all of her biggest dreams, she'd never imagined it could be this good.

"Mrs. Jackson," Emma Jane said, turning her attention to her mother-in-law. "Would you mind taking Moses into the other room so I could have a moment alone with my husband?"

Gone was the expression of contented gentility on the older woman's face, replaced by the hawk-like version Emma Jane knew so well. "This will not do. I realize you have your own mother, but do you think you could at least call me Mother Jackson? Mrs. Jackson implies we have no relationship at all."

Mother Jackson's eyes softened. "And I do hope that we can have one. Jasper tells me that you knit. Perhaps when you're feeling up to it, we could make some things for my grandson."

A twinkle filled her eyes. "And perhaps any others who might come along?"

"I would like that," Emma Jane whispered, looking over at Jasper. He'd suggested that their shared love of knitting would bring them together, just as Olivia had said that a grandchild would change their relationship.

Jasper winked at Emma Jane, then turned to his mother. "Now that we've settled that matter, I do believe my wife has requested time alone with me."

He didn't wait for Mother Jackson to leave before bending down and kissing Emma Jane. For the first time, their kiss felt absolutely complete. He loved her, and she loved him. Which was all that mattered in the world.

Epilogue

Spring had brought a flurry of activity to Leadville Community Church. And not for tragic reasons. Emma Jane had no idea where so many flowers had come from, but as she gazed around the entrance to the church, she couldn't imagine it looking any more beautiful.

Though her silk dress was brand-new, it was already starting to feel tight. She rubbed the small of her back where it was starting to ache after spending all day helping her friends ready the church for today's ceremony.

"Tired already?" Jasper asked, putting an arm around her, then placing his hand over the tiny bump that was starting to form at her waist. They hadn't told anyone of the new addition soon to be joining their family, but tonight, at the celebration at the Jackson mansion, they would share their news.

"We don't have to go through this," he said, grinning. "After all, we've already been married once."

If she didn't know the twinkle in his eye so well, she'd have thought that he was concerned about her well-being. She pulled his head down for a kiss.

"Absolutely not," she chided when they were finished. "Guests are arriving, and your mother has been looking forward to this event for so long."

Mother Jackson approached, laughing as Moses reached for her diamond necklace and tried putting it in his mouth. "Jasper, do try to behave for at least one day. I know how you hate these things, but I am determined to show off your lovely wife and son."

She pulled the diamond out of Moses's hand. "As for you, young man, I think your father needs to teach you about the proper treatment of a lady's jewelry." In a swift motion, she handed the baby to Jasper.

Then she looked Emma Jane up and down. "Although I see he has neglected his own wife's collection, and that simply won't do."

Emma Jane tried not to groan. She'd made it clear that diamonds were not what she wanted from Jasper, and they'd both agreed their money would be better spent on their projects with the church.

Mother Jackson reached at the back of her neck, then took off her necklace. "Turn around, Emma Jane. This was a gift from Henry when we were married, and now I am giving it to you."

The diamond was heavy on her neck as she looked at Jasper, questioning. He merely shrugged.

"There." Mother Jackson turned around and examined her handiwork. "Absolutely breathtaking. Just watch your son's sticky little fingers on it."

She smiled as she turned to greet the guests who were arriving, but before she could take more than a step, an older matron with an oversize hat approached her.

"Whatever kind of celebration is this?"

"My son and his wife wanted to renew their wedding vows. Apparently, people have been saying it's not a love match. Which, as you can see, is simply not true. We are absolutely delighted to have Emma Jane as part of our family."

Mother Jackson turned and gestured toward Emma Jane and Jasper. "Aren't they the most beautiful couple?"

"Yes," the woman murmured. "But the baby looks nothing like them. So dark. And…"

"I do hope you're not disparaging my grandson." Mother Jackson looked down her regal nose at the woman. "I take insults to my family very seriously, and I would so hate for you to be left off all the good invitations, like the poor Montgomery family has."

Emma Jane felt a pang of regret at her mother-in-law's threat. The Jacksons had sat down with the Montgomerys and told them that Flora's behavior toward Emma Jane was unacceptable. Unfortunately, it had strained relations between the two families, and most people in Leadville had sided with the Jacksons. Apparently, Emma Jane wasn't the only person Flora's tongue had alienated.

The woman shrank back. "Not at all. I think they're a lovely family."

Mother Jackson snapped her fan open, and the woman scurried off. With the same impish look Emma Jane had learned to love about Jasper, Mother Jackson smiled at Emma Jane, then continued on her way.

Jasper leaned in and gave Emma Jane another kiss as voices swirled around them. It wasn't until she felt Moses tugging at her necklace that she pulled away.

"*Moses James Jackson*, that is enough! You mustn't touch Mama's pretty things."

His dark eyes filled with tears as he stuck out his lower lip. Jasper smiled and ruffled his hair. "I know, son. Sometimes she's a hard one, but you'll find, just as I have, that she's almost always right."

"Almost?" Emma Jane gave him a look of mock indignation.

"Yes, almost." Jasper placed a fleeting kiss on the tip of her nose. "And it's always worth it to work through the times when she's not."

"I can live with that."

She'd been right about many things and wrong about others, but Jasper's words about it being worth it to work through them were correct. In the end, none of those things had mattered, except the time and effort they'd both put into their relationship.

Her first wedding day had been one of the most miserable of her life, and while a person should never be forced to marry someone she didn't want to marry, she would never stop being grateful for her marriage to Jasper. It was just as Pastor Lassiter had said—by trusting in the Lord and allowing Him to work in their lives, they had found far greater happiness than Emma Jane could have ever imagined.

* * * * *

Dear Reader,

Emma Jane Logan was never supposed to have a story. Who would want to read a book about a woman described as a "sourpuss"? But as I wrote *The Lawman's Redemption* and saw how Mary's friendship with Emma Jane helped Will see a softer side to Mary, I fell in love with Emma Jane, a girl who only needed a little kindness to transform into a character who deserved a happy ending of her own. But isn't marrying Jasper, the man who will solve all her problems, a happy ending? And that, my friends, is exactly where I began Emma Jane's story. Sometimes the thing that you think will fix everything wrong in your life only makes your life worse.

Like Emma Jane, I faced a time of darkness in my life when I thought I'd lost all hope. But I had a couple of amazing friends who stepped up and loved me, even in moments when I was probably pretty unlovable. More importantly, like Emma Jane, I found strength in God's Word, and between that and the love I'd been shown, I was able to grow and rise above my circumstances.

I hope in whatever darkness you face, you know that God's love is for you. I pray you will find the transformational love that not only impacted me, but Emma Jane and, ultimately, Jasper.

I love connecting with my readers, so please stop by www.danicafavorite.com and say hello.

Blessings to you and yours,
Danica Favorite

COMING NEXT MONTH FROM
Love Inspired® Historical

Available May 3, 2016

THE COWBOY'S CITY GIRL
Montana Cowboys
by Linda Ford

While staying on Levi Harding's family ranch to help his stepmother recover from an injury, city girl Beatrice Doyle discovers an orphaned child. Is the little girl exactly what Levi and Beatrice need to let their guards down and allow themselves to open their hearts?

SPECIAL DELIVERY BABY
Cowboy Creek
by Sherri Shackelford

Town founder Will Canfield and cowgirl Tomasina Stone are as opposite as day and night. But when a baby is abandoned on Will's doorstep, caring for the infant brings them together...and shows them that their differences only make their blossoming love stronger.

THE RELUCTANT BRIDEGROOM
by Shannon Farrington

Bachelor Henry Nash must marry Rebekah Van der Geld to maintain custody of his orphaned nieces. With secrets in his past, will he be able to turn his marriage of convenience into a union of love?

HIS PRAIRIE SWEETHEART
by Erica Vetsch

Jilted at the altar, Southern belle Savannah Cox accepts a teaching position in Minnesota—and quickly realizes she's unprepared for both the job and the climate. But sheriff Elias Parker's determined to help the elegant schoolmarm survive her new start.

———————

LIHCNM0416

Town founder Will Canfield has big dreams for Cowboy Creek—but his plans are thrown for a loop when a tiny bundle is left on his doorstep. With a baby to care for, the last thing he needs is another complication. But that's just what he gets, in the form of a redheaded, trouble-making cowgirl who throws his world upside down.

Read on for a sneak preview of
Sherri Shackelford's
SPECIAL DELIVERY BABY,
the exciting continuation of the miniseries
COWBOY CREEK,
available May 2016 from Love Inspired Historical.

"The name is Will Canfield," he said. "Thank you for your assistance, Miss Stone."

"You sure picked a dangerous place to take your baby for a walk, Daddy Canfield. Might want to reconsider your route next time."

The measured expression on his face faltered a notch. "Oh, this isn't my baby."

She hoisted an eyebrow. "Reckon who that baby belongs to is none of my business one way or the other." She gestured toward the child. "I think your girl is getting hungry. Better get mama."

"That's the whole problem." The man spoke more to the infant in his arms than to her. "Someone abandoned her. I found her on my doorstep just now." He glanced over his shoulder and then back at her. "The woman— the one who spooked the cattle. Did you see which way she ran? I think this child belongs to her. If not, then she might have seen something. She was hiding in the shadows when I discovered this little bundle."

"Sorry. I was focused on the cattle."

Clearly frustrated by her answers, Daddy Canfield muttered something unintelligible.

He grimaced and held the bundle away from him, revealing a dark, wet patch on his expensive suit coat.

Tomasina chuckled. The boys were going to love hearing about this one. They'd never believe her but they'd love the telling. Her pa always liked a good yarn, as well. At the thought of her pa, her smile faded. He'd died on the trail a few weeks back and they'd buried him in Oklahoma Territory. The wound of his loss was still raw and she shied away from her memories of him.

"Fellow…" Tomasina said. "As much fun as this has been, I'd best be getting on."

"Thanks for your help back there," Will replied, his tone grudging. "Your quick action averted a disaster."

The admission had obviously cost him. He struck her as a prideful man, and prideful men sometimes needed a reminder of their place in the grand scheme of things.

"Daddy Canfield," she declared. "Since you don't like guns, how do you feel about rodeo shows? You know, trick riding and fancy target shooting?"

"Not in my town. Too dangerous."

"Excellent," Tomasina replied with a hearty grin.

Yep. She felt better already.

Don't miss SPECIAL DELIVERY BABY
by Sherri Shackelford,
available May 2016 wherever
Love Inspired® Historical books and ebooks are sold.
www.LoveInspired.com